GOLDEN DANUBE

Publications of the North American Jules Verne Society

The Palik Series (edited by Brian Taves)

The Marriage of a Marquis
> Contributors: Edward Baxter, Jean-Michel Margot, Walter James Miller, Kieran M. O'Driscoll, Brian Taves

Shipwrecked Family: Marooned with Uncle Robinson
> Translated by Sidney Kravitz; Introduction by Brian Taves

Mr. Chimp, and Other Plays,
> Translated by Frank Morlock; Introduction by Jean-Michel Margot

The Count of Chanteleine: A Tale of the French Revolution
> Translated by Edward Baxter; Introduction by Brian Taves; Notes by Garmt de Vries-Uiterweerd; Afterword by Volker Dehs

Vice, Redemption, and the Distant Colony
> Translated, with an introduction and annotations, by Kieran M. O'Driscoll

Around the World in 80 Days—The 1874 Play
> Contributors: Philippe Burgaud, Jean-Louis Trudel, Jean-Michel Margot, Brian Taves

Bandits & Rebels
> Translated by Edward Baxter; Introduction by Daniel Compère

(Other volumes in preparation)

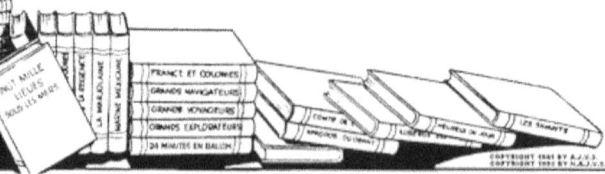

GOLDEN DANUBE

by Jules Verne

Translated,
with an introduction and annotations,
by Kieran M. O'Driscoll

Edited by Brian Taves
for the North American Jules Verne Society

The Palik Series

BearManor Fiction

2014

Golden Danube
by Jules Verne

For information, address:

BearManor Fiction
P. O. Box 71426
Albany, GA 31708

bearmanormedia.com

North American Jules Verne Society: najvs.org

Typesetting and layout by John Teehan

Published in the USA by BearManor Media

ISBN—1-59393-397-5
978-1-59393-397-5

Table of Contents

Dedicated lovingly to my late, much-loved and sadly-missed mother and father, Nora and Frank O'Driscoll; and to my late, beloved grandmother Lal.

This is also, as always, for Alice, Aiden, John and Neil O'Driscoll.

Introduction

by Kieran M. O'Driscoll

The Strauss connection

The source text of this Verne novel (of which the present volume constitutes its first rendering into English, from the original French) is entitled *Le Beau Danube Jaune*, which literally translates into English as *The Beautiful Yellow Danube*. Verne was, of course, alluding to the famous waltz by Johann Strauss II, *Le Beau Danube Bleu* (1866), a musical title which has been immortalized in the English language as *The Blue Danube*. Thus, when I began translating this novel, I considered translating its title as, simply, *The Yellow Danube*. This elimination of "Beau" or "beautiful," would achieve closer parallelism to the musical reference as recognized in English, and thus preserve Verne's allusion to Strauss and his celebrated waltz. However, subsequently it was determined that the color "golden" was a more appealing, elegant and poetic English language equivalent of "jaune," when referring to the color which Verne ascribed to the Danube, in opposition to the traditional "blue." "Golden" certainly sounds more tasteful and attractive than the more imitative, prosaic and plainer "yellow," especially considering the other, often pejorative, English-language connotations of "yellow," such as the implication of cowardice. Having agreed on "golden," the definite article was omitted—thus changing *The Golden Danube* to the more elegant and concise *Golden Danube*— as a further translational improvement. This is by way of revealing the genesis of the title of this novel; Verne explains in the opening pages his departure from Strauss's descriptor "blue": "[the Danube], that

1

famous river which is actually golden, and not blue, as the melody of the famous Strauss waltz would have us believe." (Chapter I).

One of Verne's other posthumously published novels (in 1906) is entitled *Le Volcan d'Or* (*The Volcano of Gold*, a title which has also been rendered into English as *The Golden Volcano*). The title of the current

Jules Verne in the 1890s, at the time he began writing *Golden Danube*.

volume, *Golden Danube,* will therefore undoubtedly evoke memories of, and perhaps inevitable comparisons with, the better-known *The Volcano of Gold.* Notwithstanding the similarities in the two titles, the books in question are very different and distinctive from each other, *The Volcano of Gold* referring specifically to the mineral.

VERNE *PÈRE* ET *FILS* / VERNE, FATHER AND SON

Because *Golden Danube,* a 1901 work from the prolific pen of Verne *père,* is one of the lesser-known stories within his "Voyages Extraordinaires" ("Extraordinary Journeys"), it was a natural choice for inclusion in the present Palik Series, which seeks to bring to light those less celebrated works of Jules Verne which have been, up to now, unjustly consigned to oblivion—and which had not, up to now, ever been translated into English. However, this particular novel is all the more significant and worthy of attention, in that it was reworked by Verne *fils,* Michel (though credited by him to his then deceased father) into a considerably different story, entitled *Le Pilote du Danube,* published in 1908 (and first translated by I.O. Evans in 1967 under the title *The Danube Pilot*).

A previous volume in the Palik Series—*Vice, Redemption and the Distant Colony* (2012)—has dealt, in part, with a comparison of different versions of the same stories, as originally written by Verne *père* but subsequently adapted, with significant changes yet notable borrowings from the original stories inspiring them, by Verne *fils.*[1] Various changes took place under Michel's editorial hand as he guided his father's posthumous stories to publication from 1905 to 1914, including originating some of them himself. Michel went on to become a motion picture producer-director, bringing more of his father's stories to the silent movie screen through 1920. Currently there is strong research interest in the contribution of Michel Verne in his own right to the "Extraordinary Journeys."[2]

---

1. Jules Verne, *Vice, Redemption and the Distant Colony: Stories* by Jules Verne and Michel Verne, Translated with notes by Kieran O'Driscoll (Albany, GA: Bear Manor Fiction, 2012).

2. See the articles by Brian Taves: "Michel Verne, de l'écrivain au realisateur," *Revue Jules Verne,* 19-20 (2005), 190-195; "The Novels and Rediscovered Films of Michel (Jules) Verne," *Journal of Film Preservation,* No. 62 (April 2001), 25-39, archived at <http://www.fiafnet.org/pdf/uk/fiaf62.pdf>, and translated into German by Volker Dehs as "Die Romane und wieder entdeckten Filme von

The Relationship between *Golden Danube* and *The Danube Pilot*

In the case of *Golden Danube,* Jules Verne had written a slight, but entertaining and (geographically, historically and zoologically) educational tale about an unusual, epic fishing journey all along the length of the great central European river, the Danube, a tale which contains much humor, spiced with a certain amount of mystery, intrigue and ultimate resolution. This novel clearly contains, then, the essential tropes with which we have come to associate the "Extraordinary Journeys"—adventure with a pedagogical remit—but is perhaps painted on a less sweeping, less adventurous or ambitious canvas than the more famous novels by Jules Verne such as *Le Tour du monde en quatre-vingts jours* (*Around the World in Eighty Days,* 1873) or *Voyage au centre de la Terre* (*Journey to the Center of* the Earth, 1864). For all that, *Golden Danube* is nonetheless enjoyable and engaging to readers. It is thus a worthwhile addition to the Palik Series, from the point of view of its scholarly interest and its entertainment value to Verne aficionados of all ages.

In Michel's rewriting of this novel, after his father's death, under the title *The Danube Pilot,* the story was adapted into a much more conventional, serious, humorless suspense story (with the name of the central character being altered from Ilia Krusch to Ilia Brusch), and with, therefore, the trademark humor, satire and irony of Verne *père* being largely absent. *Golden Danube* by Jules Verne is essentially an adventure story liberally laced with humor, written in 1901, just four years before the writer's death, but posthumously published in 1908 under the title *The Danube Pilot*—having been almost completely rewritten by Michel Verne, son of Jules, but attributed by Michel and his publisher, Hetzel, to Verne *père*. Indeed, the original version had been almost entirely reworked beyond recognition, into a typical detective story, by Michel Verne, at the request of his publisher, with only the first chapter of *Golden Danube* and *The Danube Pilot* bearing a notable similarity to each other. But thanks to the discovery of the original manuscript of Jules Verne's *Golden Danube,* in 1978, the text in question was republished in French under its original title *Le Beau*

Michel (Jules) Verne" in Volker Dehs, Ralf Junkerjurgen, eds., *Jules Verne—Stimmen und Deutungen zu seinem Werk* (Wetzlar, Germany: Phantastische Bibliothek, 2005), 295-314.

Michel Verne's revision changed the title of *Golden Danube* to *The Danube Pilot*.

Danube Jaune (Version d'origine), and again in 1997, with a preface and notes by Olivier Dumas, then President of the Société Jules Verne.[3] Jean Jules-Verne commented, in his 1973 biography of his grandfather Jules Verne, that, as noted in the previous paragraph, *The Danube Pilot* did not contain a single trace of the mocking humor which was a characteristic of Verne's works, and was a dominant character trait of Jules Verne himself. Michel Verne had considerably increased the detective and crime dimensions of his father's original version, thus largely omitting many of Jules Verne's descriptions of local culture and history, landscapes, fish and fishing exploits, and local gastronomic delights. Michel also darkened the original version's trope of smuggling by adding murder and arms trafficking, together with disguises and dark glasses worn by the master criminals featured in the story. This added element of criminal disguise may have been influenced by the contemporary exploits of Arsène Lupin and other characters from detective novels published at that time, the early twentieth century.[4]

Michel Verne's reworking also changes the name of the central character to Ilia Brusch, who, similarly to Ilia Krusch in the original version, undertakes an epic fishing journey down the Danube, from its source to its mouth at the Black Sea, a journey of 3,000 kilometers. In Michel's version, Brusch's journey coincides not only with continued smuggling activities along the Danube, but also with a series of murders and burglaries. As in the original version, it is police chief Karl Dragoch who is entrusted with the task of bringing the perpetrators of these crimes to justice. Dragoch also sets out to solve the mystery of who this unusual and impassive Captain Brusch really is. It turns out that Ilia Brusch is really Serge Ladko, a Bulgarian patriot who has been forced to flee the Ottoman invasion. Ladko's wife Natcha has, unbeknownst to him, been kidnapped by his worst enemy, Yvan Striga. Striga is the villain of the piece, as it were; he is a river pirate, murderer and smuggler who bears fierce hatred for his arch-enemy Ladko, and strives to have him suspected of the crimes which he himself has committed. It thus requires all of the ingenuity and detective flair of Dragoch to bring Striga to justice and to not be misled by his evil machinations.

---

3. Jules Verne, *Le Beau Danube Jaune: Version d'origine* (Montreal: Les éditions internationales Alain Stanké, 1997).

4. Jean Jules-Verne, *Jules Verne* (Paris: Hachette, 1973).

Michel Verne

One of the themes of Michel's version is that of the struggle of a country for the right to self-determination and freedom from the colonial oppressor. In this regard, *The Danube Pilot* is reminiscent in theme of several novels by Jules Verne, including *P'tit Bonhomme* (*Foundling Mick*, 1893) which has as one of its central themes, the oppression of the Irish in the nineteenth century by the British colonial rulers. In the blurb on the inside jacket of the 1970 American publication of I.O. Evans's translation of *The Danube Pilot*, Michel Verne's narrative is described as "both a story of resistance and a thriller." The description goes on to explain that:

> In the period of the story much of the Balkans formed part of the Ottoman Empire, then a byword for tyranny, corruption and inefficiency. The hero is implicated in an impending revolt and is being sought by the Turkish government.
>
> He is also suspected of being the leader of a gang of criminals who are taking advantage of the political confusion to commit a series of crimes in the Danube valley. An international police-force has been formed to deal with them and is led by a detective of outstanding brilliance.
>
> So, who is the mysterious prize-winner [of the Danubian Line fishing contest]…? Can he be the resistance-leader, the master-criminal, or even the detective? Why does he disguise himself with dark glasses and dye his hair?[5]

It is in this way that I.O. Evans's translation of Michel's version summarizes the plot and sets the central puzzling question as to the identity of the mysterious prize winner of the fishing contest, a puzzle which is shared by both Jules's and Michel's versions.

Let us briefly examine, at this point, the premise of Jules Verne's undeservedly little-known *Golden Danube* (eclipsed, as it was, up to now, by the success of the son's retelling, falsely attributed to the father). Some may prefer not to read the following summary and discussion of its plot and themes, until they have first enjoyed the novel itself, as this synopsis and thematic analysis unavoidably contain certain "spoilers."

PLOT: CENTRALITY OF LOYAL MALE CHARACTERS, MYSTERY, ADVENTURE AND A PEDAGOGICAL REMIT

To write this novel, Jules Verne found inspiration in the account by Victor Duruy (1861-1862) of his travels along the Danube, an account entitled *De Paris à Bucharest*, published by the journal *Le Tour du Monde* between 1861 and 1862. The story opens one afternoon at a tavern

---

5.   Dust jacket flap for Jules Verne, *The Danube Pilot*, Translated by I. O. Evans (Bridgeport, CT: Associated Booksellers, 1970).

called *The Fisherman's Rest,* situated near the town of Sigmaringen, on the banks of the Danube, the great Central European River which forms the geographical, natural centerpiece to this entire novel; the tavern in question is, in fact, located close to the source of the Danube. A large and exceedingly merry group of fishermen is gathered together in the tavern, following a morning of intense competitive fishing, as part of a periodic fishing contest organized by the Danubian Line, described by Jules Verne as "an international Fishermen's Society, most of whom were of German, Austrian and Hungarian nationality" (Chapter I) The atmosphere prevailing amongst the assembled fishermen is one of raucous merrymaking, as increasingly copious amounts of alcohol are poured into their gullets, but is also, as Verne says, one of "keen excitement," for the assembled fishermen are waiting, with anxious anticipation, to hear the results of the competition in which they have just partaken.

The overall winner of the contest's two most prestigious prizes turns out to be a very modest and reserved, though highly skilled, fisherman, who is, moreover, completely unknown to the assembled professional throngs from the fishing world of Central Europe. This unknown winner is a middle-aged man (about fifty years of age) called Ilia Krusch, an enigmatic Vernian hero. Verne does indeed seem to have had a predilection for creating such puzzling, elusive, reserved and solitary central characters, including Phileas Fogg of *Around the World in Eighty Days*, Captain Nemo of *Vingt mille lieues sous les mers* (*Twenty Thousand Leagues Under the Seas*, 1870), or Professor Lidenbrock of *Journey to the Center of the Earth*, to name but three of Verne's most famous fictional heroes.[6]

In *Golden Danube*, following his sensational double victory at the fishing contest referred to above, Krusch proceeds to generate an increasing degree of curiosity amongst his fishing colleagues and the general populace over the following days and weeks. This curiosity reaches fever pitch when a rumor begins to circulate that Krusch is planning to sail alone down the entire length of the great River Danube, fishing as he goes. He is extremely uneasy and embarrassed by the level

---

6. Jules Verne co-authored a stage version of his hugely successful novel *Around the World in Eighty Days*, with Adolphe D'Ennery, containing additional characters and locales, and the translation of the play for its original Broadway presentation has been included in the Palik series volume, *Around the World in 80 Days—The 1874 Play* (Albany, GA: BearManor Fiction, 2013).

of public attention which he has begun to attract. Indeed, throughout his eventful journey along the majestic Central European river with its varying landscapes and the even more varied adventures which befall the central character, Krusch seems to do all in his power to avoid the crowds of admirers gathered along the riverbank at each of his stopovers at riverside villages, towns and cities, at which he moors his boat in order to sell his catch of fish at the end of each day. Krusch seems to be, essentially, an easygoing man, accustomed to living a quiet life in his home town in Hungary and to enjoy the peaceful activity of fly fishing; understandably, then, he is ill at ease when he finds himself at the center of so much attention.

In a plot development which echoes the mystery surrounding the departure of Phileas Fogg on his journey around the world in eighty days, Krusch's departure on his epic, much-publicized journey coincides with news that police forces across Central Europe are still striving unsuccessfully to apprehend and bring to justice a highly successful though elusive master smuggler, Latzko, aged between forty and forty-five, and his gang of smugglers, who have been operating very successfully along the Danube for the past few years, dealing in large amounts of valuable contraband. Just as Inspector Fix in *Around the World in Eighty Days* wondered whether Fogg was one and the same person as the mysterious bank robber who had carried off a major heist from the Bank of England, at almost exactly the same time as Fogg hastily left London, so too does Verne implicitly pose the question of the reader, as to whether Krusch and Latzko might be one and the same—however unlikely this seems, given Krusch's seemingly kind, sincere, unassuming, self-effacing and gentle nature.

A senior police figure, who happens to be a seasoned, highly capable and apparently fearless master detective, called Karl Dragoch, a Hungarian chief of police based in Pest and aged forty-five, is appointed by an international commission to lead an extensive investigation into this river-bound, Central European-wide smuggling operation.

Around the same time, a mysterious stranger who identifies himself as an Austrian called "Mr. Jaeger," suddenly and unexpectedly approaches Ilia Krusch at the riverside, just as the latter is about to set off one morning from his mooring point near the city of Ulm. This enigmatic Jaeger has an unusual proposition for Krusch—in exchange for five hundred florins, he asks to accompany Krusch throughout the rest of his journey down the Danube, and to be allowed to pocket each day's takings from the catches of fish sold by Krusch. The amount of money offered is extraordinarily generous and seems to be weighted in Krusch's financial favor—which begs the question as to who this Jaeger fellow is and what his true motives might be.

Themes of Uncertain Identity

Verne thus cleverly sets up a number of intriguing mysteries, all centered on the question of identity—might Jaeger really be Inspector Dragoch, using the vantage point of Krusch's boat to observe all of the river fleet along the Danube and thus finally capture his prey, the elusive smuggler Latzko? Might the apparently innocent Krusch—however improbable it may appear—actually be the smuggler Latzko? Or, in another possible interpretation of these mysterious events and characters, might Jaeger even be the criminal, Latzko?

In the following passage, for instance, from Chapter V, the reader begins to wonder whether Jaeger and Dragoch might not indeed be one and the same person, thanks to the subtle hints dropped by the narrator.

> Perhaps Ilia Krusch didn't notice the care with which his travelling companion was watching not alone the boats… but also the vehicles which travelled along the river banks. Another person, more observant, or less indifferent to anything which wasn't related to fishing, would certainly have noticed.

There is a key scene in Chapter VI in which Verne gives one of the strongest hints of the entire novel, that Jaeger may be actually Dragoch, and the reader also wonders at this point whether Jaeger/Dragoch suspects Krusch of being the smuggler Latzko. This scene takes place at the Steamship Hotel in Regensburg, where Jaeger is having lunch alone, while Krusch is elsewhere in the town selling his catch of fish.

> But though Mr. Jaeger ate with a hearty appetite [...] he did not at all involve himself in the conversation. However, he listened closely to what was being said, with the air of a man who seemed to be in the habit of lending an ear to

everything that was said around him. And, the comment which struck him most particularly, was when one of the diners said to the person seated beside him:

"So, this famous Latzko, there's no news of him?"

"No more news of him than there is of the famous Krusch," replied the other.

[...] "Unless Krusch and Latzko are one and the same..."

Upon hearing these exchanged remarks [...] Mr. Jaeger had swiftly raised his head.

Verne consistently hints that Jaeger is Dragoch and, indeed, Jaeger/ Dragoch is seen to continuously make cryptic remarks to Krusch, such as "...I'm not going to make a loss [on this journey], quite the contrary... and the price at which I've bought your catch will have doubled before we get to the mouth of the river!" (Chapter VI)

Similarly, Verne occasionally plays with the reader's parallel suspicion that Krusch might just be Latzko—as unlikely as this seems, we cannot but be a little curious about Krusch and his motives for making this journey down the Danube. For instance, take the following passage from Chapter VIII:

It goes without saying that Ilia Krusch's barge could not be under suspicion, and so, with a laugh, he would say:

"And what about me? Are they really sure that I'm not passing along smuggled goods, and that once I've collected them around Sigmaringen, I'm not transporting them to the mouth of the Danube?"

"Indeed—who knows?" Mr. Jaeger would riposte, in the same light-hearted tone.

Thus, Verne—possibly in the guise of the unreliable narrator, as commented on by William Butcher, in his discussions of other Verne novels—confronts the reader with all sorts of puzzles as to the true identity of the principal characters: is Krusch really Latzko? Is Jaeger really Dragoch, or might he even be Latzko?[7]

---

7. See, for example, Butcher's *Verne's Journey to the Centre of the Self: Space and Time in the "Voyages Extraordinaires"* (London: Macmillan, 1990) and *Jules*

Indeed, when Krusch and Jaeger/Dragoch are forcibly brought on board the strange ship towards the end of the novel, we are still not absolutely certain that this mysterious, curt, violent skipper and his crew are definitely Latzko and his smuggling ring, despite the strong likelihood that this is the case... Verne thus successfully maintains the suspense, right up to the closing pages of the novel.

The enigmatic character of Ilia Krusch, who echoes the similarly impenetrable character of Phileas Fogg, is equally reminiscent of Fogg in his meticulousness, and in his certainty of a successful outcome to the journey he has embarked upon. Neither Krusch nor Fogg can countenance the likelihood of any unforeseen obstacles occurring to disrupt the smooth and timely completion of their challenging journey.

> By travelling at a rate of one league per hour, and by covering a distance of approximately ten leagues between sunrise and sunset, he hoped to arrive at his journey's end within two months, provided that he was not stopped along the way by any incident or accident. And indeed, why should he experience any delays? Would the navigation not be easier on the return journey than on the outward one? (Chapter IV)

PEDAGOGICAL FUNCTIONS IN *GOLDEN DANUBE*

As Krusch's barge, containing the two travelling companions Krusch and Jaeger, proceeds down the Danube, with Krusch catching copious amounts of fish and selling them at the various towns, villages and cities along the great river, Jules Verne takes every opportunity to offer detailed descriptions of the history, economic activities, culture and physical appearance of the various hamlets, villages, towns and cities situated along Krusch's river-bound route. At the same time, Verne describes the diversity of types of fish which populate the waters of the Danube and which are caught, always in large quantities, by master fisherman Krusch; he simultaneously describes the various landscapes passed through. Verne also provides detailed technical

---

Verne: The Definitive Biography (New York: Thunder's Mouth, 2006), for detailed analysis of Verne's themes and stylistic devices throughout his corpus of work.

Michel's revision added to the melodrama.

descriptions of the various types of fishing tackle and boats to be found among the Danube's river fleet. Thus, *Golden Danube* can be seen as characteristically Vernian in its themes and ambitions, combining as it does various pedagogical aims with a tale of adventure and mystery.

THE RELATIONSHIP BETWEEN THE TWO CENTRAL (MALE) CHARACTERS

The two travelling companions, Krusch and Jaeger/Dragoch, become increasingly bonded to each other as a close friendship develops between them over the course of their shared fishing trip along the River Danube, with Krusch feeling increasing admiration for, and loyalty to, his mysterious fellow traveller Jaeger. This male pairing is also essentially Vernian, echoing the loyalty felt by Passepartout for Fogg in *Around the World in Eighty Days*, or by Conseil for Arronax in *Twenty Thousand Leagues Under the Seas*, as well as the similar strong bonds between the central male characters in almost all of the novels within the canon of "Extraordinary Journeys."[8] Thus, Krusch is extremely disconcerted and baffled when Jaeger suddenly disappears during one of their stopovers at a Danube port, leaving him only a short note which does not explain why he has had to absent himself so abruptly.

The third-person, omniscient narrator then switches the scene of the action, with equal abruptness, to a meeting of Latzko and his gang of smugglers in the woods near the Lower Carpathians, which ends in a bloody skirmish between the police forces, led by Dragoch, and the smugglers, with Latzko once again evading capture. This incident considerably heightens the mystery and tension of the plot. It seems to make it even more likely that Jaeger is actually Karl Dragoch, the chief of police, as Jaeger is conspicuously absent from Krusch's barge at the same time that this encounter takes place between the smuggling ring and the forces of law and order; but might it not be equally possible that Jaeger is really Latzko, the chief smuggler? Verne thus skilfully builds up the suspense and uncertainty, being the consummate storyteller and weaver of mystery that he is.

Around this time, Krusch is arrested on suspicion of being Latzko, but is later released when the international commission judging him

---

8. Jules Verne, *Twenty Thousand Leagues Under the Seas*, Translated by William Butcher (Oxford: Oxford University Press, 1992).

receives excellent reports of his character from his native city of Racz. As he languishes in prison, a baffled Krusch wonders where his travelling companion Jaeger might be, and wonders if Jaeger might be in some way implicated in the smuggling operations, or whether he might even be Latzko (a question which, as we have already seen, Verne has also planted in the reader's mind) but such is the strength of Krusch's loyalty to and trust in Jaeger that he immediately dismisses his fears as groundless. He does, however, hope that Jaeger is safe and that he may appear to vouch for the integrity of Krusch, though this does not happen.

Krusch continues his journey following his release from prison, and is unexpectedly reunited, much to his joy, with the mysterious Jaeger. However, as their barge progresses ever closer to its ultimate destination at the mouth of the Danube, where the great river meets the Black Sea, the two fellow travellers are suddenly kidnapped by a group of sailors whom we presume to be the ruthless, violent smugglers, and brought on board their ship, where they are held prisoner below deck, another typically Vernian trope (as, for example, in the novel *Face au Drapeau* [*Facing the Flag*, 1896] or even in *Twenty Thousand Leagues Under the Seas*, in which a group of central characters are forcibly held on sailing vessels at the pleasure of a mysterious captain). The reason for this abduction is that Krusch's skills as a river pilot are urgently needed by the smugglers in order to steer a course along the Danube—as they try to transfer their contraband to a waiting ship on the Black Sea—because their own pilot has been swept away by the current, one night, during a heavy storm.

Once again, Jaeger disappears, this time from his water-bound prison, again leaving Krusch bereft and baffled. However, in the novel's final *coup de théâtre*, Ilia Krusch heroically uses his piloting skills to ensure that the smugglers' ship is captured by Dragoch's police officers, who—led by Dragoch, who does indeed turn out, in the final analysis, to be one and the same person as Jaeger—finally succeed in apprehending the notorious Latzko and his henchmen.

In the conclusion to the story, we are informed that Krusch and Dragoch/Jaeger remain the best of friends, as Krusch retires back to his native town in Hungary and enjoys the tranquil existence, centerd round his beloved pursuit of fishing, to which he had always been accustomed.

SYMBOLISM IN *GOLDEN DANUBE*

Olivier Dumas, in his Preface to the 1997 French language edition of *Golden Danube,* comments on the symbolism which he interprets within this novel written towards the end of Verne's life. The journey down the Danube is seen by Dumas as symbolizing Verne's final journey through the declining years of his life, as he calmly approaches and confronts his inevitable mortality, enjoying one final retrospective contemplation of the various images which have featured so much in his own life, travels and fictional works. According to Dumas, in the following quotation, Jaeger may be the alter ego of Jules Verne himself.

> All of these rivers which are travelled down in the final works, are not devoid of significance.… In all the posthumously published novels, rivers flow… in *Golden Danube,* the complete descent of the Danube… the final mouth, Kilia, which lends its name to the hero: Ilia K. from K/ilia. Rivers, symbols of life, which, in the case of the Danube, ends up at the Black Sea, the color of death. Throughout this descent, a spectator, a "voyeur," devours this spectacle with his eyes. This passive character, Mr. Jaeger, is this not the writer himself who, before his death, is building up his final visions, as a sort of "hunter of images" (*Jaeger,* "hunter" in German)?… After the Amazon and the Orinoco, this peaceful descent of the Danube enables the author to gaze upon the beautiful Hungarian landscapes, to drink and to smoke his pipe in the boat of the most tranquil of his characters, open to friendship, without any ulterior motives or ambitions, in short, a perfect, honest man, a Voltairian philosopher, such as Jules Verne takes pleasure in describing.[9]

HOMOEROTIC *INSINUENDO* WITHIN *GOLDEN DANUBE*

Throughout this little-known Verne novel, there are several telling references to the relationship between the two principal characters who are journeying down the Golden Danube together and seemingly

9. My translation from Dumas, "Pêche dans les eaux du *Beau Danube Jaune,*" in Verne, Jules, *Le Beau Danube Jaune*: Version d'origine, 14-15.

enjoying each other's company. I have isolated a number of salient quotations from the novel in order to draw the reader's attention to incidents in which Jules Verne appears to be hinting at the possibility of unusually strong male bonding between the two principal characters of this story, and, in particular, pointing to Ilia Krusch's increasingly strong affection for, and attachment to, his mysterious fellow traveller, Mr. Jaeger. Some of the following quotations also refer to affectionate physical contact and unusual physical proximity between the two central protagonists (e.g. sleeping side by side in the barge).

Verne scholars and biographers, including Marcel Moré, Herbert Lottman and William Butcher have, in the past, referred to possible homosexual and/or bisexual aspects of Verne's life, and, in Butcher's case, have conducted research into homoerotic undertones and homosexual references appearing throughout some of the novels contained within the "Extraordinary Journeys."[10] In my 2009 article on Butcher's "Queer Studies readings" of Verne's *Around the World in Eighty Days*, I note in the abstract to the article that

> The translator Butcher has reinterpreted *Around the World in Eighty Days* in the context of its author Jules Verne's life history, original manuscripts of the French novel in question [...] and textual clues themselves. Butcher's Queer Studies readings have had an important influence on his translation decisions. Examples of his translation solutions throughout this Verne novel are discussed, and are seen to purposively accentuate perceived sexual and sometimes specifically gay subtexts.[11]

---

10. Moré, *Nouvelles explorations de Jules Verne* (Paris, Gallimard, 1963); Moré, *Le très curieux Jules Verne* (Paris, Gallimard, 1963); Lottman, *Jules Verne* (Paris: Flammarion, 1996); Butcher, *Jules Verne: The Definitive Biography*; Butcher, *Verne's Journey to the Centre of the Self: Space and Time in the "Voyages Extraordinaires"*; Jules Verne, *Around the World in Eighty Days*, Translated by William Butcher (Oxford; New York: Oxford University Press, 1995).

11. Kieran O'Driscoll, "Around the World in Eighty Gays: Retranslating Jules Verne from a Queer Perspective," in Dries De Crom, ed., *Translation and the (Trans)formation of Identities. Selected Papers of the CETRA Research Seminar in Translation Studies 2008* (Catholic University of Leuven, Belgium, 2009), 1. http://www.kuleuven.be/cetra/papers/papers.html.

It should also be noted that Verne's publisher, in seeking a family audience, deliberately minimized the portrayal of romantic attachments between men and women. As a result, Verne was sometimes criticized for the secondary roles women typically played in his stories, and he was writing at a time when the opportunities for women were vastly more limited in an adventurous story. Verne's strong focus on almost exclusively male characters throughout many of his novels was typical of adventure stories of the late nineteenth century, and the introduction of female characters in his stories usually took place in a context in which the women in question were older and safely asexual, as it were (e.g. the character of Mrs Barnett in *Le Pays des fourrures* [*The Fur Country*, 1873]) or safely subsumed within the creation of a standard couple (e.g. Mary Grant and Captain Mangles in *Les Enfants du Capitaine Grant* [*The Children of Captain Grant*, 1867]).

Even taking this into account, however, it does seem that the partnership that develops in *Golden Danube* takes the standard male relationship one step further than usual; for instance, whereas in Michel Verne's *The Danube Pilot*, Brush is married and younger than Ilia Krusch's fifty years, Ilia Krusch and Mr. Jaeger/Karl Dragoch in *Golden Danube* are both confirmed bachelors. This seems to make the affection between both men, throughout *Golden Danube*, even more striking to the reader. Indeed, in other Verne novels which I have studied in recent years, including *Cinq Semaines en Ballon* (*Five Weeks in a Balloon*, 1862), *Michel Strogoff* (*Michael Strogoff*, 1876), *Hector Servadac* (1877); *Les Tribulations d'un Chinois en Chine* (*The Tribulations of a Chinese in China*, 1879), and *Le Chateau des Carpathes* (*The Castle in the Carpathians*, 1892), I have noted unusual instances of strong male bonding as well as apparaently homoerotic references, similar to the following allusions taken from the present novel, *Golden Danube.*

Despite their deepening friendship, Krusch and Jaeger remain invariably formal and polite to one another, as evidenced in how they address each other, throughout this novel, a form of address which adds to the humorous tone of this narrative.

"See you tomorrow morning then, Mr. Krusch," said Mr. Jaeger.

"Early," replied Ilia Krusch, "for we leave at dawn…"

"Weather permitting…"

"It'll permit our departure, Mr. Jaeger! Believe me…"
(Chapter V)

The following extracts reveal the homoerotic feelings of affection, felt by Ilia Krusch for his enigmatic travelling companion (an admiration which is sometimes seen to be reciprocated by Jaeger/Dragoch).

> But at a certain moment, it so happened that a hand was placed on his shoulder, and he heard somebody calling out to him in the following manner:
> "Well, Mr. Jaeger, it has to be believed that all this is of interest to you…"
> Mr. Jaeger turned round, and saw Ilia Krusch standing in front of him watching him with a smile. (Chapter VI)

> Mr. Jaeger and Ilia Krusch were enjoying a relaxed supper at the back of the barge. Then, having finished this meal, they stretched out near to each other within the tarpaulin shelter. (Chapter IV)

> [Ilia Krusch] would have been very upset if Mr. Jaeger had entered into an unprofitable deal, and all the more so because, since they had begun sharing this common existence, Ilia Krusch, with his good and sensitive nature, had been feeling strong friendship for his companion, who did not fail to notice this. (Chapter VII)

> The two friends—they can safely be described as such, as certainly from Ilia Krusch's point of view, this was now a serious friendship—the two friends, were they not due to meet up with each other again later on, to resume, together, this navigation? Was Mr. Jaeger's absence only a temporary one? (Chapter IX)

> "And where might he be now?" thought Ilia Krusch to himself as he ate. […] I'm very much afraid that I'll still be on my own having supper this evening! He's most definitely an excellent travelling companion, this Mr. Jaeger, and

I have no regrets whatsoever about having accepted his offer! [...] Mr. Jaeger's company is most pleasant..." [...] Ilia Krusch's thoughts were running along these lines, he who had taken such a strong liking to Jaeger. (Chapter X)

There are interesting sights to be seen when sailing along this stretch of the river, but how much more enjoyable it would have seemed, had Mr. Jaeger been occupying his usual place on the barge. (Chapter XI)

He dreamed [...] of Mr. Jaeger who, in his dream, had come back to the boat to rejoin him, and the two friends peacefully continued journeying downriver. But as soon as he woke up, he had to face facts and become rapidly disenchanted from his reverie, and cold, harsh reality reappeared in all the horror of its ugly head. (Chapter XII)

Darkness fell, and with that, sleep came [...] Krusch's dreams were not such happy ones this time round, and, this time, Mr. Jaeger was no longer in the barge with him. (Chapter XII)

And then, memories of Mr. Jaeger began to return to his mind. He continued to experience a feeling of self-congratulation at never having uttered the name of his companion. [...]... not once did it occur to this fine fellow, Krusch, that Mr. Jaeger could have been Latzko, not once! Such an excellent man as Jaeger, a friend whose friendship he appreciated so much! He, the head of that smuggling ring! Come on, now!

"And as soon as I meet up with him again," Ilia Krusch would say to himself, "because I truly do hope to see him again, I'll tell him all about this, and he shall thank me, and shout: 'Mr. Krusch, you are the finest man I've ever met on this earth!'" (Chapter XIII)

[Krusch] hadn't even baited his fishing hook that morning, so possessed was he by the desire to locate, and be reunited with, his dear companion. And so here he was, wandering through the streets, travelling through the various neighbourhoods, and, should he have to devote the entire morning to his investigations, he wouldn't hesitate to do so. (Chapter XIII)

Just at the moment when [...] Ilia Krusch was about to disembark, a man suddenly clapped a hand on his shoulder in a friendly manner. It was Mr. Jaeger.

"So, how's it going, Mr. Krusch?" he asked.

"Not bad... and you?"

This was all that Ilia Krusch—as stunned as he was satisfied, at the sight of his former travelling companion—could think of to say in reply!

Mr. Jaeger and Ilia Krusch hadn't seen each other since they had become parted from each other in Vienna on May 20th, that is, for a total of thirty-one days. [...] The important thing now was that both men were going to resume their navigation of the Danube, together.

Ilia Krusch's first question had been: "When are we leaving?" (Chapter XIII)

"I shall follow your orders to the letter, Mr. Jaeger." [...] Ilia Krusch didn't even notice his friend's demeanour; he could see only one thing, and that was, that Mr. Jaeger had been "given back" to him and that he [Jaeger] asked nothing more than to set off again. (Chapter XIII)

"Ah, Mr. Jaeger," exclaimed Ilia Krusch, taking both his companion's hands in his, "how long they seemed to me, those days without you! In every town or village I came to, I kept hoping to meet up with you again... and each time, nobody! I feared that you might have come to some harm..." (Chapter XIII)

"So, the time isn't dragging too much for you, then?"

"Oh, Mr. Krusch, in your company... in your company!..."

And the good man felt deeply moved by this response. Without a doubt, he would be able to push this friendship he felt towards Mr. Jaeger, to the point of devotion, should the opportunity to do so ever present itself! (Chapter XIII)

And Mr. Jaeger-Dragoch, kissing [Krusch] on both cheeks, cried out:
    "Ah! The good man! The good man!" (Chapter XVI)

It can be seen, in passages such as the foregoing ones, which span the entire novel, that the hero, Ilia Krusch, has a marked attachment and characteristically Vernian loyalty and devotion to Jaeger/Dragoch, which is reciprocated. It should also be noted that, in my translation of the foregoing segments, I have simply provided an imitative and accurate rendering into English of Verne's French words; I have not attempted to "impose" extra words or debatable meaning into the foregoing segments.

HUMOR AND OTHER NOTABLE THEMES WITHIN *GOLDEN DANUBE*

Verne scholars such as Laurent Sudret have written extensively about the admiration which Verne felt for the writings of his British nineteenth-century fellow novelist, Charles Dickens, and about the thematic similarities between some of the works of Verne and those of Dickens.[12] One of those similarities is, of course, the humor—especially the satire and irony—employed by both writers. In this section of the foreword, I wish to discuss certain examples of Verne's humor in this novel, humor being a stylistic device which features prominently throughout *Golden Danube*.

One commentator refers generally to the humor which runs consistently throughout the story, in the following manner:

In order to speak about *Golden Danube*, one must completely forget about the former narrative of *The Danube Pilot*, because the dark detective novel written by

---

12. Laurent Sudret, "P'tit Bonhomme, l'hommage de Verne à Dickens," *Bulletin de la Société Jules Verne*, Vol. 13, no. 1 (2007), 1-13.

the writer (Jules Verne)'s son (Michel Verne) quickly loses any possible connection with the ironic work written by his father. Ever present, the humor of *Golden Danube* is what gives it its force and modernity. This humor operates on two levels: the satire of line fishing—that noble sport— and the permanent, naïve affability of the good Krusch.[13]

From the very first page of this novel, Verne's tone is laden with satire and irony, setting the scene for the light, humorous tone which is to feature throughout most of this story. The opening paragraphs describe the mildly raucous and highly celebratory, alcohol-fuelled deliberations of the Danubian Line, a fishermen's professional association, following that morning's fishing contest. Verne here takes the opportunity of gently lampooning the characters, self-congratulatory nature, and actions of the fly fishermen.

> In this tavern, fishermen would drink full tankards of fine beer from Munich and full glasses of quality Hungarian wines. And during these sessions, the main room of the tavern would seem to disappear in the midst of the fumes of pungent tobacco smoke which curled in a continuous stream from the long pipes of the drinkers. And if the members of the Society could no longer even catch a glimpse of each other through the thick smoke, they could at least still hear one another; and how indeed could they not hear each other, unless they had been deaf! (Chapter I)

Continuing, at the outset of the novel, Verne goes on to say that,

> ...while fly fishermen are generally calm and silent when engaged in their activity of predilection, they are the noisiest people in the world when they are not immersed in their professional occupation, and when it comes to recounting their great exploits, they are as vocal as hunters, which is indeed saying something! (Chapter I)

---

13. My translation of the article "Le Beau Danube" Jaune on www.wikipedia.fr, (Accessed 5th June 2013).

The town of Racz, which figures in *Golden Danube*, also appeared in Verne's *Le Secret de Wilhelm Storitz* [*The Secret of Wilhelm Storitz*, 1910].

The competitors at this fishing contest are then described by the narrator as "knights of the fishing line, passionate zealots of the bait, fanatics of the fishing hook" whose "gullets had become remarkably parched during the exertions of that fine April morning." (Chapter I) The language appears to be deliberately bombastic, overblown and grandiose in a mocking way, and thus reminiscent of Dickensian style, in this and many other similar passages throughout this novel. Original, humorous metaphors are here used to describe and gently lampoon the fishermen.

When the President of the Danubian Line makes a speech at the prize-giving ceremony in the tavern, he "place[s] the line fisherman in the front ranks of humanity... [and he adds that when a fish has been caught, it is often seen to be] wriggling, and, so to speak, [itself] applauding the fisherman's victory..." (Chapter I) When Verne describes the deliberations of the International Commission, in Chapter III, the reader encounters a similar satirical depiction of political and administrative figures of authority, as we have found elsewhere in Verne's writing, including *Fact-Finding Mission*.[14] In the following extract, it is the unfailing diplomacy of the Commissioners which is satirized.

> M. Roth hastened to reply to him that this assertion was based only on rather uncertain information and that in any event, if this gang leader's name was Latzko, and if this gang leader should turn out to be a Serb, that could not in any shape or form undermine the honor of a country which counts among its dynastical leaders, people such as Stephen, Brancovitch, Czerin and Obrenovitch! M. Ouroch appeared satisfied with this response, as would have been, in a similar situation, the German, Austrian, Hungarian, Valachian and other representatives, for whom chairman Roth would have only needed to alter the names cited in his reply. (Chapter III)

Verne also satirizes national pride and cross-national rivalries among the citizens of the various Central European countries depicted in this novel. Even the hero, Ilia Krusch, is not safe from Verne's gentle

---

14. I have translated *Fact-Finding Mission* in the Palik series volume, *Vice, Redemption and the Distant Colony: Stories by Jules Verne and Michel Verne* (Albany, GA: Bear Manor Fiction, 2012).

lampooning: "In the purity of his primeval national pride, Mr. Ilia Krusch couldn't have brought himself to countenance the possibility that this wrongdoer [Latzko] might be one of his fellow countrymen [i.e. a fellow Hungarian national]." (Chapter VII)

There is also a suggestion that the good-natured Krusch may not be the most perceptive of individuals. Indeed, Dumas points out that the surname Krusch is probably a play on the French word "cruche" which, when used to refer to a person, can be translated as "ass," "idiot," "twit" or "ninny."[15] This humorous naming of characters according to their traits is another stylistic feature which Jules Verne shares with Charles Dickens, as Laurent Sudret has pointed out.[16] Is Ilia Krusch so blinded by his loyalty to, and fondness for, his mysterious travelling companion Mr. Jaeger, that it never once occurs to him that perhaps Jaeger might be Dragoch (though Krusch does eventually, briefly, wonder whether Jaeger might be Latzko)? "'Ah!' thought Ilia Krusch, 'that's a piece of news that would have been distressing for Mr. Jaeger to hear! When we spoke about Dragoch, he seemed to take a keen interest in that police chief.'" (Chapter X)

As noted in this introduction's earlier discussion of the plot of this novel, Ilia Krusch is consistently portrayed as naïve and accepting, to the extent that it becomes somewhat difficult to imagine this unlikely hero surviving in tough waterfront areas without, for example, being robbed or having his boat taken. How might he have fared if he had not been mostly accompanied along the Danube by Jaeger/Dragoch? On the other hand, Krusch becomes an unlikely and unexpected hero towards the end of the novel, when he single-handedly ensures that the smugglers are brought to justice, at the risk of his own life. One commentator on *Le Beau Danube Jaune* suggests that Ilia Krusch is a wonderful comic character as well as being a most likeable fellow (and, in this regard, Krusch is reminiscent of Passepartout in *Around the World in Eighty Days*).

> The good fisherman, naive and likeable, is a wonderful
> character. He really doesn't have a clue about anything at all;
> he doesn't realize who Mr. Jaeger is, [and] he understands
> nothing about his arrest, any more than he understands that

---

15. Dumas, "Pêche dans les eaux du *Beau Danube Jaune*," in Jules Verne, *Le Beau Danube Jaune*: Version d'origine.

16. Sudret, "P'tit Bonhomme, l'hommage de Verne à Dickens."

he's dealing with Latzko, until he is actually told! All of his touching naivety provides an amusing contrast with the virtues which are attributed to him; but ultimately, the mouse roars [...] and brings about the capture of the bandit![17]

Apart from Ilia Krusch, Verne seems to satirize line fishermen in general as being rather foolish, ridiculous characters. Dumas refers to this aspect of *Golden Danube*: "...when the author states that the fisherman's rod 'is a tool which sometimes has a silly creature at one end and always a silly creature at the other,' this is probably what he thinks, though he states the opposite."[18]

Verne also mocks the fickleness of the general public; when Krusch is arrested on suspicion of being Latzko, the former high esteem in which the fishing champion has been held all along the banks of the Danube, by virtue of his success at the fishing contest and his current unusual journey, quickly becomes transformed into hatred.

What most astonished [Ilia Krusch] were the feelings of the general public as he passed along [under police escort, having been arrested], manifestly hostile sentiments, shouts, threats, looks of indignation and horror.

"That's him!" shouted one enraged onlooker, abusively.

"He truly looks the part!" screamed another.

"What a bad face!"

"But at least they've finally got their man and they won't be letting him go!"

A number of shrewish women, fishwives—they are everywhere, even in Pest—would come over to shove their fists under his nose.

[...] the noisy, hostile escort could only grow bigger in number as it made its way onwards. (Chapter XII)

---

17. My translation of the article entitled "Le Beau Danube Jaune" on www.wikipedia. fr (Accessed 5th June 2013).

18. My translation from Dumas, "Pêche dans les eaux du *Beau Danube Jaune*," in Verne, Jules, *Le Beau Danube Jaune: Version d'origine*. For a revealing and amusing article on Verne's attitude toward the fishing by his sailors aboard his yacht, see "Hoodooed Fish," *The Youth's Companion*, 79 (August 17, 1905), 387.

Golden Danube ends with a humorous "rhetorical" question, when the narrator of Krusch's epic and incident-laden navigation ironically asks: "And after hearing this story, who would now dare to ever make fun of that wise, prudent and philosophical man that, in every era and in every country, is the line fisherman?" (Chapter XVI)   A similar final line in *Around the World in Eighty Days* asks, "Truly, would you not, for less than that, make the tour of the world?"[19]

THEMES OF OBSESSIVE-COMPULSIVE RUMINATIONS

In other Verne novels, such as *Around the World in Eighty Days,* some scholars have commented on apparent themes of psychological distress and obsessive-compulsive ruminations suffered by certain characters, such as the often tormented Detective Fix, obsessively dogged in his pursuit of Phileas Fogg. Fix's name may have been chosen by Verne to allude to the character's *idées fixes*.[20] Similarly, in *Golden Danube,* Verne affords the reader an insight into Krusch's horrendous anxiety as he waits, in his prison cell, to learn his fate.

> [Krusch]… the poor man… remained overwhelmed, crushed. A thousand terrors tormented his brain, his eyes no longer saw anything, his ears no longer heard anything, his powers of reason were dimming so that he ultimately came to wondering: "Could I, perchance, be Latzko; might I no longer be Ilia Krusch?" But he finally came out of his stupor… (Chapter X)

A further allusion by Verne to Krusch's possible obsessive-compulsive thoughts occurs as Krusch reflects on his ordeal after he has been found innocent and freed from prison.

> "…how close I came to being hanged instead of [Latzko]!"
> [He] continue[d] to sink ever-deeper into the quicksands of his distressing ruminations… (Chapter XI)

---

19. Jules Verne, *Tour of the World in Eighty Days*, Translated by Stephen W. White (New York: Belford, Clarke and Co., 1873).

20. Jules Verne, *Around the World in Eighty Days*, Translated by William Butcher.

Golden Danube, in its closing paragraphs, with its references to the penal colony to which Latzko and his fellow smugglers are sent, echoes *Pierre-Jean* and *The Sombre Fate of Jean Morénas*—another pair of stories authored by Jules, and rewritten by his son, respectively.[21]

TRANSLATIONAL LANGUAGE IN *THE DANUBE PILOT* AND *GOLDEN DANUBE*:
A Brief Contrast Between the English Target Language Usage in Both Target Texts

In my 2011 monograph, *Retranslation Through the Centuries: Jules Verne in English*, the style of various different individual translators of Verne from French into English, over a period of more than 130 years, is analyzed, together with their varying approaches to translation in terms of accuracy, simplification, explicitation, naturalness of target language use, and so on.[22] Given that the first chapter of the French source texts of *Golden Danube* and *The Danube Pilot* are very similar in content, I will briefly examine the use of English target language in the same chaper of both target texts, the one produced by I.O. Evans, and the other by myself in this present volume. Evans translated Michel Verne's *The Danube Pilot* in the 1960s, whereas I have translated Jules Verne's original version, in 2012-2013.

Idrisyn Oliver Evans (1894-1977) was an essential figure in bringing renewed attention to Verne during the 1950s and 1960s, and whose contributions have just begun to receive the attention they deserve.[23] In addition to compiling a Verne anthology, and writing a critical study, Evans edited the "Fitzroy edition" that returned to print no less than thirty-six Verne books. In addition, Evans translated nine Verne novels for the first time into English, although he was unaware, given what was known at the time, that many of these were the texts that Michel had rewritten from his father's originals, or even that Michel originated.[24]

---

21. I have translated these stories in the Palik series volume, *Vice, Redemption, and the Distant Colony* (Albany, GA: BearManor Fiction, 2012).

22. Kieran O'Driscoll, *Retranslation Through the Centuries: Jules Verne in English* (Oxford: Peter Lang Ltd., 2011).

23. Brian Taves, "'Verne's Best Friend and his Worst Enemy': I.O. Evans and the Fitzroy Edition of Jules Verne," *Verniana*, 4 (2011-2012), 25-54.

24. These titles were *The Village in the Treetops, The Sea Serpent, A Drama in*

Evans faced significant commercial pressures, having to issue books of a uniform size, intended to reach a mass market, rather than a scholarly one. Given the paucity of analysis to date of Evans's specific translating techniques, particularly using the apparatus of translation studies, this publication of *Golden Danube* offers an appropriate opportunity for some examples of his technique.

The following examples would appear to indicate that I.O. Evans's rendering is accurate and couched in natural target language, but that Evans also favors, at times, slight reduction, concision and simplification, occasionally, therefore, abbreviating some of the source language expression, but scrupulously preserving global accuracy in his rendering of the original French. This makes for a reliable and readable English translation. My own translation, on the other hand, tends to opt for more imitative target language, and rather than seeking to reduce or simplify, generally tends towards completeness and explicitation; this also makes for a reliable (accurate) though, of necessity, wordier rendering.

> Les fenêtres de ce cabaret s'ouvraient sur la rive gauche du Danube à l'extrémité de la charmante petite ville de Sigmaringen [...] située presque à l'origine de ce grand fleuve de l'Europe centrale.

Here is Evans's translation:

> The windows opened on to the Danube, where the pleasant little town of Sigmaringen almost dominates its source.

And my own:

> The windows of this tavern opened out onto the left bank of the Danube, at the edge of the charming little town of Sigmaringen [...] a town which is situated close to the source of this great Central European river.

Livonia, and the posthumously-published, Michel-inflected volumes, *The Golden Volcano*, *The Thompson Travel Agency*, *The Danube Pilot*, *The Survivors of the Jonathan*, *The Secret of Wilhelm Storitz*, and *The Astonishing Adventure of the Barsac Mission*.

The following examples of further coupled pairs of source language segments and their corresponding target text segments by Evans and myself, respectively, offer further support for my contention that Evans, in his approach to translating Verne, tends to be non-imitative and concise, to reduce and simplify, while my own translation approach tends rather to be complete, more imitative of source language and syntax, and, at times, it displays expansion and explicitation to ensure optimal clarity for the reader, which, together with simplification, are types of translation shifts which are often regarded by translation theorists as possible "universals" of translation.[25]

> Ce jour-là, 25 avril—une vive animation qui se traduisait par les chants, les hochs, les applaudissements, et le choc des verres, remplissait le cabaret à l'enseigne du *Rendez-vous des Pêcheurs*.

> On 5th August 1876 a large noisy crowd was gathered in *The Angler's Rest*. Songs, shouts, the clatter of glasses, all combined to produce a terrible din, regularly punctuated by the loud "Hochs!" which express the summit of Teutonic joy. (Evans)

> That day, the 25th April, the tavern known as *The Fisherman's Rest* was filled with a sense of keen excitement, which manifested itself in singing, spluttering, bursts of applause and the clinking of glasses. (O'Driscoll)

It can be seen from the foregoing coupled pair that Evans reduces and simplifies the original French expression, while still conveying its global meaning; he also alters the syntax of the original (as do I to a lesser extent), and even inscribes his target text with some embellishment as in "which express the summit of Teutonic joy." At the same time, Evans shows his tendency to reduce and to prefer concision, in his omission of "which manifested itself in." Both translators have differing individual styles, and thus different strategies for conveying the same

---

25. See, for example, Mona Baker's 1992 monograph *In Other Words: A Coursebook on Translation*, published by Routledge, first in 1992 and in a second edition in 2011, a classic in its field which discusses translation shift types in detail.

source text meaning, and this stylistic individual difference extends to differing choices of synonyms, e.g. Evans renders "une vive animation" as "a terrible din," whereas I choose "keen excitement."

Let us now consider a further coupled pair.

> Il convient d'observer que si les pêcheurs à la ligne sont calmes, silencieux alors qu'ils fonctionnent, ce sont les gens les plus bruyants du monde en dehors de leurs fonctions, et lorsqu'il s'agit de raconter leurs hauts faits, ils valent les chasseurs, ce qui n'est pas peu dire. .

> Calm and silent while performing their functions, anglers become the noisiest people in the world when they put their tackle away. In describing their prowess, they even rival the hunters, and that's saying a great deal. (Evans)

> It is appropriate to point out that, while fly fishermen are generally calm and silent when engaged in their activity of predilection, they are the noisiest people in the world when they are not immersed in their professional occupation, and when it comes to recounting their great exploits, they are as vocal as hunters, which is indeed saying something! (O'Driscoll)

In the foregoing example, by being more imitative of Verne's original language, syntax and style, I perhaps succeed in preserving more of his ironic humor, this being a strong characteristic of *Golden Danube*. Evans again illustrates his tendency towards some concision and omission, by eliding the phrase "It is appropriate to point out that;" he also inscribes his rendering with his own individual style and personal choice of target language synonyms, in his use of such words and phrases as "performing their functions," "when they put their tackle away" and "describing their prowess." I show alternative self-inscription in my version, through alternative choice of synonymy as in "they are as vocal as hunters" and "which is indeed saying something;" I also display some embellishment, to reinforce the irony of the source text, in my choice of "immersed in their professional occupation" or "their activity of predilection."

Here is a further coupled pair to consider:

On était à la fin d'un déjeuner des plus substantiels, qui avait rassemblé une centaine de convives autour de la table du cabaret. Tous des chevaliers de la ligne, des enragés de la flotte, des fanatiques de l'hameçon.

After a substantial lunch, a hundred or so were gathered around the tables, all of them knights of the rod, *dévotees* of the float, fanatics of the fish-hook. (Evans)

...the assembled fishermen had come to the end of a most substantial lunch, which had brought together approximately one hundred guests around the tavern table; all were knights of the fishing line, passionate zealots of the bait, fanatics of the fishing hook! (O'Driscoll)

In the foregoing coupled pair, Evans arguably loses some of Jules Verne's humor in normalizing Verne's description of the fishermen as "des enragés de la flotte," reducing it to simply "*dévotees* of the float" (I have preferred the term "passionate zealots" to try to more closely convey the ironic sense of "enragé"). In addition, I opt for a more source language-oriented, imitative translation, exemplified here in my use of "which had brought together approximately one hundred guests around the tavern table."

Set out hereunder is one final coupled pair for comparison purposes.

M. Miclesco continua son discours en mettant le pêcheur à la ligne au premier rang de l'humanité. Il fit valoir toutes les vertus, toutes les qualités dont l'avait pourvu la généreuse nature. Il dit ce qu'il lui fallait de patience, d'ingéniosité, de sang-froid, d'intelligence supérieure pour réussir dans cet art, car c'est plutôt un art qu'un métier. Et cet art, il le voyait bien au-dessus des prouesses cynégétiques dont se vantent à tort les chasseurs.

He next placed the angler at the head of humanity, extolling his patience, his ingenuity, his sang-froid, his lofty intelligence, all essential to success in an art rather than a trade, which set him far above the hunter. (Evans)

Mr. Miclesco continued his speech, placing the figure of the line fisherman in the front ranks of humanity. He emphasized all of the virtues, all of the qualities with which a generous Nature had bestowed this distinguished personage. He spoke of how much patience, ingenuity, calmness and superior intelligence the fisherman needed to succeed in this art; because it is indeed an art rather more than a mere trade. And he regarded the art of fishing as being considerable superior to the supposedly amazing feats of hunting, which huntsmen undeservedly boast of. (O'Driscoll)

In the above example, it can once again be seen that Evans offers a greatly reduced, summarizing rendering, though one which is still globally accurate, while my own rendering, being more complete and imitative, perhaps reflects more clearly Verne's humor and ironically bombastic, Dickensian language. Hopefully these excerpts will allow a greater understanding of the translating technique of I.O. Evans, whose renditions of Verne have now been widely read for several generations.

CONCLUSION

In sum, this discussion of the plot and themes of *Golden Danube* has shown that this original version by Jules Verne has indeed proven worthy of translation into English in its own right, and deserves to be enjoyed as a humorous, entertaining, educational and mildly intriguing tale of suspense.

It stands apart from the significantly different "adaptation" and "rewriting" that is *The Danube Pilot*, Michel's more action-packed, traditional detective story version. Twenty-first century readers are now invited to enjoy this hitherto little-known and under-appreciated gem from the pen of Jules Verne, which inspired Verne *fils* to write *The Danube Pilot*. Jules was, when he wrote this work, in his declining years and close to the end of his life, but was still evidently very much in possession of his strong literary powers. *Golden Danube*, the tale of the extraordinary navigation of the River Danube by the unlikely but loyal, closely-bonded pairing of fisherman Ilia Krusch and detective Dragoch/Jaeger, an "odd couple" if ever there was one, is a worthy addition to the English-language versions of Verne's lifelong corpus of "Extraordinary Journeys."

GOLDEN DANUBE

Sigmaringen

Chapter I

AT THE SIGMARINGEN CONTEST

THAT DAY, APRIL 25ᵀᴴ, the tavern known as *The Fisherman's Rest* was filled with a sense of keen excitement, which manifested itself in singing, spluttering, bursts of applause and the clinking of glasses.[1]

The windows of this tavern opened out onto the left bank of the Danube, at the edge of the charming little town of Sigmaringen,[2] capital of the Prussian enclave of the House of Hohenzollern[3] a town which is situated very close to the source of this great Central European river.

As was indicated by the tavern's name, painted in beautiful Gothic lettering on a sign above the entrance, it was here in this inn that, on that day, were gathered together the members of the Danubian Line, an international Fishermen's Society, most of whom were of German, Austrian and Hungarian nationality.[4] In this tavern, fishermen would

---

1. In the French original, Jules Verne names the tavern *Le Rendez-vous des Pêcheurs,* which is more literally and faithfully translated as *The Fishermen's Meeting Place.* However, I have opted for a more natural-sounding target culture (TC) equivalent.

2. Sigmaringen is a town in Southern Germany, in the state of Baden-Wurttemberg, situated on the Upper Danube. It is the capital of the Sigmaringen district. Up to 1850, it was in the principality of Hohenzollern-Sigmaringen, after which it became part of Prussia's Province of Hohenzollern.

3. The House of Hohenzollern is a noble family and royal dynasty of electors, kings and emperors of Prussia, Germany and Romania; the family motto is *Nihil Sine Deo (Nothing Without God).*

4. In the 1997 edition of the source text, *Le Beau Danube Jaune: Version d'origine,* Olivier Dumas here provides a footnote stating that "It should be noted that, through a misreading of the typeface, Michel Verne used the word "League"

drink full tankards of fine beer from Munich and full glasses of quality Hungarian wines. And during these sessions, the main room of the tavern would seem to disappear in the midst of the fumes of pungent tobacco smoke which curled in a continuous stream from the long pipes of the drinkers. And if the members of the Society could no longer even catch a glimpse of each other through the thick smoke, they could at least still hear one another; and how indeed could they not hear each other, unless they had been deaf!

It is appropriate to point out that, while fly fishermen are generally calm and silent when engaged in their activity of predilection, they are the noisiest people in the world when they are not immersed in their professional occupation, and when it comes to recounting their great exploits, they are as vocal as hunters, which is indeed saying something!

At the point at which this story begins, the assembled fishermen had come to the end of a most substantial lunch, which had brought together approximately one hundred guests around the tavern table; all were knights of the fishing line, passionate zealots of the bait, fanatics of the fishing hook. It would be a fair point to acknowledge that their gullets had become remarkably parched during the exertions of that fine April morning. Thus, many bottles were in evidence in the middle of the sideboard, bottles which had now given way to the various liqueurs which accompanied the coffee; raca,[5] extracted from fermented rice; taffia from the East Indies,[6] ratafia, extracted from that blackcurrant liqueur which is also known as cassis,[7] curaçao,[8] brandy from Gdansk in Poland, Dutch gin, elixir of Garus, Hoffman brandy,

---

instead of "Line" ("Ligue" au lieu de "Ligne"), which is nevertheless a more logical name for an association of fishermen as opposed to a political grouping" (my translation).

5.   This obscure word seems to refer to a type of wine known as "raca" or "arraca," a name originating in Provence, from an old Provencal word meaning a liqueur fermented from the dregs of grapes, and produced originally in that region of France.

6.   Taffia, or tafia, is a type of rum, especially from Guyana or the Caribbean; the word is derived from West Indian Creole, and its usage in French dates from about the eighteenth century.

7.   Ratafia is the name given to any liqueur made from fruit or from brandy with added fruit.

8.   An orange-flavoured liqueur originally produced in Curaçao, a Caribbean island.

Kirschwasser,[9] *keetsch-wasser*,[10] *korsoli* from Turin, *scuba*,[11] and even whisky extracted from Scottish barley, even though the Danubian fishing association did not include within its ranks any son of the Emerald Isle, green Erin.[12]

Three o'clock in the afternoon was ringing out at the *Fisherman's Rest* when the assembled diners, whose complexion was becoming increasingly red, finally rose from the table. Some were staggering, and leaned on their companions for support. But the majority of them, if truth be told, remained standing firmly on their legs. After all, were they not well-accustomed to these prolonged sessions of high festivity, which recurred several times throughout the year, on the occasion of these fishing contests organized by the Danubian Line? These fishing competitions enjoyed a large and devoted following, and were the source of much celebration and merrymaking, having, as they did, a strong and well-deserved reputation, as much along the upper as the lower Danube, that famous river which is actually golden, and not blue, as the melody of the famous Strauss waltz would have us believe. Competitors hastened to participate, coming from such regions as the Duchy of Baden, from Wurttemberg, Bavaria, Austria, Hungary and the Romanian provinces, thanks to the devoted industriousness and the widespread, positive renown of the President of the Danubian Line, the Hungarian Miclesco.

The Society had already been in existence for five years, and, thanks to the contributions made to it by the subscription fees of its members, it was prospering financially. Its ever-growing financial resources allowed it to award quite substantial prizes at its various contests. Furthermore, it competed valiantly, and not without some degree of success, against rival associations, and its banner sparkled with the medals which had been obtained following each of its

9. In the original, the name of this type of brandy is italicized and spelled *kirsch-wasser*; this is a brandy distilled from cherries, made chiefly in the Black Forest in Germany and in the Jura and Vosges districts of France (Collins English Dictionary 2003: 898). The German term literally means "cherry water."

10. Keetsch-waasser is a type of liqueur flavoured with cumin and caraway.

11. Scuba is a whiskey-style liqueur with honey and saffron.

12. In the 1997 publication of the French original, *Le Beau Danube Jaune: Version d'origine*, Olivier Dumas remarks in a footnote that, whether this allusion by Verne is an error or a deliberate pleasantry, the term "green Erin" describes Ireland rather than Scotland.

victories. It kept itself up-to-date with current legislation relating to river fishing, staunchly defending its rights, with equal vigor against the State and against private individuals, and, in all countries, as is well-known, everybody has the right to fish in rivers, large and small, and in navigable watercourses, using either a floating fly line or a bottom line. At several points along the course of the river Danube, the Society possessed various ponds and lakes, types of secluded, corralled-off areas which were patrolled by guards working on the Society's behalf, who had sworn an oath of allegiance to the Danubian Line. In short, it defended its rights and privileges with that tenacity—one might almost call it a professional obstinacy—typical of the human being whose line fisherman instincts make him worthy of being classified within a particular category of humanity all of his own.

The contest which had just taken place that day, was the first one of that year, in the 1860s. From five o'clock that morning, the members of the Line, numbering about sixty, had left the nearby town in order to reach the left bank of the Danube, a short distance downriver.

The weather was fine—quite warm, even—and it had not proved necessary to bring along protection against the rain. The competitors wore the Society uniform, which consisted of baggy woollen clothing (replaced by cloth during periods of extreme heat): a short jacket which allowed freedom of movement, trousers tucked into fishing boots with deep insoles, a white cap with a wide peak, protected, if necessary, by a hood of the same color. They were equipped with the various requisite items of fishing apparatus, exactly as they are listed in the Fisherman's Manual: fishing rods, poles, landing nets, fishing lines wrapped up in their buckskin covering, lure devices to which the hook is attached, toolboxes of fishing floats, lead lines, split lead weights in all sizes for the sinkers and supplies of artificial flies and of fishing cords. The fishing had to be "free," in the sense that all of the fish, regardless of species, should be catchable from a comfortable vantage point where the fisherman could stand and be supported, and so that each fisherman could prepare his bait in his own chosen way and designated spot, according to the species of fish, bleaks, eels, barbels, bream, river carp, chubs, sticklebacks, roach, gudgeons, red mullets, graylings, perch, tenches, plaice, trout, minnows, pike, and others which live in the waters of the Danube.

On the stroke of six o'clock, exactly ninety-seven competitors were in position, floating line in hand, poised to cast their hook.

A bugle call sounded the starting signal, and the ninety-seven lines had by now tightened themselves above the current all along the riverbank.

Several different types of prizes were designated to be awarded at this contest, but the two first prizes, of a value of two hundred florins each, would be given, firstly, to the fisherman who would catch the greatest number of fish and secondly, to the fisherman who would catch the single heaviest fish.

The contest took place in perfect conditions. Naturally enough, there were a few disputes over fishing spots which had been too sparingly measured out, or fishing lines which had become entangled with each other. These were the usual minor incidents which necessitated the intervention of the stewards on duty, but nothing serious occurred right up to the second bugle call which, at five to eleven, signalled the end of this contest.

Each catch of fish was then submitted to the judging panel, which consisted of the president of the association, Miclesco, together with four members of the Danubian Line. These were persons of the utmost integrity who performed their judging duties with the most scrupulous impartiality, to such an extent that there could be no complaint against their decisions, despite the fact that, in this particular sphere of activity, people tend to be rather hot-headed, especially when personal pride is at stake. As for the results of the competition—the awarding of the various prizes, be they based on weight or number of fish caught—these were kept secret by the judges. They would not be made known until the actual moment of the prize-giving ceremony, that is, following the meal which would bring together all of the contestants around the same table.

That moment had now arrived. The fishermen—not to mention the curious onlookers who had come from Sigmaringen—were assembled in front of the platform on which stood the president and his fellow judges.

The truth of the matter is that, if there was no shortage whatsoever of seats, benches and stools, there was no scarcity of tables either, nor of pitchers of beer, small bottles of various different liqueurs, or of glasses, large and small. During these gatherings of line fishermen, it would not be possible to listen to a speech without being seated, nor to sit down without quenching one's thirst.

After the usual din and commotion of high spirits and cheerfulness, everybody took their place, and the pipes continued to discharge more smoke than ever into these springtime surroundings.

The president then stood up and was greeted by cries of "Listen! Listen!" as numerous as they were loud.

Mr. Miclesco, a forty-five year old man, fit, robust and in early middle-age, was a perfect example of the typical Hungarian: a pleasant face, a warm and beautifully resonant voice, elegant and persuasive gestures. He truly cut a fine figure, as he stood between his two assessors, one of whom was an older man, the Serb Ivetozar, the other a younger man, the Bulgarian Titcha. He spoke perfect German, a language understood by all the members of the Danubian Line, so that not one of his words was lost on his audience.

Having drunk, to the dregs, a glass of frothy, snowy white-topped beer whose foam could be seen at the tips of his long moustache, Mr. Miclesco now began to express himself in the following terms:

"My dear colleagues, please do not expect a formal speech with a well-organized introduction, exposition and conclusion. No, we're no longer in the business of getting carried away with solemn official speeches, and I'm here only to chat to you about our various little items of business as a group of good friends; even, I would venture to say, as a brother, if this description seems appropriate to you for an international gathering!"

These two sentences, as long as all those which are generally spouted at the beginning of a speech, even when the orator claims not to be speechifying, were greeted by a unanimous burst of applause, to which were added many declarations of "Very good! Very good!" mingled with splutters and even hiccups.

Then, as the president lifted his glass, all of the full glasses in the inn clinked in approval of his gesture; those which broke in the somewhat rough clanging together of containers, were immediately replaced.

Mr. Miclesco continued his speech, placing the figure of the line fisherman in the front ranks of humanity. He emphasized all of the virtues, all of the qualities with which a generous Nature had bestowed this distinguished personage. He spoke of how much patience, ingenuity, calmness and superior intelligence the fisherman needed to succeed in this art; because it is indeed an art rather more than a mere trade. And he regarded the art of fishing as being considerably superior to the supposedly amazing feats of hunting, which huntsmen undeservedly boast of.

"Could hunting really be compared to fishing?" he cried.

"No! No!" came the replies from all sides of the assembled participants.

"And what skill is involved in killing a young partridge or a hare, when you see him at close range, within easy reach, and after a dog—

do we have dogs, I ask you?—has advantageously led him into your range of vision? That prey, you spot him in due time, you take aim at your leisure, and you then proceed to bombard him with multiple leadshots, most of which are, in any case, fired in vain! A fish, on the other hand: you cannot see him or follow his progress... he's hidden under the waters... With nothing but one single hook at the end of your Florence-made fishing rod, what skilful manoeuvers are needed, what delicate invitations, what expenditure of intellectual energy; what instinctive skill is required, in order to entice the fish to make up its mind to take the bite, in order to deftly strike him and to reel him in from the water, sometimes unconscious at the end of the fishing line; at other times, wriggling, and, so to speak, himself applauding the fisherman's victory!"[13]

This time, it was a thunderous round of applause and cries of "Bravo!" which spread like wildfire through the crowd and reached the platform. Undoubtedly, the president, Miclesco, was exactly in tune with the sentiments of the Danubian Line. He knew that it would be impossible to go too far in showering his fellow fishermen with praise, by placing their noble pursuit above all those others which bring human intelligence into play. He need have no fear of being accused of exaggeration in eulogizing, to the heavens, these most ardent zealots of the piscatory sciences,[14] and in even making reference to that superb goddess[15] who presided over the piscatorial games of ancient Rome during the piscine ceremonies!

There could be no doubt but that these esoteric words had been understood, for they triggered fresh outbursts of applause, even noisier than before.

---

13. These marks of ellipses (...) are present in the original French manuscript, but do not indicate any omission in the translation.

14. Verne here employs a deliberately bombastic, satirical style, which I have tried to mirror through the choice of adjectives such as "piscatory," "piscatorial" and "piscine," all referring to fish; in the original, he uses the phrase "la science pisciptologique" to refer to fishing, or, as explained by Dumas in a footnote to the 1997 edition of *Le Beau Danube Jaune: Version d'origine*, "the art of catching fish." Verne also here uses such adjectives as "piscotariens" and "halieutiques." The latter term, which Dumas also explains in a footnote as referring to fishing, does not, apparently, have a transparent cognate in English.

15. The fish goddess, Aphrodite Salacia, was worshipped by her followers on her sacred day, Friday.

And then, having recovered his breath through emptying another tankard which he had filled with frothy beer:

"It now remains only for me," he said, "to wreath our Society in garlands of honor; its prosperity is ever-growing; each year it recruits new members, and its reputation has become so notably established throughout all of Central Europe! I shall not speak to you about its successes, as you are already familiar with them and have your own share in them, and it is a great honor to take part in its contests! The German press, the Czech press and the Romanian press have never been sparing in their so invaluable—so well—deserved, I might add—praise of our Society, and I now ask you to join me in a toast to all those people who have devoted themselves to the international cause of the Danubian Line!"

Needless to say, the assembled fishermen joined wholeheartedly in President Miclesco's proposed toast. The contents of bottles were emptied into glasses, and the contents of glasses were emptied into throats, with as much ease as the waters of the great river and its tributaries flow between its five thousand kilometers of banks!

And that would have brought this part of the ceremony to an end, if the presidential speech had concluded on that last toast. But—and this should cause no astonishment—that toast was to be followed by several others of equal timeliness and aptness.

And, indeed, the President had now proudly raised his head and straightened back up to his full height; the secretary and treasurer were also standing. Each of them held in his right hand a glass full of a strongly Germanized vintage of champagne, while their left hand rested on their heart. Then, in a voice which grew ever more resonant:

"I drink to the Society of the Danubian Line!" the President grandly declared, as he cast his eyes over the assembled participants.

Everybody had now stood up, a champagne glass to their lips, some having climbed up onto benches, others onto tables, and all responded in perfect unison to the toast proposed by Mr. Miclesco.

The latter—once the glasses had been drunk from—started to speak yet again, waxing more lyrical than ever, after drinking some more from the inexhaustible supplies of beer which were being placed in front of him and his fellow judges:

"I drink to the various nationalities—to those from Baden-Baden and Baden-Wurttemberg, to the Bavarians, Austrians, Hungarians,

Serbs, to those from Valais, to the Moldavians, the Bessarabians and Bulgarians whom the Danubian Line numbers within its ranks!"

And the assembled Bulgarians, Bessarabians, Moldavians, citizens of Valais, Serbs, Hungarians, Austrians, Bavarians, citizens of Baden-Baden and of Baden-Wurttemberg echoed this toast as one man, as they absorbed the contents of their champagne glasses.

The president finally concluded his speech with the announcement that he was now drinking to the health of each individual member of the Society. However, as their number reached a total of two hundred and seventy-three persons, he was forced to confine himself to including them all in one single, all-encompassing toast.

Moreover, he was answered by thousands and thousands of splutters, gulps and cries which continued on for so long that people's vocal cords were worn out.

And thus came to an end that interesting segment of this ceremony, the second part of the programme following the first, which had consisted of the festive, merry-making social activities and revelries.

The third section of the ceremony was to consist of the announcement of the prize-winners of the Sigmaringen fishing contest.

As has not been forgotten, the fishermen were to be classified within two separate categories, and a number of prizes, also separate, were reserved for each category.

The first group of prizes were to be bestowed upon those among these knights of the fishing rod who would have been deemed to have caught the greatest numbers of fish throughout the hours of the contest. The prizes belonging to the second group would reward those who had reeled in the heaviest individual fish with their fishing lines. Moreover, there was a possibility that this double-result might have been achieved by the same single competitor, a fortunate victor both in the weight and the numbers categories.

Thus, everybody was now waiting with a perfectly natural and understandable anxiety, because, as has been said, the judging panel's secrets had remained closely-guarded. But the moment had now come when these secrets were finally about to be revealed.

President Miclesco took the official piece of paper, a sort of results sheet of the prize-winners which contained the names of all of the awardees under both categories.

In accordance with a customary system of prize-allocation, which was, moreover, prescribed by the standing orders of the Society, the prizes of lesser value were to be announced first. In this way, it was expected that there would be ever-increasing interest and anticipation according as the reading out of the names of the winners proceeded, and wagers would sometimes even be laid as to the names of the likely victors in such-and-such a category. Indeed, it is likely—at least in America—that such wagers would have risen to significant sums of money, as large as if it was the Presidency of the United States that was in question.[16]

The winners of the lower prizes in the category of "numbers of fish caught" presented themselves in front of the platform, and the President gave each of them an embrace accompanied by a certificate, and an amount of money which varied according to the rank obtained.

The fish which had been gathered together in the nets—having been counted—were of such types as any fisherman might catch, without distinction of species, in the waters of the Danube—sticklebacks, roach, gudgeons, plaice, perch, tenches, pike, chubs and others. Valasians, Hungarians and citizens of Baden-Baden and Baden-Wurttembergeois all appeared in the list of winners of these lower prizes. Even though the panel of judges had discharged their duties with perfect justice; even though they could not be faulted, either for unfairness or preferential treatment, there were nonetheless a number of challenges to their decisions. In relation to the third prize, for instance—for which a Moldavian and a Serb had been declared to have tied, the number of fish caught being equal—an argument broke out, which quickly deteriorated into a violent quarrel which pitted the two prize-winners against each other. They had been positioned beside each other at the river bank during the fishing competition; their top pieces and floats had become entangled. They claimed that the judges had attributed to one, the fish belonging to the other; the Serb declaring that thirty-seven fish should be credited to him, an amount which the Moldavian, in turn, sought to have ascribed to himself as his due.

In vain was it explained to them that—in accordance with normal procedure—the judges did not accept any complaint of this nature. The decisions of the assessors were final and their judgments had to be regarded as legitimate and equitable rulings. And in this instance,

---

16. This is the first of two references in *Golden Danube* evoking Verne's satire of American mores, written shortly before, the novel *Le Testament d'un excentrique* (*The Will of an Eccentric*, 1897). While the book was published contemporaneously in English in the United Kingdom, it never appeared in the United States until 2009, when the original translation was republished with the engravings in an edition edited by Norman Woolcott for Choptank Press, with an afterword by Brian Taves, and available on Lulu.com.

they had decided that both contestants had reached the same rank in the contest, so that the Serb and the Moldavian had no grounds for protesting against their ruling.

But as neither man would agree to give in and accept this ruling, their accusations developed into insults; and after these insults they came to blows. President Miclesco was obliged to intervene with the assistance of his fellow judges. What is more, as the Moldavian members of the Society had taken the side of their Moldavian compatriot as right and just, while the Serb members were supporting their own fellow countryman, there followed an unfortunate fist fight which was not quelled without some difficulty. It is true that, when it comes to these line fishermen, who come across as such calm, docile people, so far removed from human violence, anything is possible when their pride is at stake!

As soon as order had been restored, the announcement of the prize-winners was resumed, and, this time, as no other candidates were declared to have tied for equal ranking, no other incident occurred to mar the ceremony.

Second prize was awarded to a German by the name of Weber, who had caught seventy-seven fish of various different kinds, and the proclamation of this name was greeted with applause by the Society members. Besides, the said Weber was very well-known to his colleagues within the fishing confraternity; on numerous occasions already, he had been very highly placed in previous contests, and it may even be a cause of some surprise that, on that day, he hadn't won first prize for number of fish caught.

But no! Only seventy-seven fish appeared in his net, seventy-seven which had been diligently counted and recounted, while some rival contestant, if not more skilful, then at least more fortunate on the day, had caught seventy-nine fish in his net.

The name of this prize-winner was then proclaimed for the award of first prize in the first category of awards, that of number of fish caught; the winner was the Hungarian Ilia Krusch.

A murmur of surprise went through the assembled participants, who did not burst into applause. The fact is that the name of this Hungarian was hardly known to the members of the Danubian Line which he had just very recently joined.

As the winner had not appeared in front of the platform, where he was to receive the prize of one hundred florins, the judges proceeded with the awarding of prizes within the second category, that of weight. The winners within this category included Romanians, Serbs and Austrians, and as nobody tied for the same prize, the judges' decisions in this category gave rise to neither argument nor quarrel.

When the name of the winner of the second prize was announced— it was Ivetozar, one of the assessors—the proclamation of his name was also warmly applauded, just as the German Weber had been. He had triumphed with a three-and-a-half pound chub which would almost certainly have escaped his hook were it not for his coolness and dexterity. He was one of the Society's most visible, active and dedicated members and, up to then, he held the record for the number of prizes won. The announcement of his victory was thus greeted with a unanimous round of applause.

It now remained only to award the top prize in this category, and hearts raced as everybody waited, with baited breath, to hear the name of the winner.

And so, what a surprise there was—more than surprise, a sort of stupefied astonishment—when President Miclesco announced, unable to curb a sort of trembling of his voice:

"And the first prize, for the heaviest fish caught, for a seventeen-pound gudgeon, goes to: the Hungarian Ilia Krusch!"

Again, the same winner, upon whom two awards had now been bestowed, and who hadn't appeared the first time his name had been called out!

An almost deafening silence fell on the assembled fishermen; hands ready to clap remained still; mouths ready to acclaim the winner fell silent. A strong sense of curiosity seemed to have temporarily paralyzed all of these people.

Would Ilia Krusch finally make an appearance? Would he resolve to accept from the hands of President Miclesco, the certificate of honor and the hundred florins which went with it?

Suddenly, a murmur began to ripple through the audience.

One of the people present, who had up to then kept a little apart from the others, had just stood up and was making his way towards the platform.

It was the Hungarian, Ilia Krusch.

Chapter II

AT THE SOURCES OF THE RIVER DANUBE

ILIA KRUSCH was about fifty years old, of medium build and robust constitution. He had blue eyes, which were of that type of blue which could almost be called a Hungarian blue; he had hair of a blond color which was now beginning to turn yellow; he was thinly-bearded both in his moustache and sideburns; he had a rather large, strong head which was a little narrow in its upper part, wide shoulders, and arms and legs which were still sturdy.

Even though he was devoted to the calm, sedentary leisure pursuits of the line fisherman, Ilia Krusch had remained fit and robust, and he was as strong in his moral fibre as he was in his physical health; he was thus strong in body, and also stout of heart, which was an added bonus. In any event, there could be no mistaking the fact that he was a good and kind man, helpful and obliging, always ready to do a good turn for his fellow creatures, and easily and willingly making friends. With his slightly meek and easy-going appearance and his calm, gentle disposition, he was quite a good example of the typical image which people generally have of line fishermen, and was thus quite similar to, and would seem to fit in well with, most of his fellow members of the Society. But he was, above all, a modest man who sought none of the noisy, flashy pomp and circumstance of celebrity, which has been clearly seen from his reserved demeanour when he was twice proclaimed the top prize-winner of the Danubian Line.

It is true that most of his fellow fishing Society members hardly knew him or, in some cases, did not know him at all. Up to now, he had never taken part in any of the contests of this Society. He had only been admitted as a member five or six months previously. He had enrolled under the name of Ilia Krusch, of Hungarian nationality, residing in the small town of RaczBecse on the right bank of the Tisa, one of the main tributaries of the Danube. These were the names and details which he provided when paying his membership subscription. He thus belonged to the Society, enjoying the same rights as all his fellow members; but, let me repeat, this was the first time that he had actually participated in one of its fishing competitions; and yet he had done so well in both categories, weight and number!

Ilia Krusch, who had arrived in Sigmaringen just the evening before, had come only that morning to take up the position which had been allocated to him by lot on the left bank of the river, a spot which, in fact, turned out to be one of the positions which were farthest away upriver. Equipped with a comprehensive set of fishing implements, a meticulously organized, well-cared-for bag of fishing tackle, everything about him indicated that he was a serious fisherman—indeed, a fisherman who was in a league of his own, one might say, if such an expression doesn't tend towards being a play upon words—in short, a true professional. Yet none of his colleagues had paid any heed to him, so that he had gone unnoticed in the midst of this hundred-odd group of competitors.

Therefore, in actual fact, Ilia Krusch emerged from his cloak of invisibility only because he had twice been called to come up to the platform to accept, from President Miclesco, the certificates and prizes awarded to the highest-placed contestant. Even though he presented himself in a very modest light, his good-natured, round face indicated deep private satisfaction with his achievements, without, however, giving the impression that he felt any vanity as a result of his victory. He climbed up to the platform with short steps, with the air of a man who was in the habit of counting the number of steps on a stairwell; he bowed slightly before the judges' desk, shook the hand offered by President Miclesco and went back down the steps with his eyes discreetly lowered. He was, most certainly, not a man who felt at ease in such ceremonial surroundings, and his cheeks flushed slightly when he was greeted with some applause, which was the least that could be given to this double prize-winner.

To bring this afternoon to a close, it was necessary to drink one last time to the success of the Danubian Line, and this was done so conscientiously that there remained not a single drop of the various drinks either in the bottles or the glasses. And if, on that special day, the cellars of the *Fisherman's Rest* inn were not totally depleted of their stocks, it was only because the innkeeper had taken the precautionary measure of sufficiently stocking up his premises in anticipation of the extraordinary event. But the time had finally come for these drinkers—whose thirst was seemingly unquenchable—to be on their way.

Their departure occurred, indeed, towards six o'clock in the evening, after President Miclesco had shaken hands with all his colleagues and invited them to the next fishing contest, the date and venue of which were to be decided on a subsequent occasion. Given that such a diverse range of nationalities were represented amongst the membership of the Danubian Line, it was customary for these fishing competitions to be held, in rotation, in each of the states crossed by the great river. Also, a great many of the members who competed in these contests for its certificates and prizes, travelled long distances to take part, and, this time, since the contest had taken place at Sigmaringen, almost at the very sources of the Danube, there was a long return journey in store for those who lived in the farthest-flung provinces situated near to the mouth of that great river.

As for Ilia Krusch, he would have to undertake only half of this journey, as he had mentioned that he lived in one of the smaller towns in Hungary.

It goes without saying that the newspapers of Central Europe devoted many column inches to reporting on this particular contest, which was destined to go down in history, within the annals of the Danubian Line. It was rare—unprecedented, in fact—for the same prize-winner to have been awarded first place in both categories of weight and number. The sensation caused by the name of Ilia Krusch will thus come as no surprise. The newspapers from Vienna, Budapest, and Belgrade published the most highly complimentary articles about his achievements. Hungary could be proud of producing a hero of this calibre. He was celebrated not only in prose, but also in verse, and many songs were composed in his honor.

How did this modest man—and there could be no doubting his genuine modesty, judging from his demeanour throughout the awards ceremony—react to such a blaze of glory? Did he shut his ears to the resounding blasts of the hundred trumpets of renown which

now reached him from all sides? Would he return peacefully to his small home town and resume the course of what was most probably among the calmest of existences, one which was likely to be devoted to the irresistible lure of this love for line fishing? Nobody could have answered these questions. As soon as the ceremony was over, his fishing and landing nets in one hand, his rod in the other, he had discreetly gone away upriver, while his fellow members had returned to Sigmaringen.

Therefore, over the two days following the contest, it was impossible to find out what had become of Ilia Krusch. If he had gone back by train to Racz, his return would undoubtedly have attracted attention, and the newspapers would have been well able to keep the public informed of his trajectory; but, most certainly, after leaving Sigmaringen, he had not gone in the direction of Hungary.

Moreover, it is pertinent to point out that Ilia Krusch's identity had not been subject to any preliminary checks prior to the contest; in his case, as for the other members of the Danubian Line, his official declarations of identity had been relied upon and accepted, at the time of his application to take part in the contest. He had declared himself to be Hungarian, from Lower Hungary, and there was no reason to doubt what he said. His subscription fee having been paid and accepted, he was in exactly the same situation as his fellow members; the only thing required of them was that they have a love for line fishing, and that they consider that noble pursuit to be superior to all others in the "illustrious compendium of human activities"!

After the glowing success which he had recently achieved, there was thus every reason to believe that this Ilia Krusch would not neglect to take part in the future fishing contests which brought together, six times a year, the members of the Danubian Line. This man would certainly be seen to reappear, and, what is more, he would be once again within the front ranks. He was, in sum, a fisherman who was among the most adept and competent within his profession—a fact which had just been proven for all to see—and who knows whether fortune might not smile on him again, on some future occasion? In any event, it would be two months before such an occasion would again present itself, and it was quite likely that the fortunate victor was now going to return to his own country, to his native town, where his fellow citizens would give him a welcome as enthusiastic as it was deserved.

And so, there was astonishment of quite a different nature when the general public came across the following article in the newspapers of Vienna, Budapest and Belgrade, on April 26th of the present year:

> The name of Ilia Krusch is now in everyone's mouth, and escapes from everybody's lips in the midst of the general fevered turmoil of admiration directed at him. The story of his double victory at the most recent contest of the Danubian Line is well-known, and, when one has reaped such a harvest of laurels, it is permissible to make them into a triumphant bed on which to lie and savor rest following victory.
>
> But what have we just found out? It is nothing less than the fact that this astonishing Hungarian is getting ready to astonish us even more. Not content with receiving his certificates and financial prizes from the hands of President Miclesco, he is now preparing to break another record, a title of which he will probably never be stripped in the future.
>
> Yes! If our sources are correct—and the reliability of our information is well-known—Ilia Krusch now intends to travel down the Danube, fishing rod in hand, making his way along the entirety of the great river from its furthest source as far as its ultimate mouth on the Black Sea—a journey of about seven hundred leagues!
>
> It is reportedly from tomorrow onwards that Ilia Krusch is going to cast his hook into the waters at the source of the great international river, and we can only wonder whether or not he will depopulate it of all the representatives of the ichthyologic race which swim up and down its course!
>
> We will keep our readers updated on this novel undertaking, which will undoubtedly be of worldwide uniqueness!

Thus, Ilia Krusch was confident of being able to descend the Danube, fly-fishing as he went, but under what conditions this was to be accomplished, the article from the Austrian newspaper did not specify. Would he proceed by making his way on foot on one or the other of the banks of the Danube? Might he be about to abandon himself to the current in a small boat? And, as for the fish that he would catch over the duration of this extended fishing trip which could not last less than several months, what did he intend to do with all of those? Would he use them to feed himself, or would he perhaps sell them in the towns and villages along the banks of the river?

In short, public curiosity remained in a constant state of over-excitement, worked up as it was to fever pitch by this news report. Some people regarded it as nothing more than a bit of gossip, of which nothing more would come, while others, on the contrary—and these were in the majority—took the proposed endeavour very seriously. Wagers were even placed as to whether this enterprise would be carried through to a successful conclusion, or whether, after making contact with the Danube at its very source, the daring fisherman might not abandon his adventurous quest before reaching one of the Danube's numerous mouths.

When the President, Miclesco, was questioned as to what type of person this one-of-a-kind fisherman was, he could respond only in an inadequate manner, explaining himself in the following terms:

"I don't know the winner of the most recent contest particularly well, and, insofar as I have been able to ascertain, none of my colleagues know him any better than I do. He joined our Society only very recently, and none of us had previously had any dealings whatsoever with him. He seemed to me to be a very modest, unaffected sort of man, very conventional, very calm, the type of person of whom it can be readily agreed that he is a good-natured fellow. But, in the light of the feat which he has just proposed to accomplish, it must be assumed that, underneath this affability, there lies a strong character, a truly extraordinary level of endurance, an uncommon strength of will!"

And when President Miclesco was asked whether Ilia Krusch had made any direct approach to him on this matter:

"Not at all," he replied, "and it came to my knowledge only through the article in the newspaper."

"And you haven't seen Ilia Krusch since the contest?"

"I have not seen him at all since then," the President replied, "and that in itself is actually quite unusual. It would have seemed appropriate that he would at the very least have informed his colleagues in the Danubian Line of his attempted feat, given that he had just been awarded two first prizes by our Society!"

President Miclesco was right; it was indeed rather strange that Ilia Krusch had held himself at a distance from his colleagues, keeping his own counsel in this way. But after all, could not one expect anything from such an eccentric individual, and one surely had to be equipped with a strong degree of eccentricity to have come up with this plan in the first place.

But in that case, given that Ilia Krusch had said nothing of his plans to the Society committee, did that mean that he had spoken to the newspapers of his intentions, and was the news report based on the words of the fisherman himself?

No, it was a rumor which had begun like so many others, without anybody being able to guess at its origins. However, if it was true, there could be no doubt but that it had originated with Ilia Krusch himself. Nevertheless, this point remained obscure, and, amongst the general public, not many people were prepared to take it seriously.

In any event, public curiosity would very soon be satisfied on this score. People would not have long to wait to find out the lie of the land. According to that newspaper which prided itself on having such impeccable sources, it was on April 27th that the project was to be launched, and so, in twenty-four hours time, people would know the truth of the matter.

A few more impatient individuals, having earnestly sought to meet up with Ilia Krusch, had gone to look for him in the hotels and inns of Sigmaringen, but to no avail. He did not seem to have stayed on in that town after the contest. Furthermore, and as has not been forgotten, at the end of the ceremony he had set off along the right bank, going back upriver. It was even legitimate, at this point, to wonder whether he might not be making his way towards the sources of the river, with the intention of noting their exact location.

In any event, those who were interested in this project need only travel a few leagues from Sigmaringen. There, they would surely meet Ilia Krusch, unless, despite the information provided by the Austrian newspaper, the Danubian Line's prize-winner had calmly got back on the train in order to return to his Hungarian homeland, without even realizing that he had become such an object of public curiosity.

However, one difficulty did present itself: had the location of the source, or sources, of the great river, ever been determined with geographical precision? Were there maps in existence which situated these sources with a degree of exactitude with which Ilia Krusch would have to comply? Was there not, in actual fact, some level of uncertainty on this point, and when people would try to join up with him in such-and-such a spot, might he not be somewhere else?

Certainly, there is no doubt but that the Danube, known as the Ister in ancient times, springs into being within the Grand Duchy of Baden, and geographers even declare that its source is located at six degrees and ten minutes of eastern longitude and forty-seven degrees forty-eight minutes of northerly latitude. But at the end of the day, this reckoning, presuming it is correct, is calculated only to the minute of the arc of a circle, and not as far as the precise second, and that fact can give rise to variations of some significance. Yet, according to Ilia Krusch's plan, the project involved casting the fishing line at that precise place from which a first single drop of Danubian water sprang forth, to set out, and ultimately mingle with the waves of the Black Sea.

And yet after all, as it was observed by some, in the case in point, it was not absolutely necessary to attain a completely mathematical degree of precision. This project had not at all been forced upon Ilia Krusch. It was he alone who had conceived it, and nobody would think of splitting hairs with him on the question as to whether or not he would have set out on his journey from the exact point at which the great river rose. The most important matter was to catch up with Ilia Krusch at the place where the current would begin to carry his vessel downriver.

If one was to believe the legend which used, for a long time, to enjoy the status of geographical fact, the Danube apparently has its source, quite simply, in a garden, that is owned by the princes of Furstenberg. Its birthplace is apparently within an ornamental lake, surrounded by marble, to which great numbers of tourists come to fill beakers and tumblers with the water which pours forth within this lake. Could it be, then, at this inexhaustible basin that people should wait for Ilia Krusch on the morning of the 27th?

But of course, that is not the true, authentic source of the great river. It is now known that it is formed from the meeting of two streams, the Brège and the Briegach, which flow from a height of eight hundred and seventy-five meters, through the Schwarzwald forest. Their waters merge at Donaueschingen, several leagues upriver from Sigmaringen, and then flow together under the single name of the Donau, from which the name of the Danube is derived.

If one of these streams is more deserving than the other of being considered as the river itself, it would be the Brège, which is thirty-seven kilometers longer than the other and which has its source in the Brisgau.

But the wiser members of the curious public had doubtless said to themselves that Ilia Krusch's point of departure—presuming, that is, that he was indeed setting out on this journey—would be Donaueschingen, and it is there that—most of them being members of the Danubian Line—they had gone, with President Miclesco.

Thus, from early morning onwards, they were waiting on the bank of the river Brege, at the confluence of the two streams, but the hours passed without any sign of the man of the moment making an appearance.

"He's not going to show up," some people said.

"He's nothing but a practical joker!" others commented.

"And we seem to be a crowd of particularly gullible fools!" added some, in a rather bad-humored tone.

This was the cue for President Miclesco to jump to the defence of Ilia Krusch.

"No," he declared, "I can't believe for one moment that a member of the Danubian Line could have taken it into his head to deceive his colleagues! If that was the case, he would deserve to be very publicly removed from this honorable Society... It is made up of men who are too dignified and too serious for one among them to do such a thing... Ilia Krusch has probably been delayed, and we shall soon see him..."

"Unless," the secretary said, "that there's been some mistake in the date that was publicized..."

To which the reply came: "Or even—which is quite possible— perhaps our colleague never came up with this project in the first place?"

And indeed, perhaps this whole thing was nothing more than hearsay, an unfounded rumor, one of those deliberately planted false stories, designed to amuse the general public, stories which hatch underneath the wings of the daily press. In which case, if there wasn't deception at work, there would at least be disappointment, which would make the general public just as sorrowful, perhaps more so.

Just before nine o'clock, the following shout broke out from the group of people standing at the confluence of the Brege and the Briegach:

"There he is… there he is!"

At two hundred paces from where they stood, at a bend in a promontory, a small open boat came into view, driven along by means of a scull, or single oar, through a swirling eddy which was apart from the current. It followed the riverbank. A man stood alone at the back of the boat, navigating it.

This man was indeed one and the same person as the man who had taken part a few days previously in the fishing contest of the Danubian Line, the winner of the two top prizes, the Hungarian Ilia Krusch. After the prize-giving ceremony, he had gone back to the small boat which he was using as a floating residence, moored a few kilometers upriver, and that was why the searches for him in Sigmaringen had proven fruitless. And the fact that his plan to travel down the entire length of the Danube had become public knowledge, was because he had actually spoken about it to several people, hence the fact that the news had reached the paper in question, one of the regional newspapers; a report which had caused its instigator such an extraordinary stir.

When the boat had reached the confluence of the two rivers, it stopped, and was fixed to the riverbank by means of a grapnel hook. Ilia Krusch disembarked, and all of the curious bystanders gathered round him. He had probably not been expecting to be greeted by such a large attendance, as he seemed to be somewhat ill-at-ease as a result of this large group of people, and he was definitely the sort of man who was not at all keen to be the center of public attention.

President Miclesco approached him and offered him his hand, which Ilia Krusch shook with respect and deference, after removing his otter-skin cap.

"Ilia Krusch," he said, with that tone of solemn dignity which was his hallmark, "I am happy to meet, once again, the most distinguished prize-winner of our most recent contest!"

The distinguished prize-winner turned his head to the right, to the left, a little discomfited and not knowing how to respond. The President thus went on, saying: "Given that we are now encountering you at the sources of our international river, should I take it that your reported plan to make a line-fishing trip down the entire course of the Danube, as far as its mouth, must be taken seriously?"

Ilia Krusch remained silent, his eyes lowered, his tongue paralyzed by a sort of confusion which he was unable to overcome.

"We're waiting for your answer," President Miclesco went on.

A further minute of silence followed, after which Ilia Krusch finally managed to say:

"Yes... Mr. President, sir... that is my intention, which is why I've sailed back up here..."

"And you intend to begin your journey downriver..."

"This very day, President."

"And how shall you make this journey?"

"By abandoning myself to the current..."

"In this boat?"

"In this boat."

"Without ever putting into port?"

"Yes... at night."

"But it's a journey of six to seven hundred leagues..."

"At a rate of ten leagues per twelve hours, the journey will be completed in about two months."

"In that case, let me wish you *bon voyage,* Ilia Krusch..."

"My grateful thanks, Mr. President."

Ilia Krusch acknowledged the onlookers one last time, and stepped back into his small craft, while the curious bystanders hurried forward to see him setting off.

He took his fishing line, baited it and placed it on one of the benches within the boat, brought the grapnel hook back on board and pushed the boat forward by means of a hefty strike of the gaff, then, sitting down, he cast the line...[1]

Within an instant, he drew the line back in, and a barbel was wriggling on the hook; and, as he sailed round the promontory, all of the onlookers, with frenzied gasps, saluted the Danubian Line's award-winner.

---

1. The gaff, in angling terminology, is defined by the *Collins English Dictionary* (2003, 6th edition) as "a stiff pole with a stout prong or hook attached for landing large fish" (p.663).

Chapter III

AN INTERNATIONAL COMMISSION

THIS INTERNATIONAL COMMISSION comprised as many members as there are States whose borders are on, or are crossed by, the Danube, from west to east.

Its composition was as follows:

Representing Austria was Mr. Zwiedinek;
for Hungary, Mr. Hanish;
for the Duchy of Baden, Mr. Roth;
for Wurttemberg, Mr. Zelang;
for Bavaria, Mr. Uhlemann;
for Serbia, Mr. Ouroch;
for Valachia, Mr. Kassilick;
for Moldavia, Mr. Titcha;
for Bessarabia, Mr. Choczim and
for Bulgaria, Mr. Joannice.

It was in Vienna, the capital of the kingdom of Austria-Hungary, that this Commission had recently come together to meet, on April 6th. One of the great rooms of the Custom House had been placed at its disposal, and, on that day, its official business was to proceed to the election of its charirman and its secretary.

It was on this thorny issue that the first struggle got underway, a struggle which was indeed one of the fiercest imaginable, given that the question of nationality was at stake. There was nothing to even indicate definitively that these Commissioners would manage to reach a mutual understanding, even though that was apparently an easy matter amongst Germans, Austrians, Serbs, natives of Valachia, Bulgarians and Moldavians, all familiar with the various languages used in this part of Europe right up to the shores of the Black Sea.

But the mere fact of discussing or arguing various matters does not, in itself, lead anywhere: agreement must also be established on the ideas expressed.

And the fact is that, at this particular meeting—and with the smaller States not willing to regard themselves as in any way inferior to the larger ones—a fiery exchange of views was to cause all of the Commission members to end up in heated confrontation with each other on the subject of the election of the chairman and of the secretary. Under these circumstances, Baden, Serbia, Wurttemberg, Moldavia, Bulgaria and Bessarabia put forward their claims, which neither Bavaria, Hungary nor Austria felt able to accept. However, fellow feeling or antipathy between different nationalities, had no bearing on the issue submitted for the consideration of these Commissioners. Each one was there as a nominee of the government of his country, and represented an emperor, a king, a grand duke, a voivode or a hospodar. In reality, each Commission member therefore enjoyed equal rights and intended to assert them, specifically on the question of the nomination of the chairman of this international Commission.

And so, the eventual outcome, on this occasion, was what most often happens when each person obstinately refuses to concede any part of their claims. Certainly, of the various States which were represented on the Commission, the greatest, in terms of its rank within Europe, its population and history, was the kingdom of Austria-Hungary, and so it was expected that the chairmanship would devolve to either Mr. Zwiedinek or Mr. Hanish.

But this turned out to be not at all the case, and who won the most votes? It was Mr. Roth, the representative of the Duchy of Baden.

There was no other choice but to accept this result, and, when Mr. Roth had taken his place at the official desk of the chairman, there was no longer any real interest in the election of the secretary, a position won by Mr. Choczim from Bessarabia.

The real subject of debate thus began, and, contrary to what one might have feared after the heated discussions relative to the chairmanship, this new topic of discussion did not give rise to any serious incident.

Moreover, this is what it was about, and here is the purpose for which this international Commission had been brought together at the Custom House, Vienna.

For some time now, the various States crossed by the Danube had felt—not without justification—that large-scale smuggling of goods was being carried out between the sources and the mouths of the river. It appeared that there existed a perfectly-organized association of smugglers, one which operated to the utmost detriment of the parties concerned, so that the losses to the customs authorities of potential tax revenues already amounted to a considerable sum.

This merchandise which was crossing national barriers, fraudulently, consisted of highly-priced goods, including luxurious fabrics, wines of quality vintage, manufactured objects of high value and also food products, including canned food, all of which thus evaded customs duty.

Where did this merchandise come from, and where was it brought? The most intense investigations had been unable to discover the answers to these questions, and no police officer or customs official had ever been able to locate the smugglers' trail.

In addition, it was not likely that this smuggling was taking place over land, and everything seemed to indicate that it was being carried out along the river.

And yet, the coastal and inland navigation was being subjected to the most careful—indeed, extremely severe—surveillance, which caused the strongest of protests from all sides. The Danube river fleet was subjected to daily harassment; some boats were stopped, others detained, some were inspected and sometimes even unloaded when they gave rise to particular suspicion. There were all sorts of difficulties caused for the boat owners, and ultimately, significant damage was being caused to trade and to the transport industry.

Yet, despite all these investigations and the constant vigilance and intervention on the part of the various officers involved, nothing had been discovered. One thing which appeared certain was that these various goods, on which no customs duty had been paid, were arriving at the various mouths of the river, where steamships were waiting for them, ships which then unloaded the merchandise and dispatched it inland.

Neither did it seem that there could be any doubt on the following point: this fraud had already been going on for several years now, and it was legitimate to wonder whether it had been used to smuggle ammunition and weapons whenever war had broken out in the provinces bordering the Black Sea.

Whatever the case may be, the governments concerned had no idea, up to then, as to what basis this smugglers' ring had been founded on, what material it used, whether its associates were many in number and whether they were recruited only from among the ranks of nationals of Central Europe. It had not proved possible to catch any of these wrongdoers in the act. Thus, customs and police officers, realizing their powerlessness, were requesting that a new level of surveillance and of security operations—one which was stricter than ever, and which would operate by day and by night—now be established over the entire course of the River Danube.

It was thus with a view to implementing more efficient and more rigorous measures that this international commission had been formed, and, for the first time, it had been summoned to deliberate on these serious and difficult issues.

The chairman, Roth, having taken his place at his desk, proceeded to give a background review of the situation: he explained everything which had been attempted, but without success, up to that point. The intelligence which had been gathered from different sources was communicated by him to his fellow commissioners. In his view, the various States concerned had been the victims of massive fraud. It was not known where the smugglers' profits had been accumulated, or to what use they had been put. It was concluded that this state of affairs could not go on any longer, and all parties concerned expected that the international commission would be able to resolve this problem quickly.

A question was then put to the chairman by one of the commission members, Mr. Kassilick, the representative of Valachia.

"I would like to know—and I think my colleagues will share my wish—whether, since this smuggling has begun to take place over the upper as well as the lower Danube, there has been any one particular suspect."

"I can reply in the affirmative," was the reply of Chairman Roth.

"A suspect who is presumed to be the leader of the association of smugglers?"

Vienna

"We have every reason to believe so."

"And this leader, who might he be?"

"A certain Latzko, whose name has apparently been mentioned on several occasions…"

"And his nationality?"

"We don't know definitely, but he may possibly be Serbian."

This statement did not seem to be to the liking of the representative of Serbia, Mr. Ouroch, who felt obliged to express certain reservations.

Mr. Roth hastened to reply to him that this assertion was based only on rather uncertain information and that in any event, if this gang leader's name was Latzko, and if this gang leader should turn out to be a Serb, that could not in any shape or form undermine the honor of a country which counts among its dynastical leaders, people such as Stephen, Brancovitch, Czerin and Obrenovitch!

Mr. Ouroch appeared satisfied with this response, as would have been, in a similar situation, the German, Austrian, Hungarian, Valachian and other representatives, for whom chairman Roth would have only needed to alter the names cited in his reply.

And so it was, therefore, that the suspicions of the various police forces centerd on a man by the name of Latzko, but only because this name had been revealed in a certain letter which had been intercepted at the post office in Pest. But as for the person who bore this name— sufficiently shrewd and skilful to have, up to now, escaped all pursuit –he was not even known to anybody; he had never been seen. Was he the leader of this gang, whose operations he was perhaps directing from one of the inland towns, or from one of the towns on the banks of the Danube? Was he operating alone, along the entire length of the great river? Nobody could say. Furthermore, it was to be presumed that, even if Latzko was his real name, he was operating under some other, assumed name—and as to what that "alias" might be, the international police forces were completely and utterly in the dark.

The members of the Commision all knew what they were up against in dealing with this matter. In this issue which had been submitted to them for their consideration, a small amount was known, but there was a large degree of mystery, of the unknown.

What was known was that much merchandise, of significantly high value, was being smuggled right up to the basin of the Black Sea.

What was unknown was the nature of the organization of this massive smuggling operation, by what means it was being carried out and under what leader, and who were the personnel being commanded by this leader, suspected to be a certain Latzko of Serbian extraction.

It was at this point of the discussion that the Moldavian representative, Titcha, suggested that a large reward should be offered to whoever might catch this Latzko and hand him over to the police.

"Up to now," he pointed out, "the rewards promised have been low, too low, and they need to be increased, so that we might even tempt one of the smugglers themselves, from the gang!"

This was assuming that it was possible to find a traitor in the midst of the gang of smugglers, somebody who would be completely unable to resist the lure of the high reward, provided it was indeed high enough to make it worth his while to betray his accomplices and leader, and the truth of the matter was that this was perhaps not at all a bad idea, or bad reasoning, on the part of the Moldavian.

"What reward is being currently offered?" asked the Bavarian, Uhlemann.

"Five hundred florins," replied the secretary, Choczim.

"And five hundred florins—when you're talking about smuggling operations which yield profits a hundred times greater than that—is quite simply not enough," the Moldavian went on.

All of the Commission members seemed to unanimously share this view and, on the proposal of chairman Roth, the reward was increased to the sum of two thousand florins.

"And," declared the Wurttemberg representative, Zerlang, "it would be a good idea to add an honorary reward to that main reward."

"As long, however, as it's not won by one of the men from the gang," the Bulgarian, Joannice, rightly pointed out.

That went without saying.

The chairman then stated that if this gang of smugglers answered to a leader—this Latzko person or anybody else—then, the international police forces, entrusted with the task of pursuing the smugglers, ought equally to have a leader of their own. It was important that any such leader be able to centralise the surveillance operations, that he have absolute and total control over all of the police personnel under his command and that all of his police officers should be able, night and day, to make contact with him—in short, a leader who, enjoying absolute power, would assume absolute responsibility.

"Up to now," the chairman stated, "the police and customs officers have not been acting in a co-ordinated manner, they have not been singing from the same hymn sheet, given that they haven't been directed by the same leader... Manpower was deployed in different directions, with no single 'brains behind the operation' who ought to have been co-ordinating their movements... Which has resulted in mistakes being made, regrettable errors, unfortunate contradictory orders which it will be important to avoid in the future."

Everybody agreed with the chairman's statement. The Commission would nominate a leader who would be given complete authority over all of the other officers. And it would not adjourn without making its choice, which would probably lead to heated discussions somewhat similar to those which had preceded the election of chairman Roth.

But, before speaking about the candidates whose credentials would have to be discussed by the Commission, the chairman wished to read into the record of the meeting, a memorandum which he had received from the Chief Customs Officer in Vienna.

The substance of this memo was that the authorities had every reason to believe that a new smuggling operation was taking place, one which had been in preparation for some time… In the provinces bordering the upper Danube, a major movement of merchandise had taken place, especially of manufactured goods. It had been attempted, in vain, to track this movement of goods, which had been carried out with the utmost caution, and all traces of the smugglers had been permanently lost. In addition, the appearance of several suspicious-looking vessels had been noted at the various mouths of the river. These ships seemed to want to communicate with people on land, and, after long waits of varying durations, they made their way back out into the open sea, some of them heading for the Muscovite shores, others for the Ottoman shores. When they had been accosted by certain military vessels which had drawn alongside them, they had been able to produce valid documentation, and even though there was reason to be suspicious of them to a certain extent, it had proved necessary to allow them to go free to continue their journey.

The memo added that the surveillance of the waterways must now be carried out more strictly than ever, along the entire course of the Danube. All the signs seemed to indicate that this new smuggling operation was already underway, and the international commission now had to take the most rigorous measures in order to dismantle this gang of smugglers once and for all.

In sum, chairman Roth and his fellow commissioners were strongly resolved to use all possible means to put a stop to this disastrous smuggling operation, to discover the leader behind it and his accomplices, and to destroy, down to the very last man, this gang of wrongdoers.

What remained was to organise these measures in such a way as to make them effective, by concentrating them in the hands of one single person. There could be no question but that the customs authorities on one side, and the police on the other, must act in a co-ordinated fashion, and moreover, the efforts of these two public authorities were already being made in co-operation with each other. Customs vessels were surveying the Danube, and were not sparing in their inspections of the boats which sailed down its waterways. As for the banks of the river, between the towns and villages situated along the Danube, police squadrons were very actively patrolling these areas, day and night.

But, when all was said and done, these measures had proved a dismal failure, perhaps because of a lack of unified leadership and direction between officers from different nationalities, and it was this state of affairs which the Commission intended to rectify.

The chairman thus opened the discussion on the choice of a leader to whom the Commission would delegate its powers and who would have authority over all the personnel provided by the States bordering the Danube.

The discussion was inevitably a long one. Austria, Hungary, Bulgaria, Wurttemberg and others put forward their favorites from amongst the police forces of their own countries. Each one defended his choices with a tireless zeal. One would never have thought that Central Europe was equipped with such a supply of police officers of such worth. At the end of the day, what was threatening to happen was what had happened already for the election of the chairman, whereby, realizing that they were fighting a losing battle, the Commissioners had ended up appointing the delegate from the least important country.

This time, however, it was necessary to proceed differently, and though the chairman, Roth, had been elected by a show of hands, it was necessary to have recourse to a secret ballot for the appointment of the police chief.

When all was said and done, the candidates who seemed to have the strongest chances were those from Hungary, Bavaria and Moldavia, three policemen whose merit had been demonstrated and appreciated in various circumstances, a merit which was, overall, approximately equal. Thus, after a long discussion—and the names of the other candidates having been ruled out—the Commission decided to submit these three police officers' candidacy to a secret ballot. It would be sufficient for the winning candidate to obtain a simple majority after the first round of voting, that is, five out of nine votes, with no Commissioner having the right to abstain.

On the chairman's invitation, each person wrote the name of his chosen candidate on a ballot paper, and these papers were then placed into a hat. If truth be told, in this era of unending vote-taking, is it not legitimate to wonder whether hats are not intended to be used as ballot boxes rather than as coverings for the head?

"Has everybody cast their vote?" asked the chairman.

Yes, and the nine ballot papers were removed from the hat.

The chairman then proceeded to the counting of the votes, and the figures for the ballot were recorded in the official minutes of the meeting by the secretary, Choczim.

Seven of the votes had all concurred in the choice of a Hungarian national.

The name of this candidate was Karl Dragoch, chief of police at Pest, on whose name an overall majority of the Commissioners had been in agreement, following their discussions.

The name of Karl Dragoch was thus welcomed with satisfaction, and even the Valachian Kassilick and the Moldavian Titcha, who had not voted for him, stated that they willingly accepted his appointment.

One could thus say that it was a unanimous vote.

Moreover, this choice was amply justified by Karl Dragoch's profile and previous achievements, and the services which he had rendered on numerous occasions in his capacity as chief of the Hungarian police.[1]

Karl Dragoch, forty-five years of age at that time, lived in Pest. He was a man of rather average constitution, fairly thin, endowed with more mental than physical strength, yet in good health, and highly resistant to the strains and pressures of his profession, as he had proved throughout his career, being, furthermore, very brave in the face of the dangers of all sorts which his job involved. He lived in Pest because the administrative headquarters of the police force which he led, happened to be established in that city, but he was most often working in the field, taking part in some difficult or delicate mission. Furthermore, as a single man, he did not have any family concerns, and nothing impeded his freedom of movement. He came across as an officer who was both intelligent and zealous, very reliable and energetic, and endowed with that particular type of intuition which suits this profession.

It will thus come as no surprise that he was the Commissioners' choice, after his fellow countryman Hanish had made his merits known and had spoken highly of his qualities.

"My dear colleagues," chairman Roth then said, "the votes we have cast could not have concurred on a more commendable candidate, and

---

1. In the 1997 source text, *Le Beau Danube Jaune: Version d'origine*, Olivier Dumas inserts a footnote: "There remains here [in this part of Verne's original text] the original name of Karl Dragoch, "Dragonof," the correction of which is sometimes forgotten [by Verne]. This original name evokes more clearly the *dragon* of the river, killed by Saint George." (my translation)

this Commission will not regret choosing Karl Dragoch as leader of the agents who must take action in this serious matter."

It was decided that Karl Dragoch, who was, at that moment, in Pest, would be summoned urgently to Vienna before the Commission adjourned, in order to make contact with its members. He must be already aware of the affair of this smuggling ring. He would be informed of whatever he might not already know of this case. He would then give his opinion on the manner of proceeding henceforth, and would immediately swing into action.

It went without saying that total secrecy would be maintained on the choice which the Commission had just made. The general public must not know that Karl Dragoch was in charge of this police operation. It was important, in fact, that the smuggling ring were not alerted to what was about to happen, and could thus not have reason to become wary of the police chief.

That very day, a dispatch was sent to Pest, to the central police administration, inviting Karl Dragoch to make his way, without delay, to the Austrian capital. It could thus be expected that, the following day, at the earliest possible hour, Karl Dragoch would report to the Custom House where the Commission would hold its final meeting.

Before taking their leave of each other, the chairman and his fellow commissioners decided to reconvene as and when circumstances would make it necessary, either in Vienna or in any of the other cities of the States involved. At the same time, in each one of these States, the Commissioners would follow the various unfolding events of the campaign which had been undertaken; they would remain in contact with the officers on the ground, and all correspondence would be addressed to Mr. Roth, at the central office, in the capital. But it was agreed that Karl Dragoch would maintain complete independence and have total freedom of manoeuver and would never be hindered under any circumstances.

This concluded the business of the meeting, and there was now every reason to be optimistic that, thanks to the new measures about to be put in place, the police would finally manage to capture this Latzko, the elusive leader of this equally elusive smuggling ring.

Chapter IV

From the Sources of the Danube, to Ulm

And so, it was in this fashion that Ilia Krusch's journey down the great river had begun; this navigation which would transport him through two dukedoms, Baden and Hohenzollern; two kingdoms, Wurttemberg and Bavaria; two empires, Austria-Hungary and Turkey, and four principalities, Serbia, Valachia, Moldavia and Bulgaria. And the eccentric fisherman would undergo this long journey of more than six hundred leagues, without experiencing any tiredness; he would simply abandon himself to the current of the Danube which would carry him right up to its mouth, on the Black Sea. By travelling at a rate of one league per hour, and by covering a distance of approximately ten leagues between sunrise and sunset, he hoped to arrive at his journey's end within two months, provided that he was not stopped along the way by any incident or accident. And indeed, why should he experience any delays?

Would the navigation not be easier on the return journey than on the outward one? Unless, of course, the Danube climbed back upwards from its source to its mouth, which was not, in reality, something to be seriously feared—not even on the part of that celebrated but unpredictable, capricious Danube!

When Ilia Krusch had come from RaczBecse to Sigmaringen in this boat, which he usually availed of for fishing purposes, he had been obliged, most of the time, to ask the help of the steamboats or tugs which frequent the river in such great numbers, and not once had anybody refused him such help. Moreover, he used to plead his case by testifying to the fact that he was a former sailing master—

which indeed he must have been. Indeed, on several occasions, the captains had noted that he was well acquainted with the all-too-often highly dangerous channels of the Danube which have to be negotiated through the multiple islands spread out along the river's course.

It was, therefore, in this manner that Ilia Krusch had completed his previous long journey. Had it, in fact, been undertaken with the express purpose of competing with the members of the Danubian Line, to which he had belonged for some time? There was every reason to believe that this was indeed the case, and the success which he had achieved in that competition has been seen. One should not therefore be overly astonished that a fisherman who was so skilful, staunch and determined, should have come up with this truly eccentric plan to descend, fishing line in hand, these six hundred leagues of the great river.

Ilia Krusch's small open fishing boat was about twelve feet long, a flat-bottomed barge, measuring four feet in its center. To the front of the boat there was a round tarpaulin-like covering underneath which two men would have room to take shelter during the day in the event of bad weather, or, at night, they could equally take shelter there, should they wish to sleep. Bedding and blankets were spread out all along this tarpaulin shelter, which was closed off by a door. All around the barge, there were spread out a series of chests built at the sides of the boat, suitable for containing, on one side, clothes and linen; this was, essentially, a very rudimentary type of wardrobe! At the stern, another chest, which also served as a bench, contained various different types of utensils, and a small coal stove in which the boiling beef could be kept, and which could be used to grill potatoes or meat. In addition, it was very easy for Ilia Krusch to obtain fresh daily supplies of both fuel and food in the cities, small towns and villages all along the river. There would be no lack of opportunities for him to sell his fishing catch, on the days when this was bountiful. Most assuredly, throughout this river journey—which was likely to render even more illustrious the name of the Danubian Line's multiple prize winner—there would be no shortage of customers for his fish, either on the left bank or on the right.

It is hardly necessary to add that this barge was furnished with all of the various types of fishing equipment which constitute the material of the true fisherman: rods, poles, landing nets, mounts, floats, lead lines, sounding lines, hooks, artificial flies and additional reserve supplies of fibre and cord; in short, a well-furnished fishing kit, including various

Baden

types of bait for the different kinds of fish. Morning and evening, and even during the day, all the while drifting along downriver, Ilia Krusch would carry on line fishing. At the close of day, he would go off to sell his fish, from which he hoped to accrue substantial profit; then, after night had closed in, he would snuggle up under his tarpaulin shelter and would enjoy a good night's sleep until dawn once more broke, over the horizon. He would then recommence sailing along, carried completely onwards by the current, and would continue this peaceful and easy navigation, without ever having to ask for the use of a towpath along the river bank, or to be towed by the river steamboats.

The first day went by in this manner. Whenever the barge came close to the banks of the river, curious onlookers would always flock up to the boat in their droves. Ilia Krusch was thus greeted as he journeyed onwards. The boaters themselves—who are numerous on the Danube—followed his fishing tactics with interest. They exchanged remarks with him and were never sparing in their applause whenever the skilful fisherman reeled in some fine specimen of fish from out of the waters.

And in fact, that particular day, Ilia Krusch caught no less than about thirty of them, including barbels, bream, roaches, sticklebacks, and several of those grey mullets which are more specifically known as hotus. And when the valley began to grow dark underneath the veils of twilight, the boat stopped near an embankment on the left side of the river, at about twelve leagues distance from its point of departure.

Not once had Ilia Krusch's progress been hampered by those eddies which form at the bends in the river; not once had it been necessary to have recourse to the oar. He was able to use the steering oar alone in order to straighten the direction of the boat and maintain it in the direction of the current, and to thereby avoid colliding with the boats which sailed upriver or downriver in convoy.

What would he have done with all those fish which he couldn't possibly consume all on his own, if customers had not hastened towards him? For this is exactly what happened when the barge was tied fast to a tree: there were about fifty brave souls, inhabitants of the Duchy of Baden, calling out his name, surrounding him and paying him the requisite homage due to the multiple champion of the Danubian Line.

"Hey! Over here, Krusch!"

"A glass of the best beer for you, Krusch!"

"We want to buy your fish, Krusch!"

"Twenty kreutzers for this one, Krusch."

"A florin for that one, Krusch!"

And he didn't know to whom to give his attention at any given moment, such was the clamour of customers hailing him simultaneously! The result was that his catch had quickly earned him several fine clinking coins of the realm. This, in addition to the sum of money which he had already won at the competition, would ultimately represent a not inconsiderable amount, provided that the level of enthusiasm which was now beginning, at the source of the great river, maintained its momentum right up to the river's mouth!

And, indeed, why should such enthusiasm wane? Why would people cease to fight over Ilia Krusch's fish? Wasn't it an honor to possess some fine specimen from out of his hands, which, having been stuffed and preserved, would be worthy of being prominently displayed in some fishing museum? He didn't even have to go to the trouble of heading off to sell his wares to the householders living along the river: the local gourmets of fish instead bought them from him at his boat. Truth be told, it was a brilliant idea which he'd had, this worthy, honest Krusch, to set his sights on the Danube fishermen's championship!

There was most certainly no shortage of invitations to him to have supper at the home of some hospitable family or other. People would have been happy to have him as a guest at their dinner table. But he seemed to wish to leave his boat only as little as possible. Even though he was not given to refusing a nice glass of wine, beer or liqueur in the inns along the river bank, he at least consumed alcohol with discretion, being given, as he was, to a level of sobriety which contrasted, however subtly, with the natural appetites of his fellow members of the Danubian Line! And furthermore, it bears repeating that this modest man was not at all in search of personal glory!

By half past eight, Ilia Krusch was in bed, underneath the tarpaulin-covered shelter. By nine, he had fallen into a sound sleep which did not come to an end until the first rays of morning light.

As is well-known, these first hours of morning light are a fruitful time for fishing, when the weather is favorable, even when there is a gentle, warm and intermittent rainfall, with a southerly or south-westerly wind. Following the morning's fishing session, Ilia Krusch was wished a safe journey by two or three good souls who had risen early to see him off; he unmoored his boat and pushed it out into the open waters by means of a vigorous blow of the gaff, setting off in a light mist which slid along the surface of the waters.

The second day passed off in the same manner as the first. It took him five days to descend fifty leagues of the Danube, from Donaueschingen as far as Ulm. It is true that not all of those days were equally smiled upon by auspicious good luck, though this does not at all mean, of course, that the craft which carried Ilia Krusch and his winning fortune met with any accident. But circumstances were not always favorable to his getting some fishing done, especially whenever there were violent downpours of rain, in which case Ilia Krusch, well wrapped-up in his oilskin greatcoat and well-protected from the elements under his hood, sought only to maintain his course in the middle of the river, unless some particularly stormy gusts of wind forced him to seek shelter under the trees along the riverbank.

It was during the afternoon of the 1st of May that he stopped near to the dock of the largest city of the kingdom of Wurttemberg, after Stuttgart, its capital.

It was only three o'clock, and, as Ilia Krusch had sold all of that morning's catch of fish along the way, he could afford to take a break until the following day without being obliged to drum up customers and seek out buyers for his fish. And moreover, this expression is hardly accurate, since it was, rather, the customers who used to actively seek him out.

As it happened, the arrival of the famous prize-winner had not been noticed. He was not expected until towards late evening. Thus, there was not the usual bustle of over-attentive admirers and, very satisfied, overall, with being able to remain incognito, he availed of this opportunity to indulge his desire to visit the city without drawing the attention of the general public to himself. As he did not know the city of Ulm, this was, naturally, an obvious opportunity to satisfy his curiosity.

It would not, however, be accurate to say that the dock was completely deserted at the moment when the barge arrived there to moor.

In fact, for the last few hundred feet, as the barge sailed down the river, a man had been following it without once taking his eyes off it.

So, was it the case that this man had recognised Ilia Krusch as the fisherman steering the craft? Whatever the case may be, the latter had not paid this stranger any particular attention.

This man was of medium height, rather thin, wearing a tight-fitting, fashionable Hungarian garment, which was very neat and well-tailored, the type of clothing that might be worn by an amateur as opposed to a professional person. This man had a keen, sharp eye, a determined air and resolute gait, though he was certainly more than forty years old, and he seemed to be looking around, as though he was afraid that he . was being followed or spied upon. He carried a leather case.

When Ilia Krusch disembarked, the stranger appeared to experience a certain hesitation. He seemed to be thinking about what course of action to adopt. Was he going to make contact with the fisherman, or would he go back into town to make known his arrival?

While all this was going on, Ilia Krusch, who wasn't paying any heed to his observer, was securely fastening the grapnel of his boat, going back inside it, closing the door of the tarpaulin shelter, ensuring that the lid of the chests had been securely locked with a chain, then jumping onto dry land, and, enjoying a feeling of complete liberty, feeling very satisfied not to be the center of attention amidst a procession of admirers, he reached the first street which went back upwards towards the town.

Whereupon the stranger immediately began to follow him, keeping a distance of about twenty steps behind him.

The Danube flows through Ulm, rendering it Wurttemburgeois on its left bank, and Bavarian on the right, in sum, a truly German place, and, if he had been a true connoisseur in this matter, Ilia Krusch would have been able to note the differences between this city and the cities of his own country.

Perhaps the man who had been following him since he had disembarked in the northern part of the city could have acted as a guide to him? But he did not at all seek to speak to him, contenting himself with merely not losing sight of him.

Ilia Krusch thus wandered along old streets, along which were lined antiquated shops with hatches, into which customers hardly ever enter, and in which business is transacted through the glass of the display window. And, whenever the wind is whistling, what a racket of clanging, resounding metal is then to be heard, as the heavy shop signs, cut variously into the shapes of bears, stags, crosses and crowns, swing from side to side.

Ilia Krusch, his eyes wide open in amazement, his mouth gaping and agog, his good-natured, kindly face completely expressive of wonderment, wandered along aimlessly, trustingly counting on fate and luck to lead him to the most interesting, strangest places to be seen. Having reached the city's historic district, he crossed through an area in which general butchers, tripe butchers and tanners keep their drying sheds alongside a muddy stream. Having examined, approvingly and indulgently, all the displays of meat, he allowed himself to be tempted by a fine dishful of tripe, promising himself to prepare it on the little stove in his barge. Moreover, like most line fishermen, though he was not especially fond of eating fish—with the exception of carp and pike—he was not known to turn up his nose at the pork butcher's cutlets and sausages.

Ilia Krusch was not content with making just this one purchase. He was not at all unaware of the fact that this former imperial city was renowned for the delicacy of its snails, the sales of which continue to rise, year in year out, to several million. He thus treated himself to several dozen specimens of this delicacy, for which he would certainly have paid less, or perhaps not have had to pay for at all, had the merchant known the identity of the illustrious customer with whom he was dealing. But Ilia Krusch, who had little inclination for chasing recognition and fame, really hoped that he could leave Ulm without any incident occurring to "blow his cover."

As he continued to stroll along aimlessly in this way, Ilia Krusch found himself standing in front of the cathedral, which happens to be one of the most audacious, bold and striking in architectural design, in all of Germany. Its spire had nurtured the Babelian ambition of reaching a higher point in the heavens than that of the Strasbourg cathedral. But this ambition—just like so many other more human aspirations—had been thwarted, and the furthermost point of the Wurttembourgeois spire stops at the height of three hundred and thirty-seven feet.

Ilia Krusch did not belong to the family of steeplejacks. Thus, he didn't conceive of the idea of scaling the heights up to the spire, to a point from which he would have had a sweeping view commanding the entirety of the city and the surrounding countryside. If he had done so, he would certainly have been followed by this stranger, who never let him out of his sight for a single second, yet whose mysterious persistence continued to go completely unnoticed by Krusch. Thus, when he entered the cathedral, he was shadowed by this stranger, and unknowingly accompanied by him while he admired the tabernacle which a French traveller, Mr. Duruy, has compared to a stronghold with boxes and machicolation, and then as he looked at the stalls of the chancel which a fifteenth-century artist has populated with some of the famous men and women of that era.

Both men eventually found themselves standing in front of the City Hall. If Ilia Krusch had asked the age of this municipal monument—should that sort of information have been of interest to him—it is likely that the stranger would have been able to reply to his enquiry in the following terms:

"More than six hundred years have passed since this cathedral was constructed. It is older than this pretty fountain designed by Joerg Syrling, built almost a century later, and which you can admire on the Market Square opposite the City Hall."

But the worthy fisherman did not care to question anybody on this subject, neither the stranger nor indeed any other citizen of Ulm. What he had just seen was undoubtedly sufficient to the needs of his artistic leanings, and, given that—leaving from Market Square—he began to walk back downwards towards the left bank of the river, his intention was clearly to go back to what a sailor would have referred to as his "first port of call."

His mysterious follower made his way through the same streets, in the middle of the maze of a district which would have needed a guide to help one negotiate it. Thus, Ilia Krusch was unsure of which direction to take, on several occasions along the way, and was obliged to consult passers-by as to the correct route.

It was now or never that the time was ripe, and the opportunity a suitable one, for the stranger to render a small degree of service to Ilia Krusch, by giving him directions, if he wanted to make direct contact with him; for there could be no doubt but that the mysterious follower knew the city well. He did not, however, avail of this opportunity, and remained in his state of cautious anticipation without showing any outward signs of such expectancy.

On two occasions before arriving at the quay, Ilia Krusch stopped for several minutes at a time. The first time, it was to watch a group of stilt-walkers passing by, perched and teetering upon their long stilts, this being an exercise which is much appreciated in the city of Ulm, although it is not an actual necessity imposed upon the inhabitants, as it is in the ancient university city of Tubingen, where the activity first came into being, given that that city has such damp and bumpy, uneven surfaces, which are unsuited to being walked over in the normal way, by ordinary pedestrians.

In order to better enjoy this spectacle, which comprised a troupe of young men, young women, little boys and little girls, all in joyful high spirits, Ilia Krusch had sat down in a café, and the stranger thus sat down near to him, at a neighbouring table. Both men ordered a tankard of that famous beer which enjoys such renown in that region.

Ten minutes later, they had both set off again, and their onward progression was interrupted only once more, by one final stop.

Ilia Krusch had just stopped in front of a pipe shop, and the stranger could have heard him say: "Good! That's something I'd almost forgotten..."

The thing which Ilia Krusch had remembered, in a most timely fashion, was to buy one of those alder-wood pipes which come so highly-recommended in the city of Ulm. He therefore selected one of the pipes in question amongst those which the manufacturer showed him, a very simple pipe, it must, moreover, be said, one which could quite easily withstand the ups and downs of a river navigation of six hundred leagues; he then filled the pipe with great care, lit it, and reappeared outside the shop, in the middle of a cloud of aromatic tobacco smoke.

It was almost nightfall by the time Ilia Krusch found himself back on the quayside. Perhaps the news of his arrival had spread: a few

Ulm

curious onlookers were examining this barge which had avoided their inquisitive stares all along the riverside, up to now. But as the boat in question did not, in itself, offer anything of particular interest, the said inquisitive observers could only have been attracted to this place by the notoriety of its owner. Furthermore, as the said owner showed no signs of making his presence felt, they decided to put off, to a later date, the task of wishing him well and paying him their respects. And no doubt they had settled on the idea of returning the next day in order to witness the departure of the Danubian Line prizewinner.

However, it is well-known at this stage that, for one reason or another, Ilia Krusch preferred to shy away from any public displays of his celebrity. He therefore intended to leave at first light, before even the earliest risers could arrive.

As he had not been noticed when he had walked down along the quayside, nor when he had entered the barge, he was not now seen as he made sure that the mooring rope held fast and that it would not allow the vessel to float away during the night; neither was he observed as he supped on the remains of his midday dinner, thus sparing the various provisions he had just bought; neither was he seen as he slipped underneath the tarpaulin shelter to the rear of the boat, closing the door behind him. Finally, highly satisfied with his visit to the Wurttembourgeois city, he fell into a peaceful sleep, nurturing the hope that nothing would disturb his tranquil slumber.

Indeed, this tranquillity was not in the least disturbed, and yet, right up until the break of day, there was one particular man who was pacing restlessly up and down along the riverbank, never moving away from close to the barge, as if he had feared that Ilia Krusch might wish to benefit from the cover of darkness either to set off once again along the river current or to move away from the left bank in order to moor his boat at the right bank of the river.

The valley of the Danube had hardly been illuminated by the first rays of morning light than a movement became apparent on board the vessel.

The door of the tarpaulin shelter had just been opened, and Ilia Krusch made his appearance. He straightened up, stretching to his entire height, opened one of the chests to the side of the boat, took out a bottle and a glass, swallowed a few mouthfuls of *kirschenwasser,* and then, lighting the pipe which he had purchased the previous evening, he smoked several puffs with evident pleasure.

Had he noticed the stranger who was there, seemingly keeping him under surveillance? It was unlikely, as the latter kept himself, at that point, hidden within the shadows of the parapet, and there was, as yet, hardly any daylight.

Moreover, the quay was deserted, and if any curious onlookers were to come back, they would no longer find anything to satisfy their curiosity. The barge would have already been far away, carried off by the river's strong current.

The fact was that Ilia Krusch had just dragged the vessel further out into the river on its mooring rope, and all he now needed to do was to cast off in order to move away from the river bank.

But it was at this moment that the stranger came back down close to Ilia Krusch and, grabbing hold of the mooring rope which was about to be taken back into the boat:

"My friend," he said, "you are Ilia Krusch, isn't that right?"

When all was said and done, Ilia Krusch could have no reason to conceal his identity, now that he was about to depart the area, and he replied, though with some hesitation:

"My goodness… yes… sir…"

"And you are getting ready to set off again?" asked the stranger.

"As you can see, Mr.…?"

And he seemed to expect that the stranger would be willing to give his own name, given that he already knew that of Ilia Krusch.

"Mister Jaeger," came the reply. "I am an Austrian, and since you are a Hungarian, we've been made to get along with each other."

"And what does Mr. Jaeger want with me?" asked Ilia Krusch, a certain mistrust in his tone.

"Here's the thing, Mr. Krusch. I've heard tell of your exploits. I've been wanting to get to know you. This plan to sail down the entire length of the River Danube, line-fishing as you go, seemed really original to me, and I have a proposition to make to you."

"And what might that be, Mr. Jaeger?"

"What do you estimate to be the value of the fish that you will catch throughout your navigation of the Danube?"

"How much do I think my catch can earn me?"

"Yes…"

"About one hundred florins, perhaps," replied Ilia Krusch.

"Well, let me offer you five hundred for them… Yes! Five hundred, the understanding being that, each evening, I'll get the takings for that day's sale of fish…"

"Five hundred florins!" Ilia Krusch repeated.

The fisherman from Racz would undoubtedly have undertaken an excellent sales drive, by accepting an offer of this kind. The two prizes from the Sigmaringen contest which were already worth two hundred florins to him, and the five hundred now offered to him by Mr. Jaeger, this was a windfall he couldn't have ever expected. And in actual fact, he wondered whether this offer should be taken seriously.

"Your response to this offer?" asked Mr. Jaeger insistently, seeming to fear a refusal.

"It's certainly tempting, Mr. Jaeger," said Ilia Krusch… And if it's not some kind of joke… or a hoax…"

"I wouldn't dream of joking with Mr. Ilia Krusch," replied Mr. Jaeger, rather curtly, and I've never deceived anybody."

"But," Ilia Krusch went on, "you intend, therefore, to come on board my barge with me…"

"Indeed, Mr. Krusch, and that would be an essential condition of our agreement."

Ilia Krusch displayed a certain hesitation in committing himself.

"Your vessel seems to me to be big enough to carry two people…"

"Certainly, Mr. Jaeger, and there's room for two underneath the tarpaulin cover…"

"That's what I thought."

"But the journey will be a long one… perhaps two months, and…"

"I have, in this case, all of the linen and changes of clothes which I will need…"

"So, you had prepared everything with this journey in mind?" asked Ilia Krusch, looking at his interlocutor carefully.

"Yes, Mr. Krusch, I knew that you were going to arrive here in Ulm, and I was watching out for you… I followed you during your walk… I even stayed here on the quayside all night so as not to miss your departure… and I'm ready to get on board with you, and if you agree to my accompanying you…"

"And you're offering five hundred florins?" repeated Ilia Krusch, bringing the discussion of the offer back to its most serious aspect.

"Five hundred, and here's half of it," replied Mr. Jaeger, handing over a wad of banknotes.

Ilia Krusch took them, examined them, and counted them with a level of care which proved a certain level of distrust on his part, but one which did not seem to offend Mr. Jaeger in the slightest.

At this moment, several people began to appear in the distance, some coming from upriver, the others from downriver, while a certain number of them were coming down the streets of the left bank. Undoubtedly, rumors of Ilia Krusch's presence had begun to circulate, and if he wished to escape from public curiosity, he no longer had a moment to lose.

It should be pointed out that Mr. Jaeger, whose face was beginning to darken at the approach of these curious folk, seemed no less anxious to avoid them. He therefore emphatically repeated his question to Ilia Krusch.

"Will you take me on board?" he asked.

There is every reason to believe that Ilia Krusch accepted the proposition because, a minute afterwards, the barge was heading off into the current and Mr. Jaeger was on board at Krusch's side.

So it was that, by the time the curious throng arrived, the Danubian Line's prizewinner was already about twenty yards distant from them so that they could greet him only through their faraway hurrahs.

Chapter V

From Ulm to Regensburg

EVEN AT ULM, where the Danube crosses this charming little kingdom of Wurttemberg, it is still only a modest stretch of water; it has not yet had its power strengthened by the great tributaries and there is nothing to allow one to foresee that it is about to become one of the largest rivers in Europe. The current was flowing at an average speed of one league per hour. Several heavy boats, loaded to the gunwale, boats of lesser size, were sailing down the Danube, some abandoning themselves to the flow of the current, others increasing their speed by means of a wide sail which was swelled by the morning breeze emanating from some north-westerly clouds. It seemed as though it was going to be a fine day, the weather alternating between sun and shadow but with no threat of rain.

These weather conditions were about as ideal as one could wish for, and an experienced fisherman would not have neglected to take full advantage of them.

Ilia Krusch thus prepared his pieces of fishing equipment with painstaking care, without being excessively rushed, and with the air of a man whose primary quality is that of patience.

His travelling companion, seated towards the rear of the barge, seemed to take an interest in these preparations. He had declared that the art of fishing was particularly appealing to him, with all its vagaries and surprises… But whether he himself was also a fisherman, that was something that he hadn't mentioned and which Ilia Krusch didn't know.

Thus, as he continued to work, and being quite chatty by nature, Krusch brought the conversation round to this topic.

"Mr. Jaeger," he asked, "here we are setting off on a long sailing trip…"

"Oh! Not by sea, only by river."

"No doubt," replied Ilia Krusch, "and I'm not claiming that our trip will involve any danger. But it will probably last quite a few weeks, and perhaps the days will seem long to you… unless, that is…"

"Unless?" repeated Mr. Jaeger, with a questioning intonation.

"Unless you are of the same profession as I…"

"And so, what might that be, Mr. Krusch?"

"A line fisherman… I still don't know whether you are or not."

"Oh! An unworthy fisherman," Mr. Jaeger cheerfully replied, "until I become educated at your school! It will be enough for me to observe you in operation, and rest assured that I won't be bored for one second!"

Ilia Krusch nodded his agreement and Mr. Jaeger added:

"Are you not going to start fishing again this morning?"

"I'm getting ready to do so, Mr. Jaeger, but you can't prepare too carefully… Fish are distrustful by nature, and you can't take too many precautions when it comes to luring them and reeling them in. Some of them are unusually intelligent, the tench among others… You've got to compete with it in terms of cunning and craftiness, and its mouth is so hard that if it doesn't give up struggling on the hook, it risks breaking the fishing lines…"

"I believe the tench is not much sought after by lovers of fine food," observed Mr. Jaeger.

"No, because most of the time, as it's particularly fond of the muddy waters where it gets its food, its flesh doesn't taste very nice. But if, by some stroke of good fortune, a tench doesn't happen to have this fault, it's one of the finest of delicacies."

"And," asked Mr. Jaeger, "don't you consider pike to be among the tastiest of fish?"

"Absolutely," declared Ilia Krusch, "as long as it weighs at least five to six pounds, because the small ones are practically only fishbones. But, in any case, pike couldn't be regarded as intelligent or crafty fish…"

"Absolutely right, Mr. Krusch! I would have thought that those freshwater sharks, as they're called…"

"Are as obtuse as saltwater sharks, Mr. Jaeger. Real brutes, on the same level as perch or eels! Fishing for them can be a lucrative business, but never a glorious one! They are, as one fine connoisseur has written, fish which "allow themselves to be caught," not fish that "you catch"!

Mr. Jaeger could not but admire such persuasive conviction with which Mr. Ilia Krusch expressed himself, and it was no less admiration than he felt for the painstaking care which Krusch took in preparing his fishing tackle.

First of all, Ilia Krusch had taken his rod, both flexible and light, which, having been bent at its tip almost to breaking point, had straightened back up as rigidly as before. Moreover, it consisted of two parts, the first part being at its widest at its base of four centimeters, and diminishing in size until it measured only one centimetre at the place where the tip of the rod began, a tip made of fine, tough wood. Made from a pole of hazelnut tree wood, the rod measured almost four meters in length, and if the well-informed, wise fisherman that was Krusch had chosen it, it was because he intended—without distancing himself from the river bank—fishing for deep water fish such as bream, roach and other similar species; thanks to the spring and resilience of the rod's tip, he would be able to tire them out and outwit all their efforts to disentangle themselves from the hook.

And then, showing Mr. Jaeger the hooks which he had just attached with the leader to the extremity of the horsehair tip, he said:

"You see, Mr. Jaeger, these are number eleven type hooks, very fine in body. I'm going to bait them with cooked wheat, well-softened and punctured at one side only, one of the best types of bait for roach."

"I want to believe you, Mr. Krusch," replied Mr. Jaeger, "but what's one of the best things of all for the morning fisherman, is his morning drink! A little glass of brandy seems to me to be in order…"

And with these words, Mr. Jaeger took, from his suitcase, a small bottle which he caused to sparkle in the rays of the rising sun.

"Yes please, I will gladly join you in a drink," replied Ilia Krusch, "but only because it's still early morning. You see, the motto of the line fisherman is 'Sobriety above all else!' He must never partake of white wine, which can unsteady his nerves, and should consume the least alcohol possible, as it interferes with the accuracy of his vision. The preferred drink is still cold coffee…"

"Nevertheless, I hope you won't decline to agree with me on this occasion, Mr. Krusch?"

"To your health, Mr. Jaeger!"

A dampschiff

And two small glasses, filled with an excellent wine brandy, were clinked together in honor of good friendship.

It goes without saying that, while Ilia Krusch was making his preparations, the barge was tranquilly descending the river. It maintained its own steady course, so that there was no need to steer it. Moreover, the steering oar is in place on its rear wedge, and, all the while holding his fishing rod in his hand, the fisherman is able to manoeuver the oar with the other. This time, Ilia Krusch did not intend to distance himself from the left bank, but rather, intended to follow the bank at a maximum distance of two yards.

"That's the job finished," he said, once he had completed baiting his hooks, "and now, all that remains for me to do is to begin trying my luck."

And indeed, he was ready, and sat down on the bench, while Mr. Jaeger rested his elbows against the tarpaulin shelter, his landing net situated within easy reach.

The fishing line was thus launched after being lightly and methodically swung from side to side, an action which was not without a certain grace of movement; the hooks plunged deeply below the lightly golden waters, and the weight at the end of the line caused the hooks to adopt a vertical position, which is, in the opinion of fishing

A dampschiff

professionals, the preferred one. In addition, the floater consisted only of swan's feather which—as it doesn't take in water—is, as a result, excellent.

It is self-evident that a deep silence, from that moment onwards, reigned within the vessel. Fish can be frightened away all too easily by the sound of voices, and moreover, a serious fisherman has better things to be doing than making conversation. He has to listen out attentively for any movements of his floater and thereby not miss out on the precise instant at which his prey must be struck.

Throughout this morning, Ilia Krusch had every reason to be self-congratulatory on his success. Not only did he catch about twenty roach, but also several pike. Mr. Jaeger could only admire the rapid precision with which he struck his prey, this being necessary for fish of these species. As soon as he felt that he had "got a bite," he took care not to immediately bring roach or other fish up to the surface; rather, he allowed them to struggle in the watery depths, to tire themselves in vain efforts to disentangle themselves from the hook, displaying all the while that unflappable composure which is one of the characteristics of any fisherman worthy of the name.

Moreover, conversation resumed between his travelling companion and himself, as soon as the catch had been landed. He did not at all seek to be secretive about the tricks of his trade—or art—not at all being one of these egotistical people who jealously guard the benefits of their long experience. Also, it certainly seemed as though Mr. Jaeger was taking an interest in the lessons of such an eminent master, and there could be no doubting that, before long, he would try his luck by equipping himself with a second fishing line, if only to while away the long hours of this navigation.

The fishing session came to an end towards eleven o'clock. With the sun—the rays of which sparkled on the surface of the Danube's waters—practically at its zenith, the fish were no longer biting, and Ilia Krusch would set to work once more when the "glorious daytime star" set in the evening.

"Mr. Jaeger," he said, "those evening hours are the most favorable for catching fish, at least when the temperature is still warm; if we were in the middle of winter, it would be, on the contrary, in the middle of the day that there would be the greatest prospects of success."

Both men thus took the opportunity to have lunch, dining not alone on the provisions which Ilia Krusch had procured at Ulm on the previous evening, and on some of the tinned food locked up within the coffers of the barge, but also on a certain piece of ham which Mr. Jaeger took from his suitcase, and which he promised himself to replenish as many times as would be necessary. He had no intention of being fed at his host's expense throughout the entire duration of the journey, and Ilia Krusch feasted regally on this pork product of the best factories of Mayence.

During the afternoon, while Ilia Krusch allowed his eyelids to shut several times, even while he was inhaling his pipe smoke, Mr. Jaeger, for his part, was closely observing both banks of the river, the boats travelling upriver or downriver, some being towed, others floating along freely. Along the right bank, on land which had been reclaimed from the river's edge for the construction of the railway line, the trains went by, the engines puffed, their smoke sometimes mingling with that of the dampfschiffs, whose wheels beat the river water.[1]

Perhaps Ilia Krusch didn't notice the care with which his travelling companion was watching not alone the boats—which were already fairly numerous along this part of the River Danube—but also the vehicles which travelled along the river banks. Another person, more observant, or less indifferent to anything which wasn't related to fishing, would certainly have noticed.

During the final hours of daylight of this particular day, the fishing line was once more fitted with bait. About a dozen fish didn't at all decline to "take the bait." This was a timely catch, and both the morning and evening catch were conveniently sold in the little village near which the barge was tethered for the night. The takings of this sale went into Mr. Jaeger's pocket, in accordance with the terms of the agreement reached. But, in his characteristically honest manner, Ilia Krusch said to him:

"No matter, Mr. Jaeger, I imagine you're going to find it difficult to earn back the five hundred florins that my catches will have cost you!…"

"Oh, that'll be for me to worry about, Mr. Krusch, and just wait and see, my end of the bargain will work out better than you think."

It was true that, in these humble villages, there could be no grounds for counting on the sort of rush of customers which would take place in the bigger towns—just as had taken place at Ulm—when the presence of the Danubian Line's prizewinning fisherman would become public knowledge.

The days of the 3rd and 4th of May were not marked by any incidents of note. The fishing carried on in the same conditions and yielded the same profits.

---

1. *Dampfschiff* is a German word for steamship; beyond that generality, it does not specify a certain type of vessel. Jules Verne used the word in his original, French-language manuscript, so it has been retained here to preserve the intended flavor.

That evening, the anchor was cast onto the embankment at Neuburg, after the barge had crossed the two bridges which link both sides of the river. This former military stronghold has a population of about six thousand souls, and it is no exaggeration to say that if Mr. Jaeger had wished to "do a little advertising," to use a characteristically French expression, half of those inhabitants would have come up to Ilia Krusch and given him the sort of reception he deserved. But apart from the fact that that good man was not at all seeking the acclamations of the crowds, his companion—though sales would necessarily suffer as a result of his decision—maintained the same reserve, for whatever reason.

The barge had taken three days to cover the twenty-five leagues which separate Ulm from Neuburg, but it took only half a day to cross the twenty kilometers from Neuburg to Ingolstadt. It stopped at the confluence of the Schutter, one of the tributaries of the great river.[2] The reason why it didn't continue on its route was because of the bad weather, violent rainfalls, severe squalls, and a sort of swell on the surface of the Danube.

The two travelling companions considered themselves fortunate to find shelter at an inn on the quayside. This, however, did not at all prevent Ilia Krusch from going out to explore the little town. He even suggested to Mr. Jaeger that he accompany him. But the latter preferred to stay indoors, at the inn, and if on occasions he did happen to venture out of doors, it was only for the purposes of walking along the riverside, his interest still attracted by the movement of river traffic taking place along the Danube.

It goes without saying that, having lunched at the inn, Messrs. Jaeger and Krusch met up again at the same table for their evening meal, which was paid for by the former, a gesture which earned him the grateful thanks of the latter. Though the rainfall had eased a little in the afternoon, it had, by evening, begun to fall, once again, more heavily than ever. Mr. Jaeger therefore decided to reserve a room for the night at the inn. However, he was alone in occupying it: despite his entreaties, Ilia Krusch was anxious to return to his vessel.

"Once I'm under my tarpaulin shelter," he explained, "I fear neither wind nor showers, and I don't want to leave my boat unoccupied during the night."

2.　Verne gives the name of the Schutter as Shatter.

"See you tomorrow morning then, Mr. Krusch," said Mr. Jaeger. "Early," replied Ilia Krusch, "for we leave at dawn…"

"Weather permitting…"

"It'll permit our departure, Mr. Jaeger! Believe me, I'm an old hand at this river-going lark!"

And indeed, the old hand had not at all been mistaken. The gusts continued throughout half of the night, under the force of the west wind. But the wind then changed to a northerly direction, and, by the time the first rays of morning sunlight reappeared on the horizon, the sky was completely clear to the left bank of the river.

Mr. Jaeger arrived at the crack of dawn, just as Ilia Krusch was cleaning out his barge, and emptying it of the rainwater which had begun to gather at the bottom of the vessel.

"You were right," said Mr. Jaeger to him, "and here's a fine clear sky."

"And one that's very conducive to fishing," replied Ilia Krusch. "We're going to get plenty of 'bites' today!"

A quarter of an hour later, the vessel was moving away from the quayside and this time, instead of making for the left bank, it crossed the river, and sailed down with the current along the right bank. Given the wind direction, conditions would be more favorable at this side.

The direction in which the Danube flows, from Ulm onwards, is, generally speaking, in a line drawn from south-west to north-west. After straightening up a little between Neuburg and Ingolstadt, it goes up again and reaches its highest degree of latitude at the city of Regensburg.[3] The latter city is only about a hundred kilometers distant from Ingolstadt, and it was not inconceivable that the barge might reach it during this evening of the seventh of May.

Just as Ilia Krusch had confidently predicted, the catch of fish was bountiful. Thanks to his accomplished experience, he knew how to vary the types of bait most opportunely, sometimes using midges in order to catch trout, chubs or gudgeon, at other times using little balls of meat for barbell, while on yet other occasions using slugs for eels, or tadpoles for pike.

The result of this expertise was that, in the course of the morning, the landing net brought on board about forty of these different fish, and about the same amount in the afternoon. And perhaps the speed of the barge had been detrimental to the potential for catching an even greater amount of fish; the current was flowing quite rapidly. This enabled the twenty-five leagues to be travelled in forty-eight hours. But it was already late, past nine in the evening, by the time Ilia Krusch stopped at the Regensburg bridge.

---

3.   Verne gives the name of Regensburg as Ratisbonne.

It was therefore better to postpone, till the following day, the sale of the fish. Moreover, Ilia Krusch had no intention of spending the whole day of the 8th in this city; he had already visited it several times, and felt that it was better not to hang around for no good reason.

But, though he was not at all inclined to wander around Regensburg, it seemed that Mr. Jaeger, for his part, was indeed anxious to do so, because he suggested to his companion that they stay there for twenty-four hours.

"Seeing as the opportunity presents itself," he said, "it would quite suit me to spend all day tomorrow visiting this city. I can use the day to sort out a few bits of business, which will spare me having to come back here at a later stage, and if it's not inconvenient to you, Mr. Krusch..."

"Not in the least, Mr. Jaeger, apart from being a little delayed as a result... But if I can be of any service to you..."

"Thank you very much, Mr. Krusch, and it only remains for us to bid each other good night."

With these words, and having had supper and smoked a pipe, both men, half-undressed, stretched out underneath the tarpaulin shelter, and nothing had disturbed their sound slumber by the time the rising sun cast a spot of fiery light on the sharp gable end of the cathedral of the *Gesandtenstrasse.*[4]

It is timely to mention at this point that, since leaving Ulm, the Danubian Line's prize winner had no longer been greeted by the sort of enthusiastic reception with which he had been honored in the Baden city. How could it be that such a famous character could be able to pass unnoticed between the banks of the river? Thus, neither at Neuburg nor at Ingoldstadt, had there been any gathering of curious folk, nobody watching out for his arrival from the river bank, entrusted with the duty of letting people know that Ilia Krusch had arrived?...

And yet, the newspapers of Ulm had announced his departure on the morning of May 7th. Moreover, it was not known that he was no longer alone in his journey down the Danube. By the time the curious throngs had arrived to cheer him off, the barge had already left the river bank, and his travelling companion had avoided being seen. Otherwise, one can only imagine what the gossip would have been like! Who was this mysterious newcomer travelling alongside Ilia Krusch, and under what circumstances had the latter consented to accept him

4.   Ambassadors' Street.

Ratisbonne

on board? And the local paper of Ulm would have immediately gotten involved also… And the fact would have been reported in turn by the German, Austrian and Hungarian newspapers, with commentary of varying degrees of accuracy. But what was most singularly noteworthy was that, from that moment onwards, there was a shortage of news of Krusch. People no longer seemed to know what had become of the hero who had been, up to then, the subject of so much acclamation. And so it was that he went unnoticed at Neuburg and Ingoldstat and that nobody witnessed him passing alongside the townships and villages of both sides of the river.

Besides, Ilia Krusch had no desire to be conspicuous, at Regensburg any more than elsewhere. He undoubtedly preferred to travel incognito, and that Mr. Jaeger felt likewise. It would be sufficient for his companion to have his presence attested at the mouth of the Danube in order to get all due credit for—and also to reap the rewards of—his eccentric journey.

It was likely that nobody would notice this modest vessel in the midst of the numerous barges which were moored at the quay at Regensburg, where the ferry traffic is very busy. The water starts to become deep at this part of the river, into which pour liberally the waters of the Naab and the Regen, level with the city, and boats of two hundred tons can thus navigate effortlessly.

As for the barge, Ilia Krusch had towed it under the first of the fifteen arches of the bridge which joins both sides of the river—the longest bridge in all of Germany, three hundred and sixty feet in length, supported upon two islands, and which was constructed towards the middle of the twelfth century.

It was thus to be supposed that the inhabitants of this city, which for fifty years was the seat of the Imperial Diet, would discover, too late, that after Charlemagne and Napoleon, the prize winner of the Danubian Line had been their guest for twenty-four hours in the course of his journey.

Chapter VI

FROM REGENSBURG TO PASSAU

THE FOLLOWING MORNING, at the breaking of the day, Mr. Jaeger, the first of the two to get up, came out from underneath the tarpaulin shelter, performed his morning ablutions with the cold water of the river, straightened and adjusted his clothes and, having put on his wide-brimmed hat, stood squarely upright at the back of the boat.

From that vantage point, and looking both upriver and downriver from the arch, his watchful observations noted, in turn, the boats which were sailing along the river as well as those which were still moored to the quays of the two banks. This sight seemed to be of strong interest to him. His eyes followed the preparations for departure which were being made here and there; sails being hoisted, funnels of tugs plumed with blackish smoke. But what attracted his attention, above all, were the barges which descended, or were preparing to descend, the Danube.

For about ten minutes, Mr. Jaeger thus remained in watchful, close observation. He was then joined by Ilia Krusch who was coming out, in his turn, from underneath the tarpaulin shelter.

"Well! So how have you slept?" his travelling companion asked him.

"As deeply as your good self, Mr. Krusch, just as if I'd spent the night in the best room of the best hotel. And, now, I'm going to take my leave of you until supper, for I shall come back before evening."

"As you wish, Mr. Jaeger, and while you're going about your business, I'm off to sell our catch at the Regensburg market."

"For as high a price as possible, Mr. Krusch," was Mr. Jaeger's advice to him, "because it's my profits which are at stake…"

"As high a price as possible, indeed. But I fear that you will have some trouble in recuperating all of your five hundred florins…"

"That's not my opinion of the matter," Mr. Jaeger contented himself with replying.

The barge was then towed in near to the quay, and he disembarked, after taking leave of Mr. Krusch.

It was obvious that Mr. Jaeger knew the city well, because he didn't hesitate over the direction to follow in order to reach the city center district. At only a short distance from the bridge, he was standing opposite the Dom, the cathedral with unfinished towers, and was only looking rather distractedly at the interesting great door which dates from the end of the fifteenth century. He set off through the silent streets of this city which, in the past, had been noisy and boisterous, and which was still flanked, here and there, by feudal keeps, ten stories high, and is no longer livened up by a population which has fallen to twenty-six thousand souls. Most assuredly, he would not be going to admire, at the Palace of the Prince of Tour and Taxis, the Gothic chapel and cloister, or the library of pipes, which comprised part of this former convent. Neither would he visit the Rathaus, the City Hall, once the seat of the Diet, the great hall of which is decorated with old wall hangings, and in which the torture chamber, with its various devices, is shown, not without pride, by the caretaker of the premises. Mr. Jaeger would not spend a single trinkgeld, the German tip, on the services of a tour guide. He didn't need anybody's help in getting to the Dampfschiffshof Hotel which he reached by following streets whose houses are sculpted, on their facades, with the weapons of the imperial nobility.[1]

After he had crossed the threshold of the hotel, Mr. Jaeger sat down at a table in the parlour and asked for the local city newspapers, as well as the foreign papers, the reading of which took him an hour. Then, having notified the staff that he would be back for lunch, he left the hotel without giving his name; not that this was necessary, in any case, since he was not due to be accommodated there.

If Ilia Krusch had followed his companion in the course of that particular morning, he would have seen him making his way straight

1.   Dampfschiffshof Hotel is German for "The Steamship Hotel."

Ratisbonne

to the Post Office. There, Mr. Jaeger asked whether there were any general delivery ("poste restante") letters under the initials "XYZ."[2]

Two letters had been waiting for collection for several days past, one dated from Belgrade with a Serbian stamp, the other dated from Ismail, a Moldavian town at the mouth of the Danube.

Mr. Jaeger took these letters, read them attentively without betraying the least feeling in his facial expression, and then put them back into his pocket, after first placing them back in their envelopes.

Having done this, he was getting ready to leave the office when a rather shabbily-dressed man accosted him at the door.

Mr. Jaeger and this man evidently knew each other, because, just as the newcomer was about to speak, he was stopped in his tracks by a gesture, which evidently meant: "Not here... someone might hear us."

Both men went out, walking close to each other in the direction of the nearby square.

---

2.   These same initials were used by William J. Hypperbone while in disguise in *The Will of an Eccentric*.

There, they would not be bothered by passers-by. They would be able to speak to each other in complete security, which is what they did for about ten minutes. Mr. Jaeger even took one of the letters, which he had just removed from his pocket, and read several lines of it to the other.

And, if he had been there, Ilia Krusch would have heard him say:

"So, the boat which was spotted has arrived at Nicopoli?…"

"Yes, but no matter how widely we've searched, we've found nothing…"

"Okay. Are you returning to Belgrade?"

"Yes."

"It looks like I'm going to be there in three or four weeks."

"Should I expect you there?"

"Probably… unless you receive orders to the contrary between now and then."

And just as they were about to take their leave of each other, Mr. Jaeger asked: "Have you heard tell of a fellow by the name of Ilia Krusch?"

"That fisherman who's embarked on a fishing journey, sailing down the Danube?"

"Precisely. The thing is, when he arrives in Belgrade or anywhere else, if I happen to be with him, don't pretend to know me."

And with those words, they went their separate ways; the shabbily-dressed man penetrated into the hilly districts of the city while Mr. Jaeger took a street which would lead him back to the Steamship Hotel.

It was now lunchtime. But, before taking his place at the communal dining table, Mr. Jaeger went back into the parlour, and there wrote two letters, doubtless in answer to those which he had received; then, having gone to post them in the nearest postbox, he sat down to lunch.

Five or six diners were already seated, chatting about one thing and another. But though Mr. Jaeger ate with a hearty appetite, and more copiously than he would have done had he merely been feasting on the provisions of the barge, he did not at all involve himself in the conversation. However, he listened closely to what was being said, with the air of a man who seemed to be in the habit of lending an ear to everything that was said around him. And, the comment which struck him most particularly, was when one of the diners said to the person seated beside him:

"So, this famous Latzko, there's no news of him?"

"No more news of him than there is of the famous Krusch," replied the other. "He was expected to pass alongside Regensburg, but he hasn't yet been spotted..."

"Indeed, it's most peculiar..."

"Unless Krusch and Latzko are one and the same..."

"Are you joking with me?"

"Well, my goodness, who knows?..."

Upon hearing these exchanged remarks, which were most certainly just trivial conversation, what might be called remarks of a vague, speculative kind, Mr. Jaeger had swiftly raised his head. But there was a sort of hardly noticeable movement of his shoulder, and he finished his lunch without saying a word.

Towards half past twelve in the afternoon, Mr. Jaeger, having settled his bill at the hotel, was setting off through the streets which lead back downwards towards the quayside. Most probably, he had very little interest in visiting the higher-placed districts of the city further uphill, and he seemed, rather, attracted by the movement of river-going traffic which, at Regensburg, is fairly high in volume. Yet it is rare that outsiders visiting this city would neglect to travel through the suburban district of Stadt-am-Hof, adjoining the city; but this did not at all attract Mr. Jaeger's interest, and he returned towards the river bank.

Once he had arrived at this spot, instead of rejoining Ilia Krusch, who, having completed his sales of fish, would now be back in the barge, he went over the bridge and travelled along the right bank of the river.

At this place there were moored a certain number of barges, some of which were about to sail away. In fact, several of them, situated in a line, one behind the other, took the towrope of a tugboat and continued their navigation towards the upper course of the River Danube.

But it didn't seem that these vessels were likely to be of interest to Mr. Jaeger. The boats which he was continuing to observe with extreme attention were those whose destination was downriver.

The boats which were there included about half a dozen with a capacity to carry about a hundred tons. At most, they drew three or four feet, which allowed them to navigate through the shallowest channels, sometimes narrowly compressed between islands and river banks.

Mr. Jaeger remained at this spot for a good two hours, observing what was happening on board these barges, watching the loaders who were bringing along new parcels to top up the cargo, and the final preparations of those who were about to leave Ratisbonne in the afternoon.

Moreover, the comings and goings were rather lively and bustling on the quayside, and, apart from the assistants of the inland water shipping services, quite a few curious onlookers were coming and going.

Among these spectators were some who had not at all been brought there by a simple feeling of curiosity. In the middle of the groups of people, it was easy to recognize certain customs officers; Mr. Jaeger was not at all mistaken in this regard. Moreover, he could not be unaware of the fact that, since the meeting of the international commission, the most stringent measures had been decided upon in order to maintain surveillance of the Danube over its entire course. These customs officers, whose boats operated night and day on the river, didn't fail to visit a single boat, either when it dropped anchor at the cities or small towns along the river, or during its navigation.

In any event, it certainly wasn't on that day or in that spot that they were able to get their hands on that uncatchable Latzko, and this serious case of smuggling hadn't made any progress whatsoever, when Mr. Jaeger left the river bank.

Once he was on the bridge, he walked extremely slowly, stopping whenever a barge sailed underneath the central arches without dropping anchor at Regensburg. His eyes darted very quickly from the first bend in the river to the last one, and he paid hardly any attention to people passing near him.

But at a certain moment, it so happened that a hand was placed on his shoulder, and he heard somebody calling out to him in the following manner:

"Well, Mr. Jaeger, it has to be believed that all of this is of interest to you..."

Mr. Jaeger turned round, and saw Ilia Krusch standing in front of him, watching him with a smile.

"Yes," he replied, "all of this river traffic is interesting! I don't tire of watching it."

"Well, Mr. Jaeger," said Ilia Krusch, "that will interest you even more when we're on the lower course of the river! There will be more boats there! Wait till we're at the Iron Gates... Do you know them?"

"No," replied Mr. Jaeger.

"Well," declared Ilia Krusch, "it's something that has to be seen! And if there isn't, in the whole wide world, a more beautiful river than the Danube, there isn't, along the whole course of the Danube a more beautiful place than the Iron Gates!"

Decidedly, this worthy line fisherman was an enthusiastic admirer of his river, and, whenever the opportunity arose, he would sing its praises, with which his travelling companion would readily concur. But as for Mr. Jaeger, it may be that, deep down, the Danube was less interesting to him as a river than as a "moving road," to use an expression which has long been very well-known.

By now, it could be seen, upriver, that the sun was setting; Ilia Krusch's large watch indicated that it was almost six o'clock, and he said:

"I was down there in the barge when I noticed you on the bridge, Mr. Jaeger... I gestured to you but you didn't notice me or respond... So I came to get you... You know we'll be leaving very early tomorrow morning, so do you want to come and have your share of supper?"

"Gladly, Mr. Krusch; I'm coming after you."

The two men went down towards the left bank in order to reach that part of the river bank at which the boat had docked, and as they were turning at the end of the bridge, Mr. Jaeger said:

"And the sale... the sale of our fish, Mr. Krusch? Are you satisfied?"

"It's been rather poor today, Mr. Jaeger... There are loads of goods for sale at the moment, and the Regensburg market was very well-stocked... Perhaps we'll make higher profits at Passau, Linz or Pressburg..."

"Oh! I'm not worried," declared Mr. Jaeger. "I'll say it to you again, I'm not going to make a loss on this, quite the contrary... and the price at which I've bought your catch will have doubled before we get to the mouth of the river!"

A quarter of an hour later, Mr. Jaeger and Ilia Krusch were enjoying a relaxed supper at the back of the barge. Then, having finished this meal, they stretched out near to each other within the tarpaulin shelter. Sheltered as they were under the first arch of the bridge, they had nothing to fear should it begin to rain, and in fact, they didn't even hear the rain falling in large drops during part of the night.

By half past five in the morning, the boat was already three-quarters of a league from Regensburg, sailing along close to the right bank where the action and strength of the current made itself felt more rapidly. The fishing line brought on board white roach and red roach; the latter had not yet gotten back to the stony or grassy depths where they meet the colder waters which they seek out as a matter of preference.

Moreover, Ilia Krusch had equipped himself with a view to benefitting from this potential catch, and here he was, saying to his companion:

"Do you see, Mr. Jaeger, I've baited my little hooks with cooked wheat, flavoured with assa-foetida! These fish are partial to that type of bait… Each to his own, don't you think? In winter, I would have used, as bait, stale bread soaked in fresh blood… But we're a week into the month of May and the roach must be given what they prefer… It's likely that it's easier to catch them when the float remains motionless, as they have a straight mouth and bite quickly… Nevertheless, I hope to catch a few dozen of them, which will sell well, I hope… Rest assured that I won't neglect to do anything which may prove profitable to you, Mr. Jaeger…"

"I know that, Mr. Krusch, for you are the most honest man in the world… But don't be worrying yourself, and let things take their course!"

Ilia Krusch had not at all advanced too far on the river, and in the course of that morning, his rod brought in about forty roach which he had struck briskly, and without having to use too much force.

That day's catch of fish proved very profitable in the revenue it yielded. And, in truth, Ilia Krusch showed that he was completely happy with the day's results. He would have been very upset if Mr. Jaeger had entered into an unprofitable deal, and all the more so because, since they had begun sharing this common existence, Ilia Krusch, with his good and sensitive nature, had been feeling strong friendship for his companion, who did not fail to notice this.

Upriver from Regensburg, the riverbanks have very different appearances. On the right, there is a succession of fertile plains as far as the eye can see; rich and productive farmland with no shortage of either farms or villages. Many boats come to this area to load with cargo, and it was not beyond the bounds of possibility that the smuggling operations were being actively carried out along the south of the Danube. Therefore—at least during the crossing of Bavaria— this riverbank was subject to high surveillance, and the agents working under Karl Dragoch, the chief of police, must have been constantly travelling the length and breadth of this stretch of river.

To the left are masses of deep forests, and hills, in the direction of the Böhmerwald. As they passed, Mr. Jaeger and Mr. Krusch saw, above the village of Donaustauf, the summer palace of the princes of Tour and Taxis and the old episcopal castle of Regensburg; then, beyond that, on the Salvatorberg, there appeared in view a sort of Parthenon, which had a wild, lost, haunted appearance under the Bavarian sky, which is not at all the Attica Parthenon, and which in this case was built by King Louis. It is also a museum in which are displayed busts of the heroes of Germania, though this museum is less admired within than it is outside, for its beautiful architectural layout and arrangements. Though it cannot rival the Parthenon of Athens, it is superior to the Parthenon with which the Scots have adorned one of Edinburgh's hills, Old Smoky.

The current was now carrying the barge onwards, on the right-hand side of the river, along islands shaded with beautiful trees. There were numerous bends in this part of the river, all of which revealed the same, unvarying landscape. Ilia Krusch had occasion to stop at Straubing, both to sell his fish in the usual conditions and to stock up on provisions. After passing the mouth of the Isar—one of the tributaries of the left bank—he moored the boat, for the night, in front of the village of Deggendorf, where the Danube—which at that point is twelve hundred feet in width—is traversed by a bridge of twenty-six arches, eleven more than the Regensburg bridge. The Deggendorf bridge is, however, made of wood, and can even be dismantled; and, each year, it is taken away, as it might risk collapsing at the end of the winter. Afterwards, it is then restored to its original position, and the numerous pilgrims who come to this region, in procession, thus find a means of travelling between the two banks of the river; these same pilgrims who come to this country where religious legends, of miraculous memory, are so piously preserved, at Ober-Altaich, at the old Bogenberg church, and at Deggendorf.

One thing which Ilia Krusch couldn't help noticing—although it did not occur to him to be unduly astonished by this observation—was that, in the principal towns and sometimes even in the smallest and humblest of villages where they had occasion to stop over, Mr. Jaeger would meet people with whom he was acquainted. Certain

individuals, probably locals, would come and exchange a few words with him. Neither did Jaeger ever neglect to make his way to the local post office, where, almost always, there were letters waiting for him.

"So," said Krusch one day, to Jaeger, "you have contacts just about everywhere, Mr. Jaeger?"

"Indeed, Mr. Krusch. It's down to the fact that I've often travelled the length and breadth of these regions all along the banks of the Danube."

"Really? For the purposes of sightseeing, Mr. Jaeger?" asked Ilia Krusch, in whom his travelling companion had not yet at all confided on any matter—not that Krusch was unduly concerned by this, it must be added. Perhaps he even thought that his question might be construed as being somewhat indiscreet. But it was nothing of the sort, most assuredly, as Mr. Jaeger immediately answered him:

"No, it wasn't at all as a curious sightseer that I used to visit these regions, Mr. Krusch. I used to be a commercial traveller for a firm based in Pest, and, as you know, when you're doing that type of job, not only do you get to see the countryside but you also build up contacts with lots of people."

No further detail was required to satisfy Ilia Krusch's curiosity, and Krusch would never even have entertained the slightest suspicion where Mr. Jaeger was concerned.

As the boat approached Passau, the right bank revealed itself to be less flat than it had been upon leaving Regensburg. Along this stretch of countryside, there began to appear the first ramifications and foothills of the Rhetic Alps. At this point, the Danube begins to contract within a narrower valley. A journey along this stretch of the great river is a delightful experience for tourists, and truly justifies the throngs of sightseers who hasten to visit this area. The waters of the Danube no longer flow along tranquilly and at a regular pace; in the past, quite dangerous rapids used to form there, and it was not a rare occurrence for the river fleet to suffer serious damage to its boats. It is, in fact, at this point of the Danube that rocks begin to appear on the river bed, and, as the current here rushes along tumultuously, it makes it very difficult for boats to avoid these dangerous reefs. During periods of significant increases in the water levels, the difficulties and dangers were lessened; but at the usual, low water level, navigating this stretch of the river was never less than perilous.

Nowadays, the dangers are greatly reduced. The most precarious of these rocks, which used to be spread out from one side of the river to the other, have been blown up through controlled minefield explosives. The rapids have lost some of their violence; the swirls no longer fatally attract boats into their eddies and whirlpools; the surface of the river is relatively calm, and the number of catastrophic accidents has therefore diminished.

Nonetheless, there are still several precautions which must be taken, both by the larger barges and the small boats. But these treacherous rocks did not prove awkward to Ilia Krusch; and Mr. Jaeger could not but be satisfied with the manner in which he steered the barge. Anytime it tended to drift off course, a judicious use of the oar invariably put it back in the right direction, and Ilia Krusch, at all times, manoeuvered with a remarkable steadiness of both eye and hand.

On the morning of May 9th, Mr. Jaeger and Mr. Krusch had left Regensburg. It was on May 11th, one hundred and forty kilometers from Regensburg, that they reached the village of Vilshofen.[3] They were now only an hour away from Passau, the last Bavarian town of the right bank.

As soon as the sun had risen, two hours were given over to fishing, which yielded several dozen chub, carp, roach and barbells. When this catch was added to the fish which had been caught the day before, and which had not been sold—as they had dropped anchor for the night in a deserted place—the merchandise was likely to sell well and in favorable conditions, unless, that is, the Passau market was excessively well-stocked.

As it happened, it didn't prove necessary to even go as far as the town's marketplace. This time, Ilia Krusch's arrival was expected that particular day, and a piece published in that morning's papers had announced his imminent appearance. Ilia Krusch's tracks had, finally, been found again!

Indeed, about fifty curious onlookers were hastening to greet the barge's arrival with their acclamations. This caused Mr. Jaeger to cry out:

"Aha! You won't be able to travel incognito, Mr. Krusch, and you'll have no shortage of customers! Just think of it, fish caught by the prize winner of the Danubian Line! You understand, I've gambled a little on

---

3.   Verne gives the village name of Vilshofen as simply Vils, actually a tributary of the Danube.

your sales, which means I'll make a profit on you, and you're going to sell, for the price of gold, your barbells, carp, roach and chub! But I'm not a huge fan of these noisy gatherings of people; I have no claim on all these tributes, and I'm going to leave you to your admirers!"

Thus, having spoken these words, Mr. Jaeger jumped off the boat down onto dry land, as soon as it had drawn alongside the quay. The truth was indeed that all eyes were on Ilia Krusch and nobody even noticed that the triumphal victor of the fishing contest had a travelling companion.

Chapter VII

FROM PASSAU TO LINZ

IT IS QUITE OBVIOUS that a city which is situated on the right bank of the Danube, at the confluence of two not inconsiderably-sized rivers which bring to it their watery tribute—the Ils, whose water comes from the Bohemian mountains, and the Inn, filled by the Tyrolean mountains—is not going to be lacking in ready supplies of freshwater fish. If the Society of the Danubian Line ever happens to be seeking a vast network of rivers in order to bring together, in one single fishing contest, several thousand fishermen, its President, Mr. Miclesco, will only have to choose the BatavaCastra of the Ancients. Given that the pastoral letters emanating from the Bishops of Passau—who are still known by the title of Archbishop of Lorch—preach the observation of fasting from meat each Friday or on the eve of the major religious holy days, it would be unforgivable for the faithful not to conform to the Church's commandments—those among them who are Catholic, that is. Thus, it should come as no surprise that the fish market is always amply supplied with pike, carp, barbells, goujons, bream and chub. The market stallholders have no need to wait for fresh deliveries of fish from outside their area, and, in the three watercourses of their city, they find more than is needed to satisfy the needs of lovers of fish.

It is thus likely that, if Ilia Krusch had come to offer his fish to the housewives of Passau, without his identity becoming known—and if he had wandered through the different districts of the city, and had even resigned himself to climbing the two hundred and forty steps of the Mariahilf, a flight of steps built on the city's high hill, in order to sell his wares to the many pilgrims who recite prayers at each stage of the climb—he would have been unable, even at a very low price, to sell so much as a common bleak.

But the arrival of Ilia Krusch at Passau had indeed become known to the public, and it was thus to be a very profitable visit for him—or rather for Mr. Jaeger—from the point of view of fish sales.

Moreover, Ilia Krusch and his companion had decided that they would spend the entire day at Passau. It was not as though Mr. Jaeger had any intention of visiting the city; though its location makes it as picturesque a spot as one might wish for, it does not possess, in truth, a single monument worthy of attracting tourists. Furthermore, Mr. Jaeger already knew this city well, and though he was no longer a commercial traveller for the Pest-based company he had spoken of, it seems that he nonetheless had business of a different nature to transact there. Thus, he and Ilia Krusch wouldn't see each other until supper time, which came very close before bedtime. Ilia Krusch would have all the time in the world to bask in the enthusiastic reception which awaited him. And, out of the population of twelve thousand inhabitants, which the city contained at that time, half of them, at the very least, would wish to turn out to pay him homage.

Indeed, the throngs of people were already growing in number. There were already several hundred natives of Passau who had turned out to greet him, including all of those natives of the city who belonged to the Danubian Line, and who were happy to have this chance to cheer the contest winner who was about to hold the record for line fishermen.

So it was that, from the outset, Ilia Krusch didn't know whom to give his ear to, so many were there who wished to claim his attention. Some wanted to bring him off to the City Hall to offer him honorary glasses of wine, and if the good man had drank even one drop of all of those wines which feature on hotel menus, he would have been brought back in a state of complete drunkenness. One traveller has counted 180 different wine vintages in this region, "from the Baden Affenthaler at 48 kreutzers a bottle, to the Schloss-Hohannisberg at 9 florins." Well, if he were to drink just 180 single drops, Ilia Krusch wouldn't have needed any more than that, for him to lose the use of his reason as well as of his legs!

There were others among these fanatics who were persistent in wishing to drag him off to the Castle of Oberhaus, which appears as it has been conceitedly constructed on the hill overlooking this city, a hill at the foot of which—at one hundred and twenty meters below—the waters of the three great rivers merge.

Others would have liked to take him for a walk—or, it would be a more accurate word to say that they wished to exhibit him—through the three suburban districts of the city, to the accompaniment of bugles and drums.

Finally, there were others who wouldn't think of agreeing to allow him to leave Passau without his having first visited the valley of the Inn, a marvellous spot in this Bavarian region which contains such beautiful valleys!

In truth, now that he had sold all of his fish, Ilia Krusch's only desire would simply have been to escape from this overweening display of enthusiasm, and he cursed the indiscreet person—whoever that might be—who had exposed him to these crowds. And to think that he would have to spend a whole day in these conditions, he who was so resistant to all of the noise and fuss with which the world surrounds its triumphant champions! Undoubtedly, if it hadn't been agreed that they would postpone their departure until the following day, if he hadn't been obliged to wait for the return of his travelling companion, he would have cast off his moorings—or cut them if necessary—and as soon as his barge had been launched into the river's current, he would have quickly slipped away.

It was only just nine o'clock. He was being pulled and dragged in the middle of all this crowd, men, women and children, and all these invitations were deafening him, as they were as noisy as they were pressing.

"This way, Mr. Krusch…"

"We're going to bring you to the City Hall…"

"Come to Oberhaus Castle!"

"No… to the Mariahilf!"

"Come with us, Ilia Krusch!"

"Come with us, champion of the Danubian Line!"

And so it was that people began to argue over him, this being followed and added to by outright quarrels, with people eventually coming to blows, and the hero of the hour would not be likely to escape from this adventure without leaving behind a few tatters of his clothing.

Passau

Then, the church bells began to ring out in his honor, fireboxes started to explode and the rockets of firecrackers crossed and intersected over his head… And so, it seemed as though police officers would be forced to start making arrests to extricate the unfortunate knight of the oar from the madding crowd!

However, a particular circumstance which Ilia Krusch couldn't have counted on, happened to occur at this precise moment, and in a very timely fashion.

A man, pushing his way through the crowds of people, had just approached Ilia Krusch, and, with the assistance of the police officers, he took Krusch to one side, away from the crowd, and said to him:

"A message for you from Mr. Jaeger, on whose behalf I'm acting… if you want to leave here this instant, he will meet you down below, a little outside the city!"

Ilia Krusch didn't need to be asked twice! This was all he wanted. It mattered little that this messenger was not known to him. This man had spoken Mr. Jaeger's name, and that in itself was sufficient.

And thus, with the help of the police, he succeeded in extricating himself at the very moment that some people were persistently seeking to carry him off to the Oberhaus, others to the Mariahilf.

This did not at all suit his legions of admirers, and, if this reinforcement of police officers hadn't arrived when it did, it is hard to say what might have happened. But at the end of the day, there is no law which allows a citizen to be detained against his or her will, even on the border between Bavaria and Austria; it was necessary that the full force of authority be asserted, even if it meant calling in the Bavarian army.

The police thus acted forcefully and vigorously, and Ilia Krusch, escorted by police officers, like a common criminal, went down to the place where the barge was moored. The curious throngs had to resign themselves to letting him continue his journey. Hungary would certainly have begged indulgence for one of its own citizens, and most decidedly, the king of Bavaria would never have wished to give rise to a *casus belli* pertaining to a Hungarian against whom no judicial complaint had been made. Krusch was not at all a guilty party, but rather, a victim—the victim of his own celebrity.[1]

Finally, Ilia Krusch took his place on board the barge, which was pushed off again into the current of the river by means of a strong blow of the gaff.

There was no doubt but that if the famous fisherman Ilia Krusch had arrived in a carriage, his supporters would have unharnessed the horses from the coach… Indeed, it could even be envisaged that they might rush headlong into the waters of the Danube to tow the boat, like a group of Tritons, or even of water nymphs, escorting the triumphant galley.

Half an hour later, Ilia Krusch was rejoined by Mr. Jaeger who had been waiting for him a little beyond the city, and his travelling companion said to him:

"When I realized what was going on, I sent to you this man whom I had met, and as there was nothing else to detain me in Passau any longer…"

"You did the right thing, Mr. Jaeger, and you've got me out of a terrible spot of bother!… Those people are fanatical! But you could have come to me yourself…"

"I still had something left to do, and if you had delayed setting off downriver again, I really don't know what would have happened…"

"You were right, Mr. Jaeger," replied Ilia Krusch. "If I hadn't left when I did, where would I be now!…"

"Well, be careful that the same thing doesn't happen again somewhere else… at Linz… at Pressburg…"

"Don't say that to me, Mr. Jaeger!"

---

1. A casus belli is defined by the *Collins English Dictionary* (2003: 6th edition, page 265) as "an event or act used to justify a war" or "the immediate cause of a quarrel." It is a Latin expression, the literal meaning of which is "occasion of war."

"Bah! You might end up getting used to all these accolades!..."

Ilia Krusch would never get used to them; he could be taken at his word on that matter. He then changed the subject of conversation:

"I thought, Mr. Jaeger," he said, "that your business dealings were to detain you all day at Passau..."

"Business dealings?" replied Mr. Jaeger. "But I don't have any, in the strict sense of the word... A few old acquaintances to catch up with again... Nothing more! And precisely, this person I sent to you..."

"No doubt he was one of the travelling sales representatives from the Pest-based company you worked for?..."

"Exactly so," replied Mr. Jaeger, "I had met him, and I repeat to you, if I hadn't had one last thing to attend to, I would have come back... myself..."

"And it would have been in the nick of time, Mr. Jaeger, just in the nick of time!" declared Ilia Krusch, who was not at all the type of man to press home his point more than was necessary.

As they were having this conversation, the barge was travelling along the river rapidly, and when they turned round, Mr. Jaeger and Ilia Krusch were able to contemplate Passau in all the glory of its picturesque location.

The boat would probably take no more than three days to cover the thirty-odd leagues which separated Passau and Linz. The Danube, once it had become Austrian, contracted within a narrower channel beyond the border. In these conditions, the current acquires a higher speed, which is taken advantage of by the boats which sail downriver towards the Austrian capital.

However, upriver from Passau, the left bank is still within Bavarian territory, as far as the mouth of the tributary known as the Dadelsbach. Beyond this point, the navigation of the Danube takes place through charming countryside, valleys watered by smaller rivers which plunge downwards in waterfalls, forests rising gradually in tiers over the hillsides. Rolling, verdant countryside sometimes extends as far as the horizon, closed by the circular line of the sky; the riverbanks are livened up by the coming and going of aquatic birds, herons or loons.

On this subject, Ilia Krusch mentioned that sometimes this game is caught by a fishing line.

"Yes, Mr. Jaeger, it bites at the hook like a simple chub or a voracious pike! But this sort of catching of game is not worthy of a fisherman, and he wouldn't be winning any prizes for it in a contest!"

The banks of the river were also embellished by some ancient historical ruins which a tourist could visit, not without some pleasure. However, there was no question of Ilia Krusch or his travelling companion delaying at these ruins. Over the three days which was the duration of this part of their journey, they could, by stopping at night, preferably in those villages in which people couldn't have known of Ilia Krusch's arrival, enjoy a complete and uninterrupted view of the delightful sites which this crossing of middle Austria presents, by turns, to the traveller. Such historical attractions included the ruins of Hagenbach Castle, just before Neuhaus, a castle which, thanks to the bends in the river, can be seen from all its angles, or the magical-looking valley which comes into view near to this small town of Neuhaus.

From this point onwards, the descent of the barge down the river was a little less rapid. Beyond the market town of Aschach, the river banks are also lower in height. Here there are no more hills or valleys, and instead, a vast succession of drearily uniform plains leave the viewing traveller indifferent.But a large number of islands obstructed the course of the river.

Despite the difficulties of the navigation—which were, besides, reduced since the last improvement works had been carried out—the barge was able to sail along in complete safety, and the steering oar protected it against collisions and from running aground. Without a doubt, while Mr. Jaeger was well acquainted with the regions of the upper Danube, Ilia Krusch was equally familiar with the bends and channels of the river itself, and it would not have bothered him to have to steer a fully loaded boat, or one of those long rafts which drift along the river.

After Regensburg, the Danube flows in a south-easterly direction as far as Linz, and it was a little upriver from that town that the barge stopped on the evening of May 14th.

The catch of fish had only been fair enough throughout those three days, as fish do not willingly bite when the line is carried along by a fairly strong current. It would have to be a stupid and avaricious, gluttonous pike which would allow itself to be tempted by the young carp or wriggling gudgeon used to bait the hooks.

"It's true," as Ilia Krusch remarked at one particular moment when, after allowing it to swallow his prey instead of quickly striking it, he was bringing on board a fish weighing fifteen pounds, "when you've got a jaw containing seven hundred teeth…"

"If we had as many as that, we might be just as gluttonous as him!…" said Mr. Jaeger.

"That's it exactly," replied Ilia Krusch, agreeing with Mr. Jaeger's response.

It so happened that, on that particular evening—at the home of a fish wholesaler whose house looked out onto the riverbank, and who supplied the Linz market—the catch of fish had been able to be reasonably well sold, with the two men, Krusch and Jaeger, all the while maintaining the secrecy of the fisherman's identity.

It will come as no source of astonishment, then, that Ilia Krusch asked Mr. Jaeger the following questions:

Did Mr. Jaeger know Linz?

Mr. Jaeger did indeed know Linz, having actually lived there for a while.

Did Mr. Jaeger have business to transact at Linz?

Mr. Jaeger did not see any reason for sojourning twenty-four hours in this administrative capital of the region of the Muhl Circle.

Since the fish had been sold, might Mr. Jaeger have any problem with leaving the following morning at daybreak?

Mr. Jaeger had no problem with that. The barge would therefore set off along the river once again, as soon as Mr. Ilia Krusch wished to leave.

"Which will spare you," he added, laughing, "the bother of being acclaimed or carried shoulder-high in triumph. But there are twenty-three thousand inhabitants of Linz who won't be too satisfied when they learn that the famous Ilia Krusch has omitted to pay them an official visit!"

As one might suspect, this argument was not at all the sort which could influence that most modest of line fishermen, and it was agreed that the barge would set off again before the first of the curious visitors and passers-by would have begun to appear on the bank.

Moreover, Linz does not at all enjoy the privilege of being a tourist attraction, and, of itself, the city does not at all boast any especially curious features. It is a military city, which had been destined to become such as a result of its strategic position on this part of the Danube. It was surrounded by fortifications which would probably be more vulnerable to modern canons than the Austrian government imagined, and this despite being protected by thirty-two massive towers, which can cross their gunfire—twenty-two towers on the right bank, nine

Linz

on the left. It is, in short, a sort of vast entrenched camp commanded by the powerful citadel of the Postlingberg. As for monuments, there was no shortage of hills on which to have placed them in the past, in various picturesque sites, as the city is laid out in rows or layers over five or six of these hills, and there would have been no lack of a mirror in which the city could reflect itself, as the river, strewn with islands, crossed by a wooden bridge, takes circular form at the foot of the city like a calm and limpid lake. But, apart from the old royal castle, with its red-brick walls, destined to become, one day, a barracks and prison, architectural riches are rare at Linz.

Linz is not a strong trading city, and, when he used to travel for the Pest-based company, Mr. Jaeger probably did little business there. In any event, he had no intention of finishing his evening in one of the city's cafés, and he walked along the river bank until bedtime.

The next day, daylight had only just begun to appear when the boat set off from the riverbank, to set off once again into the current, and, while Mr. Jaeger remained lying down underneath the tarpaulin shelter, Ilia Krusch, fishing rod in hand, remained close to the length of the river bank.

Chapter VIII

From Linz to Vienna

Between Linz and Vienna, there are a certain number of towns and cities along the Danube. But none of these is as large or important as those which the barge had already encountered up to that point, and could not be compared to Regensburg, Passau or Linz. Even if Ilia Krusch had been able to travel without being noticed by the public, up to then, it would probably be difficult for him, in Vienna, to escape the various troubles and annoyances associated with his new found celebrity. The Danubian Line was represented, in this Austrian capital, by quite a large number of members, and they would wish to honor the champion whose fame was reflecting so brilliantly on their association.

As for merely stopping in Vienna for one night only, would this be possible? Though the great river does not actually flow directly through the imperial city, it does come so close to it that the distance between the Danube and Vienna can be crossed in less time than it takes to go from one suburb to another. There was thus every reason to believe that Mr. Jaeger would suggest staying there for twenty-four hours. And, with the help of the newspapers, the local population would be tipped off... And moreover, Ilia Krusch was an honest man, so that if his catch of fish was to fetch the price of gold at Vienna, he could not deprive Mr. Jaeger of such profit.

All things considered, the best course of action was to wait and see. They would act in accordance with circumstances, and wisdom recommended postponing any decision until later.

As it flows out of the city of Linz, the Danube justifies, with mathematical precision, what one poet has written about it in his Oriental texts:

> "...it flows
> From West to East."

It only deviates above the forty-eighth parallel of latitude in order to bathe the city of Krems, a little to the north, from where it then flows back downwards, to bring to the capital its watery tribute, between two Austrian banks.

From Linz to Vienna, the river bed takes shape over a length of about fifty leagues, taking account of its many bends and meanderings, a distance which could probably be covered in the space of four or five days, as long as no obstacle occurred. And what obstacles might present themselves, anyway? It is, of course, possible to envisage that the navigation of a large boat might be impeded, either by a mishandled manoeuver or by congestion in narrow channels; but for a light boat, drawing barely one foot of water and steered by such a careful and experienced, cool customer as Ilia Krusch, this was a possibility which didn't need to be worried about.

A further cause of delay for the great river craft of the Danube was, at that time, the frequent, and strict, visits by customs officers. No sailor could avoid such inspections, and much time was lost as cargo was intensively searched through. However, since the meeting of the International Commission at Vienna, not an iota of progress had as yet been made in the smuggling case. There was no doubt that this smuggling continued to take place, nor could there be any doubt as to the methods employed by the smugglers. As for their leader, this Latzko fellow, it was sought in vain to locate his "scent," to set off in pursuit of him and to track him down. He was able to give the most skilful sleuths the slip. There were also reasons to believe that he himself did not go on board the smuggling ships, but, from some unknown hiding place, he must be overseeing the smuggling operations. What was certain was that all of the barges visited up to now by police and customs officers had turned up no leads, so that the inspections and searches had thus far proven fruitless.

It goes without saying that Ilia Krusch's barge could not be under suspicion, and so, with a laugh, he would say:

"And what about me? Are they really sure that I'm not passing along smuggled goods, and that once I've collected them around Sigmaringen, I'm not transporting them to the mouth of the Danube?"

"Indeed—who knows?" Mr. Jaeger would riposte, in the same light-hearted tone.

Beyond that charming little town of Krems, built on the left bank of the river, a thunderous, violent tumult of water could be heard, as though there had been a dam a few hundred yards upriver.[1]

"Those are the whirlpools of the Strudel," said Ilia Krusch. "In the past, it was very dangerous for the larger river fleet to pass through this stretch of the river, and there's been more than one disastrous accident along here. But the public works have already brought about great improvements, and they're still being continued, over the last hundred years or so, ever since they were first undertaken."

Indeed, these improvement works date back to the reign of Marie-Thérèse, and their outcome has been to guarantee two meters of water to vessels, when sailing through the Strudel, even during periods of the most severe drought.

When the barge had arrived at the rocky island of Werden, almost one kilometre long and four hundred meters wide, Mr. Jaeger asked his companion which branch of the river he would now take:

"If I had a larger barge to pilot, Mr. Jaeger," replied Ilia Krusch, "I would take the left branch, where the shallows aren't as dangerous. But with our barge, there's nothing to fear and we will take the right branch, as the current carries us along more directly to our destination."

"So the larger boats never sail along the right branch?"

"Never, for it would be foolhardy."

"Well, Mr. Krusch, if it doesn't bother you, I would prefer to sail downriver to the left of Werden Island... As you know, I'm always interested in this question of the river craft... I'm even thinking of going into some kind of business along these lines, myself, if I can get an idea for myself of what might be involved..."

"No problem!" answered the obliging Mr. Krusch, always willing to do a good turn for Mr. Jaeger. "We'll hardly even lose half an hour!"

So this is what was done, and the barge set off through the left branch of the river.

---

1. Verne gives the name of Krems as Grejn.

Three barges were floating along the river at that moment, each following the next. Making fast, their movement was powered only by the action of the current on its own, as the narrowness of the river bed makes the flow faster at this point. As Mr. Jaeger watched them operate along the surface of the waters, he seemed to be simultaneously observing their crew with particular care.

The sailors, for their part, didn't pay any attention to this barge which had two men on board. These small boats are numerous, as they constantly go from one bank of the Danube to the other. And at this particular moment, these sailors were too busy steering their vessels through the deep waters in such a way as to avoid the shallows and shoals. The pilot's orders rang out and the only thing to be done was to follow them meticulously. Whenever the direction of one of these boats had to be altered, it was done by means of strong boathooks, which were supported against the notches and grooves of the gunwale. But it was an onerous task which required great skill, and a deep familiarity with the Strudel's difficult stretches of water.

And so this is what happened: while Mr. Jaeger was, for some reason, mainly observing the sailors, Ilia Krusch was more interested in the pilot's manoeuvers. He seemed to be personally taking part in these operations, and the following types of words escaped from his mouth, as though instinctively:

"A little to the left, or it's going to run aground onto the stones! Good manoeuver, that one... Rudder to the right, to the right!... Good... there it is, back on the right course... The boat in front is doing well... the others just have to follow it! But they should all take particular care at the Wirbel bend!... That one is the most dangerous of all!"

Moreover, the current was carrying Ilia Krusch's barge along faster than this succession of boats, and furthermore, it was able to sail through stretches of the water which those boats couldn't have negotiated, which shortened its route. Thus, within about twenty minutes, it was further upriver.

Mr. Jaeger, who had been standing on the tarpaulin shelter so as to better be able to see, now came back to take his place beside Mr. Ilia Krusch at the rear of the barge.

This part of the Danube is, what's more, quite difficult, for large boats heavily laden down, to cross. It is not only on the sandy shallows that they run the risk of running aground, and what is more,

Vienna

they wouldn't be able to resume their course after such a collision until they had jettisoned half of their cargo. The river is sometimes scattered with enormous rocks, some of which tower along the river banks, while others barely break the surface of the water. Because of the violence of the current, if a barge is swept towards these rocks, it is no longer the danger of running aground which has to be feared, but total destruction, the loss of merchandise and perhaps of life; and it bears repeating that many catastrophic accidents had occurred in these conditions.

"Therefore, Mr. Jaeger," said Ilia Krusch, "it's necessary, above all else, to seek the services of an experienced, accomplished sailor, and there are some good ones on the Danube…"

"But, Mr. Krusch," replied Mr. Jaeger, "it seems to me that you yourself would have made an excellent pilot…"

"I have been a pilot, Mr. Jaeger, I have been, and, before retiring to Racz, I did that job for about fifteen years."

"Really, Mr. Krusch, and would you be able to sail one of those boats to its destination?"

"Certainly, Mr. Jaeger; on the Danube, you understand, and not on the smaller rivers which flow into it… I don't think the river bed has changed in the four years since I stopped piloting boats… for it shall shortly be four years since I retired… and I went from being a pilot to becoming a line fisherman…"

"A job which seems to quite successfully suit you, Mr. Krusch…"

"But yes, Mr. Jaeger, and what better thing to do after your retirement!"

After the Strudel, there were still more dangerous straits to be negotiated, including the Wirbel, where the waters form violent whirlpools, from which a boat—if it became trapped—could no longer escape. Then there was that sort of dam of Haustein, a formation of great rocks, always difficult to negotiate, even though the public works have significantly improved it. Moreover, with a slope of four feet per hundred fathoms, which the river bed has retained, it is hardly surprising that the Danube, along this stretch of water, can bear comparison with certain rapids of the great American rivers.

Once these dangerous straits have been crossed, the sailing once more becomes easy for the river craft along quite a long stretch of the river, and, as far as Vienna, at least, there are no longer any obstacles. The barge thus continued along its way under the impetus of a fairly regular current, and without any incident occurring. Ilia Krusch's fishing was proving quite successful, and he was making acceptable levels of sales of his fish in the small towns or villages along both banks, such as Spitz or Stein, to the left, where his presence was not at all noticed, to his extreme satisfaction, which, it seemed, was shared by Jaeger.

At this point, the river was flowing as if through a sort of canal. There was a lack of any unusual or interesting places to see, and the mountains, which stood far away in the distance, towards the horizon, allowed the plain to stretch out widely, with complete ease.

Nonetheless, there are some picturesque sites which are worth viewing; among others, the castle of Persenburg, the imperial residence, solidly built upon that powerful foundation of rocks which bear it with grace and strength. Similarly, there is the little town of Maria Taferl, to which pilgrims flock, each year, in their thousands. And as soon as their pilgrimage is completed, they can enjoy a superb and imposing view, in the setting of the northern Alpine mountain range. Finally, before reaching Vienna, there was still a place to be admired, in the form of the Abbey of Melk.

This Abbey was built by Benedictine monks, at a height of almost two hundred feet on a granite promontory. Behind the two elegant towers which stand out above its front wall, can be seen the curve of an enormous copper dome, which is dominated by a pinnacle and which seems to be covered with shards of gold whenever it is flooded by rays of sunlight.

At Krems, which is a small town on the left bank, the tourist finally loses sight of the mountains of Bohemia and of Moravia, which up to then have followed the right bank since Regensburg.

Before leaving Krems, Ilia Krusch had gone to offer for sale about thirty quite fine fish, caught the previous evening, and which yielded him a good price.

Mr. Jaeger had remained in the barge, which was due to set off again as soon as Ilia Krusch would have gotten back.

When the latter had come back, he once again took his place at the rear, and launched the boat in such a way as to sail along the middle of the river bed, where the speed of the current is stronger.

And, as they were chatting about this and that, Ilia Krusch happened to say to Mr. Jaeger:

"If you had come with me to Krems, you would have heard a piece of news which is causing a bit of a stir in the town."

"What news is that?"

"They're saying that the notorious Latzko has finally fallen into the hands of the police…"

"The notorious Latzko… the head of the smuggling ring?" asked Mr. Jaeger, rather excitedly and sharply.

"The very same."

"And where might he have been caught?"

"In an encounter with customs officials."

"And whereabouts?"

"Somewhere around Gran…"

"In Hungary?"

"In Hungary, Mr. Jaeger, but that doesn't necessarily imply that he's Hungarian!"

And, in the purity of his primeval national pride, Mr. Ilia Krusch couldn't have brought himself to countenance the possibility that this wrongdoer might be one of his fellow countrymen!

Mr. Jaeger, after several moments of reflection—and while Ilia Krusch thought that this subject of conversation was done and dusted—said:

"So, people were talking about this capture at Krems?"

"They've been speaking about it since yesterday, Mr. Jaeger."

"And was this news being given as a certainty?"

"Twice or three times, the people of Krems assured me it was true."

"And where had the news come from?"

"From Vienna."

"I'm sorry I didn't go with you this morning, Mr. Krusch… I could have verified this news for myself… checked what the newspapers had to say about it…"

"It's of that much interest to you, Mr. Jaeger?…"

"Yes and no, Mr. Krusch. But this is a case which has been causing quite an amount of public interest… this smuggling case, and if it's finally come to this conclusion, everybody has reason to be happy…"

"As you say, Mr. Jaeger!"

There followed a few moments of silence, during which the fishing line brought on board a superb specimen of those hotus which are sometimes called mullets—but incorrectly so. Hotus are easily caught in the rapid waters, in which it swims in large shoals, and it is thus fairly easy to fish for it, on condition that it is rapidly struck, which is what Mr. Krusch had done in this instance. Having noticed the presence of a certain number of these fish, he had consequently chosen the most appropriate hooks, without overly concerning himself with the type of bait to be used, as the voracious hotus will bite just about any kind of bait.

"I'm coming back to the topic of Latzko," Mr. Jaeger then went on. "If he really is—as people claim—the head of this smuggling ring, the police have certainly carried off a fine feat by catching him."

"Yes, Mr. Jaeger, and it's worth as much as catching a twenty-pound pike."

"But might not the news have been fabricated?"

"That's what we'll find out for definite at Vienna, tomorrow, Mr. Jaeger. In any case, even if they haven't yet seized this Latzko fellow, I imagine they'll get him in the end…"

"Oh! People say he's quite a cunning fellow!" retorted Mr. Jaeger. "It has never been known where he lived, and perhaps he hasn't even got a fixed abode… As for his nationality, it's also unknown… For as long as the police and customs officers have been searching for him, they haven't been able to discover anything about him up to now…"

"Undoubtedly so, Mr. Jaeger, but a wrongdoer like that always ends up getting caught," replied Ilia Krusch.

"It's unfortunate," added Mr. Jaeger, "that this isn't the first time that the rumor of Latzko's capture has spread, and falsely so. And for starters, we don't even know anything about whether Latzko is even his real name…"

"I like to think it's not at all his real name," stated Mr. Krusch, "because it has too much of a flavour of its Hungarian origins, and I'd prefer him to have a German name…"

"Ah! You are a patriot, Mr. Krusch!"

"Yes, and Hungarian to the core, right into my very soul. But, I repeat, what hasn't been done today will certainly be done tomorrow."

But Mr. Jaeger contented himself with simply shaking his head to indicate that he doubted this.

"And what's more," Ilia Krusch went on, "it mustn't be forgotten that a reward has been promised for Latzko's arrest… and what a reward… two thousand florins, no less!"

"And what if they were to land in your own pocket?" asked Mr. Jaeger, laughingly.

"They'd be as welcome in mine as in yours, I expect."

"Assuredly, Mr. Krusch."

"It's true," remarked Mr. Krusch, "that Latzko would be the type of man to offer double, or three times that reward, to escape, if he was caught… His gang must have become rich over the several years that it's been involved in smuggling activities…"

"But," said Mr. Jaeger, "you're not the type of man—a former Danube boat pilot, an honest line fisherman—who would ever accept such a bribe, if good fortune caused this smuggling gang leader to fall into your snare…"

"No, certainly not, Mr. Jaeger," replied Ilia Krusch, "and as they say, that's not the sort of bread I eat!"

The circumstances which led to this conversation between the two travelling companions, have been seen. Whether the news which had been brought back from Krems was true or false, this is a question they would shortly be able to answer for definite, at Vienna. It would also be found out whether the arrest was due to the chief of police, Dragoch, who had been placed in charge of new investigations of this case by the international commission. Was this arrest the work of Dragoch or of one of the police officers under his command—if indeed such an arrest had even taken place? If some sort of stand-off had taken place between the police and the smugglers, had it been managed to seize the boat, or boats, on which the contraband had been transported to ships on the Black Sea? If the arrest had taken place in the outskirts of Gran, Mr. Jaeger and Ilia Krusch would have the opportunity to gather the necessary information in that very place, as soon as they would reach this town on the Hungarian part of the Danube.

It was completely natural, as they concluded this conversation, that Mr. Jaeger and Ilia Krusch were led to mention the name of Karl Dragoch.

"It seems," Ilia Krusch said, "that the choice of this man has been a very fortunate one… They couldn't have enlisted the services of a more intelligent man than Pest's chief of police…"

"He's a Hungarian, I believe?" asked Mr. Jaeger.

"Yes… a Hungarian man… truly Hungarian," replied Ilia Krusch, not without a certain touch of pride.

"Do you know him, Mr. Krusch?"

"No, Mr. Jaeger, and I've never had the honor of meeting him…"

"They say he's a very skilled policeman…"

"Very skilled, and he has proved it on many occasions, in numerous circumstances, paying with his person, at the risk of his life."

"Well, Mr. Krusch, let us hope that he will be sufficiently capable, and above all, favored by fortunate circumstances, in order to finally get his hands on this Latzko fellow…"

"He'll succeed, Mr. Jaeger," replied Ilia Krusch with such conviction that his companion could not prevent himself from smiling.

Upriver from the little town of Korneuburg, the river craft encounters difficulties of quite a different order than in the channels of the island of Werden, the bends of the Wirbel and the whirlpools of Haustein. The Danube becomes considerably wider, the sandbanks hamper smooth navigation, and though instances of running aground are not very dangerous, it is prudent to steer one's boat in such a way as to avoid such groundings.

The barge even met, at one point, one of those long rafts on which live, it may be said, an entire floating population. This raft had awkwardly ventured into the waters, between the sand banks. Ilia Krusch's advice did not at all go amiss. He offered it of his own accord—

together with his services—and the sailors were right to follow it. He was thus easily recognizable as a man who knew his Danube well, something which no longer came as any source of astonishment to Mr. Jaeger. After a few hours delay, the barge was able to set off again along the river current, as it headed towards the capital of Austria.

Already, it could be sensed that they were coming close to a major city. The surrounding countryside seemed much more lively and busier. The sky was growing darker due to the smoky emissions of several factories. The number of boats was increasing, especially the dampfschiffs which were on duty on the outskirts of Vienna. In the distance could be seen the huddles of villages, with the bell tower of their churches pointing upwards into the skies. Country houses and villas were dotted along the gently rolling hills in the hinterlands, away from the river banks.

That afternoon, the barge reached the base of the Kahlenberg, whose summit, to the right, had been visible since morning. It is over a thousand feet in altitude, and, from its summit, there is a view which commands and stretches over not only the Austrian capital itself, but also as far as the mountains of Hungary and the Styrian Alps.

Finally, towards nine o'clock in the evening, having sailed down, upriver from Nussdorf, where the steamboats stop—in this place, the branch of the river which comes closest to the city, cannot allow them passage as there is not enough water—the barge put in and moored near to a small wharf in a narrow inlet of the river bank.

It had been twenty-two days since Ilia Krusch had cast his fishing line at the source of the great river, and he had just travelled down the Danube, covering a distance of about seven hundred kilometers.

Chapter IX

AT THE EXIT OF THE LOWER CARPATHIANS

A FEW DAYS LATER, two men were chatting, drinking and smoking, inside an isolated inn on the road which winds its way down towards the Danube at the edge of the Lower Carpathians. The last ramifications of these Hungarian mountains come to an end at the left bank of the river, a little upriver from Pressburg, a large city within the kingdom, situated between Vienna and Budapest.[1] It is there that the mouth of the Moravia is found, this being one of the main tributaries of the great river.

These two men were seated at a table at the back of a low-ceilinged room, where nobody could either see or hear them. A window to the side, with large chained glass patterns, allowed them to observe, through sidelong glances, people or animals that were passing along the road outside, along the left bank of the Moravia, whose current was carrying several boats towards its confluence.

This inn had few customers apart from sailors and carters, whenever they stopped there, either to down some extremely strong alcoholic drink or to have their meal. Travellers, easy to satisfy, could spend the night there without dispensing too much money from their purse. But it was rare to find the innkeeper, his wife and his manservant having company on any particular night. A narrow stable, adjoining the inn to one side, provided enough room for one or two horse-drawn carriages.

That morning, two carts, their loads protected by a thick tarpaulin covering, had arrived at the inn. The master of the house had probably

---

1. Pressburg is now Bratislava, the capitol of Slovakia.

been expecting them, and was acquainted with the two carters driving them.

The first question which had been posed by these men—specifically, those two who were now drinking in the low-ceilinged room—was the following:

"They're not here yet?"

"No," replied the innkeeper. "He won't come till tonight."

"Well, let's unharness our horses," said one of the men. "The carts in the yard, the horses in the stable…"

"And enough to eat and drink," added the other man, "for this business of waiting for him makes you hungry and thirsty. Nobody in the inn at this time?"

"Nobody."

Things had been done in this way, just as they were usually done, it seems, and, from outside, the two carts could be seen sheltered under a wide sloping roof in the yard. As for the six horses—three per team—they were generously supplied with unsparing supplies of fodder. Their legs had travelled a long stage of their arduous journey along these hard roads of the Lower Carpathians, and they had an equally long road ahead of them before they reached the Danube at the confluence of the Moravia. Their strength needed to be built up, as they had been dragging a heavy load for several days already.

Thus, since morning, and having travelled throughout the whole night, the two men had been settled at the inn. From time to time, one or other of them would cross the threshold of the main door to have a look out at the road. But the atmosphere, which was then a little misty, made it impossible to see far into the distance. In any case, as the innkeeper had stated, the man whom these two men were expecting for this rendez-vous would not arrive until nightfall.

The best thing for the two carters to do, after putting their carts into a safe place, was, firstly, to have something to eat. Having travelled all night, they were ravenous with hunger and parched with thirst, just as one of them had said upon arrival, even though the flasks which they carried underneath their woollen cloaks had allowed them to liberally quench their thirst along the way. They thus sat down at the table to eat in the low-ceilinged room. In addition to the rather meager provisions offered by the inn, they also partook of the substantial supplies of food with which their coaches were provided. They thus

ate copious amounts of food while chatting to the innkeeper and his wife—a couple whose appearance had nothing very appealing about it, though carters are generally far from expecting winning smiles from their hosts.

The most pressing enquiry which the two men made was whether squads of police officers or customs officials were wandering about the countryside. It was understandable enough that they hadn't run into any of them along these meandering roads, off the beaten track, between the last ramifications of the Lower Carpathians. Through these deserted regions, far from any town or village, officers did not willingly choose to venture, nor, moreover, did wayfarers. But in the place at which they had just stopped that very morning, in the corner occupied by the inn, the plain was beginning to become clearer; a more widely-travelled road followed along the left bank of the Moravia. It crossed through quite deep forests, and served several farms whose farmers used to go to sell their produce in the neighbouring villages, and as far as Pressburg. And, as that road was the only one leading to the meeting point of the smaller river and the Danube itself, it would be necessary to follow it, and it was possible that it was under surveillance since the new measures which had been taken by the international commission with a view to cracking down on the smuggling, through arresting the smugglers.

Moreover, even though they had come from the earliest gorges of the Carpathians, the carts had only trundled along under cover of darkness, and this is what they would continue to do until journey's end.

After one final drink which had been preceded by a good many others, the two men felt an irresistible desire to sleep. They had no need of beds; a few bales of straw, thrown into a then empty stable, would amply suffice for their needs, and, having asked the innkeeper to wake them "if there was anything new," they stretched out beside each other, and five minutes hadn't gone by before they were already dead to the world, sleeping profoundly.

While they were resting, on several occasions, passers-by came into the inn and were served drink, but they left the inn almost immediately afterwards. These were farmers from the local area, returning to the nearest farms, or vagabonds, their beggar's pouch on their back and stick in hand, who were travelling towards Pressburg.

One of them, in the course of his conversation with the innkeeper, happened to mention that the police were trawling through the surrounding countryside, and that, most definitely, honest people could no longer feel safe.

The innkeeper contented himself with shrugging his shoulders and expressing his wish that the vagabond in question would not be caught by the police or anybody else of an unwelcome nature. But he noted this piece of information, and promised himself that he would mention it to his current guests. It was rare for police officers to travel through these Lower Carpathians, and if they were currently doing so, it could not be without some serious reason.

Towards five o'clock, when the two men were awake, they returned to the main room of the inn, and their first question was, once again, the one which they had already asked that morning: "They are not here yet?"

"Not yet," replied the innkeeper, "but, as I've told you, he won't be here until evening time… I've been tipped off by one of his cronies… He'll do well to be cautious, what's more, because there are police and customs officers wandering about the Moravia area."

This news seemed to worry the two men, one of whom immediately enquired whether any of these policemen had turned up at the inn.

"None of them," replied the innkeeper, "but I've been tipped off by a tramp who had met them as he travelled along the road."

The two men then ordered dinner and sat down to eat at the table in the main room of the inn. As they ate, they conversed in low voices—probably out of sheer habit, for they had no reason to be wary of the innkeeper.

"Provided he can throw them off the scent," one of the men was saying. "He's bound to have been tipped off that the banks of the Moravia are being watched…"

"Yes," replied the other, "the police believe that the smuggling of the contraband is taking place along that river, and that the Danube barges have already sailed down this tributary."

"It's essential that they continue to think that, and if necessary, that's the rumor that must be spread…"

"That's exactly what he's done, with the result that, up to now, the roads have remained free for our carts to travel through them."

"As for the boat which is supposed to be waiting for us…" the first man went on.

"No worries there," declared the second man. "It's at the Kordak creek, at the confluence of the Moravia, for all the world like some respectable merchant ship which is just waiting until it's completed its load of cargo before it makes off towards the mouth of the Danube."

As soon as they had finished their dinner, both men left the dining room and came out onto the road, where they began pacing up and down.

It was now 6:30 p.m. The sun had already disappeared in the north-west behind the mountain range of the Lower Carpathians. It was becoming duskier; the oncoming night would be pitchblack, a moonless night, and thick clouds covered the sky. But there was no threat of rain, and this was a favorable circumstance which would enable the carts to reach the confluence of the Moravia before dawn. As for finding their bearings along the road, this would not prove in any way awkward for the two carters, even in the midst of deep darkness, as they knew this countryside well, and had made this journey from the inn to the left bank of the Danube under similar conditions on previous occasions.

During their comings and goings on the road—which they went down over a distance of two hundred yards—the two men saw nothing suspicious. The countryside was absolutely deserted. With the last puffs of the breeze which was dying down, from the south, one would have heard the sound of any voices or of any footsteps which might have come from that direction. But there was nothing: absolute silence reigned. Moreover, there was reason to believe—on the basis of the information furnished—that the officers must be carrying out their surveillance along the banks of the Moravia, upriver, and thus, at a distance of at least a league from the inn.

The two men returned, therefore, to the inn, and went to have a final look at the teams of horses resting in the stable.

At a few minutes past seven, the door of the room suddenly opened, and the innkeeper immediately cried out:

"Here he is!"

The two carters rushed out of the stable and ran up to meet up, once more, with the newcomer.

This newly arrived individual was a very robust man, between forty and forty-five years old, with a face bespeaking much energy, hard features, clean-shaven, the appearance of a man who was accustomed to the open air, experienced in strenuous physical exercise. He looked, simultaneously, like a typical countryman and a typical sailor. He wore a round, wide-brimmed hat, boots which reached as far as his knees, a jacket underneath which there appeared a red belt which tightened his trousers at the waist, and was enveloped in a wide woollen cloak which fell from his head to his feet, which allowed him, should he so wish, to completely avoid being recognized.

Was this man Latzko, head of the smuggling ring, for whom the police had been searching for several years? Neither Karl Dragoch nor any of the police officers would have been able to say, as he had never been seen. In any case, if this man was indeed Latzko, then the news of his capture—which had been greeted with visible disbelief by Mr. Jaeger—was untrue. Perhaps there hadn't even been any stand-off between his cronies and the officers on the outskirts of Pressburg and, most certainly, the President of the Commission, Mr. Roth, must not have received any report along those lines from Dragoch. Moreover, since their arrival in Vienna, Mr. Jaeger and Ilia Krusch must know what the lie of the land was regarding this alleged arrest.

What is certain is that, for some time already, the newcomer had been in the company of a number of the smugglers on the other side of the Danube, on the right bank, where part of the smuggled booty had been brought. After loading this booty—without this loading having come to the attention of the police—the barge, crossing the river, had berthed a little upriver, almost at the confluence of the Moravia. About fifteen of the men had then gone along the right bank to complete the loading of the cargo, and they had then come to the inn, under the leadership of this chief, in order to escort the two carts throughout the final stage of their journey.

As for the items which the carts were transporting, fabric, expensive wines, tobacco, preserves and canned food of various kinds, these had been transported into the Lower Carpathians area, and as soon as the barge would have received this final cargo, all of the men would embark upon it, and the vessel would be well able to escape the investigations of the Customs officials and of the police, over the few hundred leagues still separating the barge from the mouth of the Danube.

Moreover, the setting up of this smuggling ring was truly the work of this Latzko person, who was not a man to retreat before any plight or obstacle. His gang members, just like their leader, feared neither God nor the devil, as they say. This gang had widely-spread branches and tentacles throughout all of this long valley of the Danube; as for the fear of being betrayed by one of their own, no, for all of them were being made rich by these fruitful contraband operations. Up to now, the boats had always reached their destination, without the smuggling having ever been discovered.

But at the end of the day, everbody's luck runs out at some point. From being good, it can become bad, and would good fortune continue to smile upon Latzko for much longer? Even though people didn't know this Latzko to see, his name was known, and nobody could have said how it had reached the ears of the police. It is true, however, that people's names are not inscribed on their faces; and a man doesn't get caught because people know his name.

As soon as he had entered the main room of the inn, this chief— Latzko's second-in-command, perhaps—proceeded to ask concise questions, which produced equally concise replies:

"Are the two carts here?"

"They are."

"You have not been stopped en route?"

"No, but the area is definitely being patrolled and watched by officers…"

"Yes… I know, but along the Moravia. Has all the merchandise arrived?"

"All of it."

"And you've been here?…"

"Since this morning."

"The horses have been given a good supply of fodder?…"

"It only remains to hitch them up."

"Let's hitch them."

It will be noted that, though about fifteen smugglers had come to this side of the Danube, this newcomer had come on his own to the inn. It was better this way, so as not to arouse the suspicions which would inevitably have been caused by the arrival of a whole band of men armed with cutlasses, large knives and revolvers. Instead, they were dispersed over all the length of the road, and as soon as the carts would set off again, these men would escort them at a distance, in such a way as to be able to regroup in the event of the slightest alert or signal of danger.

Moreover, they were very much aware that the police were scouring the surrounding countryside under the leadership of Karl Dragoch, whose presence had been signalled the previous evening. They were thus keeping very much on their guard. With the costumes they were wearing, they could very easily have been taken for Hungarians from the Carpathian locality. As for this Latzko fellow, skilled in altering his appearance and disguising his face, he had already managed to pull the wool over the eyes of police officers on several occasions. How many times had the best sleuths met a local countryman in the fields, or a sailor on the banks of the river, with the most ordinary, nondescript appearance and kindly face, sometimes leading a horse, at other times a boat, without suspecting that they only had to stretch out their hand to seize him! The truth of the matter was that Ilia Krusch would have been more likely to awaken their suspicion!

And whenever any of his fellow smugglers would speak to him about this Dragoch fellow, whom the Commission had set on his tail:

"Leave him to me; I'll be able to deal with him," he would reply. "Even if he was on board my boat with his officers, he wouldn't recognize me on it, and as for the boat, as you well know, he can rummage through it and scour it down to the very hold, but he wouldn't find in it so much as a smuggled carpet!"

Eight o'clock had rung out by the time the teams of horses, hitched once again to their carts, were ready to leave.

It's worthwhile adding that, as regards the supposed arrest of Latzko, this wasn't the first time that rumors of this kind had been doing the rounds about him. This information, repeated by the newspapers, was always as false as that which Ilia Krusch had shared with Mr. Jaeger when he had come back from the Krems marketplace.

Everything was ready, and the men, not one of whom had appeared at the inn, were just waiting for a single sign to form the escort.

The gates of the yard were opened. The carts, each drawn by three vigorously strong horses, exited the yard one after the other. As they travelled along, they would not be perceived from a distance, either through being heard—on this partly grassy road—or visually, as it was by now pitch dark. Moreover, part of the journey would be made through thick woods grouped along the road.

The distance to be covered was now only between six and seven leagues from the inn as far as the confluence of the Moravia, and there were hardly even any farms to be encountered in this direction.

As soon as the carts had exited the yard, and leave had been taken of the innkeeper, the carters at the head of their horses began to travel down the last ramifications of the Lower Carpathians.

The leader was about twenty paces in front of them. At times, as he walked alongside the lines of trees, he would stray a little from his path, either to the right or to the left and would exchange a few words with the men forming the escort, to make sure that they hadn't seen or heard anything suspicious. It was a silent, dark journey. The carts were not lit by any lantern, but their drivers were familiar with the slopes and twisting inclines of a road which they had travelled over many times, so that there was no fear of any mistake on their part.

In this way, it thus seemed that the journey would take place without incident. By the time the convoy arrived near to the first farms, the evening was already sufficiently advanced for the farming families to have gone to bed. Only a few dogs barking gave any indication of the passage of the carts. But not a door opened in enquiry, and, after all, nobody would have been surprised by this movement along the road, of a group of horses and men.

The atmosphere had considerably thickened since earlier in the evening, becoming heavier, as though the air had been saturated with electricity. But there was no threat of a storm, and moreover, in this region of Upper Austria, there is little fear of storms in springtime. A fortunate circumstance, for when the season is more advanced, they are sometimes quite terrible. They sweep through the valley of the Danube, sometimes hindering the progress of the river fleet, sometimes even halting it. And it was important that the barge should have its full load of cargo within a few hours, so as to be able to set off before daybreak.

It was midnight when the convoy came to a halt. The horses had been journeying along for the last four hours, and it was now timely and prudent to let them have some rest. Not only were they dragging vehicles which were quite heavily loaded, but the road surface, only barely maintained, was broken up with ruts and potholes, which forced the beasts to strenuously put their back into their task.

The halt was due to last one hour. There were now only three leagues left to travel over, and along roads which would not be in such

poor condition as they got nearer to the river. The smugglers were thus certain that they would have reached the confluence of the two rivers and even have all of their cargo loaded while the river bed of the Danube would still be drowned in darkness.

It was in a clearing, outside and to the right of the road—a place well-known to them—that the carters had hidden away and sheltered their carts. In this pitch blackness, under the thick ceiling of trees, they could not have been seen unless somebody actually came into the clearing. Therefore, in the event of somebody passing by, there was nothing to fear.

After giving some initial sustenance to the horses, all of the men had gathered around their leader. There were—including the carters—about twenty robust men, accustomed to danger, having proved their mettle on many occasions.

Throughout this period of rest in the forest clearing, the men talked in low voices so as not to draw attention to their presence, and didn't even smoke, as they sat at the foot of the trees. Two or three of them, who were on closer terms with the gang leader, conversed directly with him. The subject of their conversation was that this expedition needed to finish as a matter of urgency… The surrounding countryside was under too much surveillance… Instead, another part of the river would be chosen, at which the boats could wait, with greater safety, for the merchandise sent towards either bank of the river. The essential thing was, therefore, to thwart the efforts of the police in the area of the Lower Carpathians and to leave before officers were at the confluence of Moravia.

An hour went by, during which all had had an undisturbed rest. On the giving of a signal, the teams of horses were about to set off again when one of the men, who had been stationed at the outside edge of the clearing, hurried back, saying:

"Alarm!"

The leader came forward.

"So, what's going on?" he asked.

"Listen!"

Upon hearing this answer, everybody cocked their ear.

The sound of footsteps could be heard along the road in an upriver direction, the sound of a group of people coming down the road in this direction. Soon, a few voices could even be heard in addition to the footsteps, and they couldn't be any more than about two hundred yards away.

"Let's stay in the clearing," ordered the leader, "those people, whoever they are, will pass by without seeing us!"

And indeed, most certainly—given the deep darkness—the convoy of smugglers wouldn't be spotted. But there was one very serious aspect to all of this: if, by some stroke of misfortune, it was a squadron of police officers travelling along this road, they must be on their way to the river. Assuming that, once daylight came, the police didn't discover the boat at the end of the creek, it would not be discreet to drive the carts there, at least not that night. Obviously, if the police officers took it into their heads to inspect the said boat, they would find nothing suspicious there; nevertheless, they could decide to remain on in the area of the confluence, so that their presence there would make impossible any attempts to load the smuggled goods onto the boat.

In the end, it was decided that they would wait and see how circumstances evolved and act according to whatever happened. After waiting in this clearing until the following night, if necessary, a few of these men would then travel down as far as the banks of the Danube, and would verify that the customs officials and police officers were operating along this area.

But for now, the essential thing was for the smugglers not to be tracked down under any circumstances, and for this group of people coming nearer, to continue along their way without having their attention drawn to the hiding gang members.

The group of strangers passing along the main road, very quickly reached the place where the road passed right alongside the clearing. Despite the pitch blackness of the night, it could be distinguished that this group consisted of about ten men, and at times, a certain jangling, clashing sound seemed to indicate that these men were armed. So, was this a group of these police officers who, according to the vagabond, were scouring the countryside and were, as a matter of fact, in pursuit of Latzko's smugglers?

There could no longer be any doubt on this score. Two names were uttered, one after the other, by a few of the men who—ahead of the others—were walking alongside the edge of the forest. The first of these names was Latzko's, in answer to a question which somebody had asked. The second name uttered was as part of the answer to that question: "I think we shall arrive in time, Dragoch!"

It was the police chief in person who, having received a fairly accurate tip-off, had travelled with a certain number of his officers to this part of the country, situated at the corner of Moravia and the Danube. For two days, he had been operating a surveillance team at the entrance to the Lower Carpathians; but his investigations having proved fruitless, he had sent half of his men upriver to the left bank, and was now making his way to the confluence with a twelve-man squadron. And by following the same route as the convoy of smugglers, he must, inevitably, run into them.

The leader immediately decided on the only course of action which could now be taken: to stay in the clearing, not betray their presence, let the squadron keep going, have it followed at a safe distance so as not to be spotted, check whether or not it would take up position at the approaches to the confluence: if so, put off till later the loading of the merchandise; if not, change nothing of their plans and drive the carts to Kordak Creek. The distance was not such that the leader would not be able, if necessary, to observe Karl Dragoch's operations for himself.

The squadron had already gone past the pathway along which the clearing is entered, when something happened to completely change the situation.

One of the horses, frightened by this passing-by of men on the road, snorted and began a prolonged whinnying which was taken up by the others.

Karl Dragoch and his officers immediately came to a halt. The smugglers' hiding place had been discovered. A struggle would now certainly get underway and so, now, the smugglers prepared to fight.

"Halt!" Karl Dragoch had shouted to his men, who gathered round him.

And then, moving forward to the entrance to the clearing, he shouted: "Who is there?"

There was no answer.

One of his officers then struck a match and lit a resin torch which he held in his hand.

Although, by this insufficiently bright light, the police and smugglers could not recognize each other's faces, the light had at least

allowed the police chief to notice the two carts, behind which a certain number of men were grouped together.

"Who are you?" shouted Karl Dragoch again.

"Who are you, yourselves?" was the answer he got.

"We're police officers… Those carts being hidden can only contain smuggled goods, and those escorting the carts can be none other than smugglers!"

There was no response.

"We're going to take away these carts," said Karl Dragoch, speaking a final time.

He went into the clearing, followed by his squadron, without having been able to notice that the smugglers would have the advantage of greater numbers, outnumbering his own men by about twenty against twelve.

But hardly had the police chief advanced five or six steps when he was stopped in his tracks by these words uttered by an authoritative voice:

"One more step and we open fire!"

This threat could not at all stop Karl Dragoch and he responded:

"If this is Latzko in person speaking to me in this manner, I'll make it my personal business to shut his mouth!"

And the police squadron continued to move forward towards the carts. But the next instant, the resin torch was snatched from the police officer's hand, and the darkness once again became absolutely deep.

Not a shot had yet been fired on either side. There was a hand-to-hand combat which opposed the officers and the smugglers. The former realized, though too late, that they would not be in the majority; the struggle would go against them. As it had now been going on for several minutes already, and since it was necessary to get it over and done with, gunshots began to ring out; revolvers had now become part of the action. A few of the smugglers and police officers were hit by gunfire in the midst of the blackness. But this skirmish could not continue indefinitely, and, after an attack which was as violent as its resistance, Karl Dragoch had to gather his men together and abandon the scene. After leaving the woodland clearing, the police squadron travelled back up the road so as to rejoin the other officers who were spread out upriver of the Moravia.

A quarter of an hour afterwards, the convoy of smugglers, two of whose men had been slightly wounded, was setting off again. Just before four o'clock in the morning, it had almost reached the Kordak creek. There was no police surveillance apparent in the vicinity. The merchandise was immediately loaded onto the waiting vessel. With the exception of the leader, who stayed on dry land, all of the gang went on board. Then, the barge moved off and sailed down the Danube under the impetus of a fairly rapid current, just as the sun was casting its first rays of light on the golden-hued waters.

Chapter X

From Vienna to Pressburg and Budapest

THE DISTANCE WHICH SEPARATES VIENNA from Pressburg amounts to approximately twenty-five leagues and Ilia Krusch had covered three quarters of this distance by the evening of May 21st. After spending the night within the shelter of a headland, near to the mouth of a small course of water, at a stone's throw from a few isolated houses, he had cast his line into the waters, and had caught about twenty good-quality fish which he intended to sell that very evening as soon as he arrived in Pressburg.

Ilia Krusch was now alone in the barge, and his travelling companion was no longer travelling down the course of the great river in his company.

What had brought about this change in the situation? Had this separation been intentional or accidental? The two friends—they can safely be described as such, as certainly from Ilia Krusch's point of view, this was now a serious friendship—the two friends, were they not due to meet up with each other again later on, to resume, together, this navigation? Was Mr. Jaeger's absence only a temporary one?

In summary, here is what had taken place.

As the reader will remember, Ilia Krusch and Mr. Jaeger had dropped anchor on the evening of May 18th, near to a wharf at the back of a narrow creek at the Nussdorf branch of the river. The reader will also be aware that the barge was not in Vienna itself, as the river flows a little to the north of that city. And, as it was by now already quite late—a little after nine o'clock—Mr. Jaeger had postponed, until the following day, his planned visit to the capital of the empire of Austria.

As far as Ilia Krusch was concerned, that good man was not there to get to know Vienna. He had already travelled several times through that city which is not very large in size, and had visited on several occasions, then, its thirty-four suburban districts, which substantially increase the city's population. Though he had only ever seen from the outside, the imperial castle, the palaces of the chancelleries, the City Hall, the arsenals, the Royal Mint, the Custom House, the theatre, and the Esterhazy, Lichtenstein and other palaces, he had not neglected to respectfully genuflect in the churches of Saint Stephen, Saint Peter and Saint Charles, nor had he failed to take a walk at the Prater, at Augarten or at Volksgarten, or to salute, on the Old Market square, the commemorative plaque to Emperor Leopold, or to admire the superb views which provide a feast for the eyes from the terraces of the Belvedere gardens.

The reader will therefore fully understand why Ilia Krusch was not at all predisposed to leave his barge, in which he was sheltered from all of the indiscreet reports which the Vienna newspapers could publish about him. And, indeed, he would have risked being a victim of all of the inconvenience and annoyance which word-of-mouth Renown would have heaped upon his head, for he was not due to set off again until two days later.

This was exactly what had been agreed between himself and his travelling companion: that is, various different items of business would detain Mr. Jaeger in the capital for the whole day. He would leave in the early morning and would be back in the evening, promising to keep Ilia Krusch's arrival in Vienna a secret, upon the express request of the latter.

As soon as the night was over, then, Mr. Jaeger left at eight o'clock and, without fail, he would be back for supper.

"I can rely on you, Mr. Jaeger?"

"Absolutely, Mr. Krusch."

Mr. Jaeger disembarked from the barge and, with an agile step, set off along the Donau-kanal, between the two districts of the Alsergrund and Leopoldstadt, through a maze of streets with which he was thoroughly familiar and that would bring him to the city center.[1]

Though the day proved to be an eventful one for Mr. Jaeger, it was as monotonous as it could possibly have been for Ilia Krusch. And

---

1. Verne gives the spelling of Alsergrund as AusterGrund.

Pressburg

yet, the local newspapers had announced that he would be passing by Vienna at around this time. He was even able to verify this reporting for himself, by reading a newspaper in a small café not far from the wharf. And none of the regular customers seated around him had any idea that the Danubian Line's prizewinner was sipping his bock in a corner of the room.

Ilia Krusch then returned to the barge, which he proceeded to wash thoroughly. The rear and the benches were washed with lots of water, and the bedding of the tarpaulin shelter remained exposed to the rays of sunlight, after being shaken and beaten; and, in carrying out this work, he was thinking much more of his friend Jaeger than of himself. Finally, for his midday meal, he settled himself down on the bench to the rear of the vessel, and ate with that moderation which is appropriate for properly-cared-for stomachs, and the calmness which results from having a clear conscience.

"And where might he be now?" thought Ilia Krusch to himself as he ate. "It's hardly surprising that a former travelling salesman should have lots of acquaintances in this big city. Has he met them?… He's probably had lunch at the home of one of them, dinner at the home of another, and I'm very much afraid that I'll still be on my own having supper this evening!… He's most definitely an excellent travelling companion, this Mr. Jaeger, and I have no regrets whatsoever about having accepted his offer!… Although it's not as though I would have been bored during this river journey!… But when all is said and done, Mr. Jaeger's company is most pleasant… He seems to have a certain taste for fishing-related matters, and by the time we get to the end of our journey, I shall have recruited one additional member for the Danubian Line!"

Ilia Krusch's thoughts were running along these lines, he who had taken such a strong liking to Jaeger.

"Ah! I do declare," he said to himself, "as long as he doesn't prove to be too big-mouthed and doesn't say anything about our arrival here!… Because I know, it's in his interest and the sales of fish benefit from such a thing being public knowledge!… But, we have none of our fish left, since yesterday!… It's all been sold!… So it's pointless…"

Yes, that was the perpetual, constant fear of Ilia Krusch. But, at the end of the day, Mr. Krusch had solemnly promised to remain silent, and it would be a thing unheard of for a former travelling salesman to renege on a firm promise.

In the afternoon—all the while smoking his long pipe—Ilia Krusch went off to renew some of the provisions which were beginning to run out, fresh bread, eggs, beer. As he went back up the river bank, the passers-by whom he encountered were few and far between. Rather, the hustle and bustle was to be found on the branch of the river, furrowed as it was by many vessels. But nobody paid any attention to the modest barge moored at the back of the inlet.

The day came to an end, and evening came; Ilia Krusch was now waiting with a certain degree of impatience for the return of his companion. The time seemed long to him. He was counting the minutes. Night came, but Mr. Jaeger did not come with it.

Seven o'clock was ringing out in the churches of Vienna, and the north wind carried the tinkling of their bells through the night air.

Mr. Jaeger didn't show up.

Eight o'clock came, and Mr. Jaeger made no appearance, either upriver or downriver from the bank.

"What can have happened to him?" wondered Ilia Krusch. "It must be some piece of urgent business that's detained him… some accident perhaps! Will he not arrive until sometime in the middle of the night?… Will he be delayed until tomorrow morning?… And yet we were supposed to leave at the very break of day… Well, I'll wait! Yes! I'll wait… without going to bed, and in any case, I wouldn't be able to sleep!"

For a character as composed as the true line fisherman has to be, it will perhaps come as a surprise that Ilia Krusch was displaying such nervousness and anxiety. It is not possible to give any other explanation for this, other than to say that that was just how things were. Moreover, having resolved to wait, he would wait, without making the fatal error of setting off in search of Mr. Jaeger. And anyway, where might he find him in this vast city?…

Ilia Krusch thus sat down at the rear of the barge, and in order to help pass the time, he took his fishing rod in hand and baited it suitably. And yet, night-time is not very favorable for catching fish—fish seem to find their food more easily between sunset and sunrise. That is the reason why it is so much harder to "get a bite" during the first hours of the morning, because fish are no longer goaded by hunger at that time. But Ilia Krusch wished to "kill the time," and he couldn't have done so with a surer hand.

And so, he had already struck a barbell and two sticklebacks, and half-past eight had just rung out, when he heard himself being called from above on the riverbank.

"Mr. Krusch… Mr. Krusch?"

He straightened up and caught sight of an individual who was coming forward, towards him, on the wharf.

"Oh dear," he thought, "here's somebody who knows my name!"

And, feeling very disconcerted and ill at ease, he was hesitating to answer, when the individual once again shouted out, straining his voice:

"Mr. Krusch?… Mr. Krusch?… Are you not there, Mr. Krusch?"

Ilia Krusch then stood up and answered:

"What is it you want of me, Sir?"

"To deliver a letter to you…"

"A letter to me? And from whom?"

"From Mr. Jaeger."

At last, Ilia Krusch was about to get some news of his companion. But how could Jaeger have been so indiscreet as to write to him under his real name—and, thereby, breaking his cover—when he was supposed to keep his identity secret. So it must be something really urgent, and who knows? Perhaps it was something truly serious that Mr. Jaeger was now communicating to him.

In a moment, he would know what it was all about.

"Give me that letter," he said, stretching his arm out towards the individual.

"But... I presume you are indeed Mr. Ilia Krusch?" repeated the bearer of the letter.

"Yes! I am he!" retorted Ilia Krusch, his voice revealing strong displeasure.

As soon as he held the letter in his hands, he asked, in a softer tone: "How much do I owe you for your message?"

"Oh! Nothing... I have received a florin from the person who sent me here."

"And who is not known to you?"

"Who is not known to me!"

During this exchange, Ilia Krusch had sat down near to the tarpaulin shelter, had taken a small lantern, lit it, and read the letter which was worded as follows:

Vienna, 8 p.m.

My dear Mr. Krusch,

An unexpected occurrence has forced me to leave Vienna in a few moments... I don't have time to go to the barge to let you know in person... I don't even know at this stage either where or when it will be possible for me to rejoin you... But rest assured that I will do so, sooner or later... perhaps at Pest, perhaps at Belgrade.

Until then, continue our journey without me, and I wish you all the success you desire of it.

I have entrusted this letter to a messenger, and it was unfortunately necessary to make known your name and address. Let us hope that that shall not cause you undue inconvenience, and that you shall be able to extricate yourself from any difficulties.

And now, I wish you *bon voyage,* and also happy and productive fishing, for you know how much of a stake I have in the results of your fishing endeavours, and I shall not have occasion to regret the price which I have paid you in advance for your fish.

With all the apologies of your companion,

Jaeger

Such were the terms of this letter, which came as quite a surprise to Ilia Krusch. What business could have forced Mr. Jaeger to leave Vienna with such haste? That would indeed provide food for thought from now on, but as he noticed that the messenger was still standing on the wharf:

"It's fine, my friend," he said, "you may go… there is no reply…"

But the other remained standing there and said:

"So, you really are Mr. Ilia Krusch?"

"Yes… Ilia Krusch."

"Krusch the fisherman?"

"The fisherman… Good evening…"

"Well, when they hear about this in the city, you can expect to see your barge invaded by hoards of curious people."

"Ah! Really…"

"You will still be here tomorrow morning?"

"By all means, my friend!"

"Good evening, then!"

"Good evening!"

And the man went running off at some speed, delighted to be going to spread this major piece of news!

At three o'clock the following morning, while it was still dark, Ilia Krusch had untied his barge. Half an hour later, it was sailing off into the waters of the Danube at the Imperial Mills, two lines of twenty boats each, the wheels of which rotate in the current, and by the time the crowds of admirers, the following morning, were hurrying onto the wharf and the riverbank, the barge was already a good league away from the capital.

The reader has now seen, therefore, the sequence of most unexpected circumstances which had caused Ilia Krusch to be now sailing downriver alone. Having passed Essling and Lobau, a round and uninhabited island, two names which are famous in the historical annals of the First Empire, he continued his peaceful navigation towards Pressburg.

The journey between Vienna and Pressburg seemed very long to Ilia Krusch. He was so well acquainted with the great river that its various scenic landmarks no longer held any interest for him. So it was a monotonous navigation between quite low banks, mainly on the right as far as the village of Fischament, banks which rise around

Pressburg from 1700 meters during a 1907 balloon ascent,
photographed by Anton Schlein.

the village of Regalsbrun. And, further on, Hainburg mountain only barely attracted his absent-minded attention. He used to fish in the mornings, sailing downriver all day, would fish again in the evening, would go off to sell his fish in the hamlets, preferably in the villages and towns, would then spend the night there and used to sail off again at dawn.

It was in this way that Ilia Krusch reached the border separating the archdukedom from the Magyar Kingdom, a border which the Leytha delimits on the left and the March on the right, these being two large tributaries of the Danube.[2] A few barges were exiting from the March, which is the first navigable watercourse of the left bank; those of the right bank, the Inn, the Enns, and the Traise being already in the service of the river fleet.

Having crossed the gorge which bears the name of the Gate of Hungary; having sailed round the multiple headlands jutting out into the river, which the Lower Carpathians thrust into the river like so many teeth of a saw or jagged edges, one of which is crowned by the legendary tower of Theben, having sailed alongside the island which

---

2.   "March" is the German name for the Morave, which gives its name to Moravia.

seems to obstruct the Danube at this point, Ilia Krusch crossed the boat bridge, and came to spend the night in front of the very last house of the town of Pressburg.

And all the while, he was thinking about Mr. Jaeger. No! According to the letter from this absentee, it wasn't in this official capital of the Magyar Kingdom that they would be once more reunited. And would it even be at the Hungarian part of the river, at Comorn, at Budapest that both men would meet up once more with each other? Perhaps if Mr. Jaeger had been there, he would have wanted to stop over for a few hours in this city of forty-five thousand inhabitants, which does not truly "come to life" until the period during which the Hungarian Diet is in session, a city which is much sought after by persons leading a peaceful existence, people of independent means with small private incomes, where it is possible to live quite cheaply, for this part of Hungary is fertile in wines and crops. True, Pressburg does not at all boast any buildings of architectural interest for sightseers, but its location—with the vast quadrangular castle with its corners elevated in turrets—is endlessly picturesque.

But when all was said and done, Mr. Jaeger was not there, and didn't turn up there, and so the following day, May 23rd, it was on his own that his companion once more set sail along the Danube's current.

About thirty leagues from Pressburg to Raab, about fifteen from Raab to Comorn, the same distance from Komárom to Gran, about twenty leagues from Gran to Budapest, in total, almost eighty leagues, such was the distance that the barge would have to navigate before reaching the capital of the kingdom of Hungary. At least a week, such was the time that it would take Ilia Krusch to travel from Pressburg to Pest. There are interesting sights to be seen when sailing along this stretch of the river, but how much more enjoyable it would have seemed, had Mr. Jaeger been occupying his usual place on the barge.

All the while, the barge was passing along close to the left bank, in a south-easterly direction. A flat but lush, fertile countryside stretched out on both sides.In many places, the river bed is dotted with islands, some of which are of considerable size, including, amongst others, the island which is known to Hungarians by the name of the Golden Garden.

As Ilia Krusch passed along down the river, his navigation was not marked by any untoward incident, something which he was not likely to complain about! His anonymity didn't have any adverse effects on the sales of his fish, which readily found buyers. He seemed to have a talent for finding them under the flowing waters—the fish that is, not the customers. But with what wisdom, what talent, was he able to choose his hooks for their size and thickness, and his baits for their quality! The infamous old saying –false, like most such sayings—could certainly not have been applied to Ilia Krusch: the fishing line is a tool which sometimes has a dumb beast at one end, and always a dumb beast at the other!

At Raab, the Danube is joined by the waters of a tributary which bears the same name as the fortress. This county town of the comitat or local administrative area of Hungary, has a population of between fourteen and fifteen thousand inhabitants, and that day, though this number was increased by one person, thanks to the temporary presence of Ilia Krusch, it was not increased by two, since Mr. Jaeger did not arrive to resume his customary place underneath the hospitable tarpaulin shelter of the barge.

The stronghold of Raab was followed by the stronghold of Comorn, which is no less famous. Ilia Krusch had to go as far as the marketplace in order to sell his catch of fish. It was there that he heard people talking about a skirmish which had taken place in the Lower Carpathians between Latzko's gang and a police squadron led by Karl Dragoch in person. In this encounter, the police officers had been defeated. Since then, there had been no further sightings of Karl Dragoch and nobody knew what could have become of him. There was no precise declaration on this subject.

"Ah!" thought Ilia Krusch, "that's a piece of news that would have been distressing for Mr. Jaeger to hear! When we spoke about Dragoch, he seemed to take a keen interest in that police chief."

But at the end of the day, this was no more than a hypothetical observation on the part of Ilia Krusch, which his companion would have perhaps confirmed, if, at this very moment, he was not...

"Where?" Ilia Krusch unceasingly wondered, "Yes! Where?"

And he began to think that, most definitely, this absence had something very mysterious about it.

It has already been mentioned that the Hungarian countryside is extremely lush and fertile, and its richness is principally due to its vineyards. It is on these hills, whose exposure to beneficial climatic conditions is equal to those of similar hills in Burgundy, that the vine stocks of the famous Tokay and other great wines of top-quality labels, grow in abundance and prosper. At the same time, the Hungarian land produces cereals and tobacco in enormous quantities. Without a doubt, if Latzko were to come to this region to stock up on fresh supplies of contraband, he would be able to fill his boats to the brim.

And what is more, they would have had no shortage of water in order to sail down the Danube. From this point onwards, the river, nourished by its tributaries to the right and to the left, is sufficiently deep for warships of medium tonnage to be able to sail through it without risking scraping the river bed, on conditions that it chooses its channels carefully.

The mountains came into sight once again at the city of Gran, the seat of an archbishopric which is one of the most important in the Kingdom. It is possible that, on that particular day—which was a Friday—that the archbishop saw, on his table, a pike weighing fifteen pounds and a pair of superb carp which Ilia Krusch's fishing rod had deftly extracted from the Danubian waters.

It goes without saying that the river fleet was now very active on the Danube, and, as Mr. Jaeger was so fond of observing the boats sailing along, he would have found much to satisfy this very particular, personal curiosity of his. At times, there was even some obstruction of boats on the river, as the course of the Danube became narrower between the first branchings of the northern Alps and the Carpathians. Thus, there sometimes occurred incidents of ships running aground, or collisions, which did not, however, cause much damage overall. The main misfortune incurred amounted solely to loss of time. The attention of the clients and pilots could not afford to falter for a single second. But whenever a collision did take place, what shouts, curses, torrents of abuse and rows broke out, and, as one can well imagine, Ilia Krusch took care not to get involved.

However, he did not fail to notice a larger barge, of a capacity of two hundred tons, which appeared to him to be better piloted than the others. As the wind was favorable, the skipper had hoisted a large sail, with a raised mast, above the rig. These types of barges are covered by a sort of superstructure, consisting of an upper bridge which extends right to the rear, covering the cabin occupied by the crew members, with a small mast at the front of the bridge containing the national flag which unfurls from the bridge into the air.

Most of the time, two long large-spaded sculls, attached to the rear of this bridge, allow the barge to be steered by combining their joint forces, especially when the barge goes floating along freely downriver. But such was not the layout of the particular boat of which we are now speaking, which took advantage of the breeze, anytime that the direction of the river allowed it to do so. A rudder with a wide blade, possessing in width what it lacked in height, given the shallow draught of water, allowed the pilot to maintain the boat in the right direction.

The boat was thus steered by a prudent and safe pair of hands. It managed to slip in and out skilfully between the other boats which it easily overtook. If, from time to time, it cut across those other boats or made things awkward for them, its sailors paid little heed to the recriminations which they provoked as they passed along.

"There's a good pilot on board," said Ilia Krusch to himself, "and that reminds me of my own former profession!… There were a few of us like that, at Racz, where piloting is held as an honorable profession, and if it were ever necessary, my eyesight is still as keen and my arms as strong as ever, and I wouldn't be found work shy as a pilot!"

This little outburst of vanity on the part of this good man should be excused. Furthermore, he did not forget his comrades and countrymen from Racz, and the truth of the matter is that, amongst these former pilots, this way of life "is in the blood" and remains in their blood, right up to the very end of their lives.

Accordingly, as the Danube was continuing to flow upwards, the physical appearance of its banks was becoming harsher. There also reigned a certain hustle and bustle which was becoming ever more lively, which is always the case as one approaches the larger towns and cities. There was an ever-increasing multitude of shady and verdant islands, between which there were sometimes only narrow channels. But, while the barges chose navigable branches of the river to sail on, these channels were sufficient for the sailing requirements of pleasure boats. Light vessels, powered either by sails or by steam, filled with strollers or tourists, slipped between the islands.

The weather was fine, and the breeze favorable. Rays of sunshine pierced the little clouds which sped southwards, the direction followed by the Danube from the village of Waitzen below Gran.

"And what a pity Mr. Jaeger's not here!" thought Ilia Krusch. "A sight like this would be a source of absolute delight to him… But after

Gran

all, who knows, perhaps I'll catch up with him again soon?... At Buda or at Pest, it's all the same, and that gives me two bites of the cherry instead of one, two chances of meeting him again!"

Indeed, on one side, to the right, is Buda, the former Turkish city, and to the left, Pest, the Hungarian capital. These two cities face each other, just as—about one hundred leagues downriver—the cities of Semlin and Belgrade, those two historic enemies, similarly stand opposite each other, on opposing sides of the great river.

Ilia Krusch intended to spend the night at Pest, and perhaps, also, the following day and night, still in the hope of getting some news of his absent friend. Thus, Ilia Krusch's barge sailed closely and peacefully alongside the left bank, in the midst of this flotilla of cheery boats.

But if he had been a little less absorbed by the delightful spectacle offered by those two cities; their houses with arches and terraces, situated along the quaysides, the church bell towers tinged with gold by the last rays of the five o'clock evening sun; yes, if all of these magical sights had not claimed the attention of his admiring eyes, perhaps he would have noticed a certain something which, most assuredly, Mr. Jaeger would have observed: that is, that for some time already, a vessel with three men on board, two at the oars and one at the tiller, seemed to be following the barge, keeping itself at a certain distance behind.

Since Ilia Krusch knew a little corner of the river at the very edge of the city, where he would be very cosy and peaceful during his twelve to thirty-six hours of putting in at port, he continued his journey, and the other vessel accompanied him, about twenty feet distant.

The barge finally reached the location which Ilia Krusch intended it to occupy during his period of respite, a recess where it would have to fear neither a crash nor any undesirable attention.

But, to the great annoyance of Ilia Krusch, a group of about fifty people, men and women, were gathered at this section of the quayside.

"Oh, great!" said Ilia Krusch to himself. "I've been caught!"

And perhaps he was about to continue en route, when the mysterious vessel which had been pursuing him drew up alongside his barge.

As for the throng of curious bystanders and onlookers, they seemed to be motivated by malevolent rather than benevolent intentions, and a muffled murmur ran through this crowd.

The man who was at the rear of the vessel jumped into Krusch's barge with one of his companions. Then, addressing the newly-arrived fisherman: "You are Ilia Krusch, is that right?" he asked.

"Yes"… murmured that good man.

"So… follow me!"

Chapter XI

The Pro- and Anti-Krusch Factions

Though Buda had been, for a century and a half, the location of the official residence of a pasha and one of the largest fortified towns of the Ottoman Empire, and though it had once had to resign itself to being Turkish, it is now well and truly Austrian in identity, even more so than it is Hungarian, even though it is officially considered to be the capital of Hungary. But it possesses only fifty thousand inhabitants; its public buildings, cathedral, churches and palaces are not at all considered to be leading examples of architectural art; business and industry there are practically non-existent. It is a military city, a town of "regiments which pass through," a city of patrols which go through the streets at all hours of the day and night. It has a castle, a military arsenal and a theatre, and is also the official residence of the governor and of the military and civil authorities. Yet despite all of these singular advantages, it is, understandably, jealous of Pest, which stands opposite it on the other side of the great river.

Pest, on the other hand, is a city where life is lived with maximum intensity; with a population of one hundred and thirty-one thousand inhabitants, there is much lively commercial bustle, it is the city of the Magyars, which is tantamount to saying that it is a city of gentlemen. In Pest, the Diet takes place, and the superior courts of the jurisdiction administer justice in this city. Its theatres and walkways are frequented by many people, and tourists find that time goes by too quickly in a city where people are crazy about music and dancing. And then there are the four fairs per year held there, where millions of forints worth of business is transacted. Though its monuments are not at all superior in artistic value to those of its rival, its public park, the Stadtvallchen, is a delightful set of public gardens with cool shady spots, white-waters, lawns of beautiful greenery and small lakes on which elegant boats sail over the surface of the water. With so many tourist attractions to boast of, it will be easily understood that Pest is somewhat scornful of Buda.

It is thus not alone the Danube which separates the two cities in question; it's a whole complex of customs, mores and personal characters, between which the contrast is striking.

Though it has proven possible to construct, between the two cities, a boat bridge which has since been replaced by the current superb bridge suspended by two midway supports, it would be a completely different ball game to try to construct a moral or mental bridge which would reconcile both cities in a similar feeling of friendship.

And, at the end of the day, if a traveller wishes to gaze on each city from its most picturesque angle, he or she should go to see Buda from the vantage point of Pest, and Pest from that of Buda. He or she will not regret their excursion to either side of the Danube.

Moreover, at this particular moment, Pest manifested an eminently singular hustle and bustle: there were crowds of foreign visitors thronging into the city; country folk from the surrounding areas were crowding the market places; on the quaysides, there was a long line of four-wheeled vehicles, surmounted at the back by a little tent with many-colored canvases, under which were spread out baskets of fruit and vegetables and crates of poultry. The flow of traffic was becoming very slow and blocked up, throughout the streets, even in the most out-of-the-way districts. Many boats, not to mention large barges and dampfschiffs, were sailing up and down the river. Ilia Krusch would have found it difficult to find a suitable spot to shelter his barge near the left bank, if he hadn't already been familiar with this little deserted corner at the edge of town, where the barge was not, in fact, being closely guarded by a policeman.

And what was the reason for all this hustle and bustle in this county town of the administrative district known as the comitat? The reason was that the Diet was, at that moment, gathered in Pest, in this first week of the month of June. Radicals, resistant to Austrian influence, would enter into struggles of varying levels of courtesy, with jurists who represented the moderate party. Above the palace, there unfolded the long green, white and red folds of the Hungarian flag.

But, it so happened that, over several days, the passions awakened by the Diet were to be temporarily suppressed by the inflamed passions of a case which enjoyed its brief period of sensation under the name of the "Krusch affair." The reader is about to discover the conditions under which the two rival cities fought for, or against, the cause of the ill-fated prize winner of the Danubian Line. And, from the very outset of the Krusch affair, and before knowing the slightest thing about it, people were pro-Krusch at Pest, and anti-Krusch in Buda.

Upon hearing the command which he had received, without even asking the official position of the man who had arrested him, nor why he had been arrested, Ilia Krusch, being an obedient and submissive man, had set foot on the quay.

"Let's go—best foot forward and march!" were the words immediately addressed to him.

And so, Ilia Krusch had marched off, between the two authentic police officers, for he was truly obliged to recognize them as such. And what's more, he could consider himself fortunate that he hadn't been handcuffed; but in any event, he would have borne this without saying a word, given his nature which had so singularly mellowed through his long years of line fishing.

What most astonished him were the feelings of the general public as he passed along, manifestly hostile sentiments, shouts, threats, looks of indignation and horror.

Budapest along the Danube

"That's him!" shouted one enraged onlooker, abusively.

"He truly looks the part!" screamed another.

"What a bad face!"

"But at least they've finally got their man and they won't be letting him go!"

"And he won't have gotten away with the fate now awaiting him!"

A number of shrewish women, fishwives—they are everywhere, even in Pest—would come over to shove their fists under his nose.

As one can well imagine, the noisy, hostile escort could only grow bigger in number as it made its way onwards. *Cresciteundo,* Ilia Krusch would have thought wryly to himself, if he had had any knowledge of Latin, and if his stupefaction had not also been growing. These Latin words mean "It grows bigger as it moves forward;" this expression is used to describe rivers.

To cut a long story short, having crossed through several crowded districts of the city, the police officers and their prisoner arrived outside a building which singularly resembled those special houses which you go into when you don't want to, and from which you don't come out when you want to. It was the city jail. The door opened, the prison warden appeared, greeted Ilia Krusch as though Krusch were a guest whose arrival was expected, and the door closed once more in the midst of the clamour and protests of a crowd which easily numbered, by that time, about one hundred people.

A few moments later, Ilia Krusch found himself alone in a cell, furnished only by a bed and a bench; he had been put behind bars, placed under lock and key and the bolts firmly shut behind him, though neither his jailer nor the police officers had yet told him the cause of his arrest. What's more, so utterly dumbstricken was Ilia Krusch at this stage, that the poor man hadn't even asked this question. Nevertheless, he wasn't being condemned to death by starvation or thirst. On a little table top embedded in the wall, was a piece of bread, which he ate, and near the piece of bread was a pitcher of water, of which he drank a few drops.

While all this was happening, the daylight, which penetrated into the cell through a narrow loophole with bars, in the wall, was becoming gradually dimmer. Night quickly fell, and the little cell was plunged into complete darkness.

Ilia Krusch then stretched himself out on his bed, fully dressed, while questioning himself as conscientiously as possible: "Oh dear,

Budapest

all of this! But what is it I'm supposed to have done?"... he said to himself.

What sad hours he then had to spend alone in his cell, and how long did that night seem to him! But he finally managed to fall asleep, and, as he didn't have anything to feel guilty about, he didn't have any bad dreams. Quite the contrary. He dreamed of a pike weighing twenty-one pounds, caught with tadpole bait, and also of Mr. Jaeger who, in his dream, had come back to the boat to rejoin him, and the two friends peacefully continued journeying downriver. But as soon as he woke up, he had to face facts and become rapidly disenchanted from his reverie, and cold, harsh reality reappeared in all the horror of its ugly head.

The guard came in the morning, then again in the evening, to renew the prisoner's supplies of food and water. On both occasions, Ilia Krusch politely asked why he had been incarcerated within these four walls. But, most probably, the jailer had been ordered not to make any reply, and so did not give any answer.

"Well... is it something serious?" the prisoner innocently ventured.

An affirmative nod was all that he got by way of reply, and this nod alone seemed to indicate that the case was of the utmost seriousness.

Darkness fell, and with that, sleep came—quite late, admittedly. Krusch's dreams were not such happy ones this time round, and, this time, Mr. Jaeger was no longer in the barge with him.

Budapest

"And what have they done with my boat?" Ilia Krusch had repeated to himself several times, "and my fishing lines, and my hooks, and all my fishing tackle, what's going to become of all of it?... and also, are they going to keep me in this prison of theirs for long?"

And finally, there was this distressing question which he unceasingly posed to himself, and which came constantly back into his mind under this form: "What does it all mean? What does it all mean?"

But Ilia Krusch was to very quickly discover the answer to this question.

The next day, June 2ⁿᵈ, at about two o'clock, the door of the cell was opened and then, a short while later, the entrance door to the prison was opened in its turn and out of it came the prisoner, who crossed the prison threshold in the company of the jailer. A coach was waiting for him in the street; he climbed into it, with two officers. There were many curious onlookers, who were just as hostile as the previous evening.

"It's him... that's him!" people were shouting from every direction.

"Who? Who is 'him'?" wondered Ilia Krusch.

The coach sped hastily onwards and, a quarter of an hour later, it stopped in front of—not at all the local courthouse—but the City Hall. The prisoner alighted and was shown into a low-ceilinged room where the two officers had orders to keep him under surveillance.

If the Diet was, at that time, meeting in Pest, in accordance with constitutional requirements, so was the international commission, having received an urgent summons to an Extraordinary General Meeting. Not all of the commission members had been able to attend this meeting at such short notice, some being away, others having been notified too late to get there on time. The commission was thus composed—at this meeting—only of its Chairman, Roth, from the Duchy of Baden, the secretary, Choczim, from Besserbia, Mr. Hanish from Hungary, Mr. Ouroch from Serbia and Mr. Titcha from Moldavia. A total of five members was thus present, this being a quorum, legally entitled to hold an official meeting and make statutory deliberations. As the reader will not at all have forgotten, the Commission members had unanimously chosen the police chief Karl Dragoch to organize fresh proceedings against the smugglers who were carrying out their trafficking operations along the Danube. Karl Dragoch had immediately swung into action. He had been granted complete freedom of manoeuver to act as he saw fit and to take responsibility for his own decisions, and he had to refer to the Commissioners only when he judged it appropriate to do so. What was he doing? The conditions under which he was operating were not known, and in any case, any indiscreet actions on his part might have compromised the success of his investigations. So there had been no news of him, until the day when a rumor began to circulate of a skirmish between the squadron which he was leading, and Latzko's gang at the entrance to the Lower Carpathians. In this encounter with forces which had proved more than a match for his own, he had had to retreat and, since then, nobody had any idea what had become of him.

It was a short time after these events that Roth, the commission chairman, got such a serious tip-off that he believed he must urgently assemble the international commission in the city of Pest, where the suspect would assuredly be placed under arrest as soon as he got there. This tip-off drew the commissioners' attention to a series of incidents, which were such as to lend much seriousness and credence to the informant's claims. Moreover, this was no anonymous "whistleblower," as the tip-off had come from no less a personage than Belgrade's chief of police, who stated that his information had been received from the most reliable of sources.

It would have been contrary to all logical reasoning for the chairman, Roth, to ignore a tip-off of this nature, and, having discussed the matter with those of his colleagues whom he was able to meet up with, it was resolved that a meeting of the Commission would be called for June 2ⁿᵈ in the Hungarian capital. And so it was that, out of the ten members that made up the totality of the Commission, five of them were, on this very day, holding a meeting in one of the rooms of Pest's City Hall.

This sitting of the Commission was not statutorily bound to be held in public, but, as is usually the case with sittings which are not required to take place in public, the room was packed with "privileged people" from nine o'clock in the morning. Moreover, the Commission was not at all required to pass final judgement—without a right of appeal—on the accused. But, having been set up expressly with a view to hunting down and prosecutingLatzko and his gang, it would simply make a ruling as to whether the man who was now about to appear before it was, or was not, to be brought before the courts, which would then apply the full rigours of the law to him.

At half past ten, the Commissioners had taken their seats at the bench, and, upon the order of Mr. Roth, the accused man was shown into the courtroom.

Ilia Krusch appeared; he really looked more dumbfounded than ever, his eyes lowered, looking ashamed, and, it must be admitted, having for all the world the appearance of a guilty man. He stood upright in front of the bench, and the cross-examination went on between Chairman Roth and himself in the following terms, while the secretary, Choczim, was noting down the questions and answers.

"Your name?"

"Ilia Krusch."

"Your nationality?"

"Hungarian."

"Your place of birth?"

"Racz, on the Theiss."

"Your current residence is at…?"

"Racz."

"Your age?"

"Fifty-two."

"Your profession?"

"I was a pilot on the Danube for about twenty years."

Budapest

"And now?"

"I'm now retired, and I'd probably never have left Racz if I hadn't had the idea of going to take part in the Danubian Line's contest..."

"At which you won two prizes?"

"Yes, Your Honor, the prize for the greatest number of fish caught with my catch of seventy-nine fish, and the prize in the weight category for a pike weighing seventeen pounds."

Ilia Krusch had, little by little, bucked up and become more spirited as he spoke, and, moreover, to such specific questions, he had been able to give equally specific answers. Up to that point, his attitude to the tribunal had been rather to his advantage, and, even if he were to end up being charged with the gravest of misdeeds, it has to be acknowledged that he didn't at all have the air of a criminal.

What is more, he still had no idea why he had been arrested upon his arrival in Pest, or for what reason he was now appearing before this international commission.

"So," the chairman resumed his questioning, "it was purely in order to compete in the fishing contest that you left Racz to go to Sigmaringen."

"Purely for that reason," replied Ilia Krusch, "and that decision earned me two prizes amounting to two hundred florins in value."

"Indeed," replied the chairman, but in a tone which seemed somewhat mocking. "But after that success on your part, it would seem that all that would remained for you to do was to go back quietly to Racz to enjoy your moment of triumph!..."

"And that's what I did, Your Honor," replied Ilia Krusch, who made no attempt to conceal the surprise caused to him by this remark.

"That's what you did, yes... but not under ordinary conditions. Instead of travelling by rail, which would have brought you back from Saxony to Hungary, or taking the dampfschiffs which carry passengers along the Danube, you had this eccentric idea of sailing downriver, fishing line in hand, from the source of the river as far as its mouth."

"And so, is that forbidden, Your Honor?"

"No, admittedly not, unless you used your eccentric behaviour to conceal certain plans, which is something we are only too certain of!"

"What do you mean, Your Honor?" asked Ilia Krusch, who seemed perturbed by this response. "Yes! I had the idea, while I was in Sigmaringen, of travelling the entire course of the River Danube... I had a barge... I went to the source of the Danube, at Donaueschingen. I cast my fishing rod into the waters... I've arrived in Pest, fishing all the way here, and by now I'd be on my way to Belgrade, if, for the past

A dampschiff

two days, I hadn't been held in custody, without anyone wishing to give me the reason..."

"Oh, I'm going to give it to you," said chairman Roth. "But first, please answer this question once more: your name really is Ilia Krusch?"

"Yes, indeed."

"Well, no it's not! You're not Ilia Krusch, not at all."

"And who am I, then?"

"You are Latzko, the leader of the smugglers."

"Me... Latzko!"

And though Ilia Krusch might well have wished to protest against this preposterous declaration, he couldn't make himself heard, for the uproar and clamour in the public gallery drowned out his voice.

The chairman then proceeded to read out the letter he had received. It was truly damning for the so-called Ilia Krusch. What man in his right mind would have ever conceived this idea of going off line-fishing along the entire stretch of the Danube... unless this plan was intended to mask other, more sinister ones... The reason that this Latzko fellow hadn't been apprehended was that he was hiding under the false identity of Ilia Krusch. He knew that he was being hunted down from all sides, he didn't dare go on board one of his own boats as these were exposed to the risk of police and customs inspections. To travel over land was as difficult for him as to travel by water. He had thus come up with the idea of coming to the Sigmaringen contest; then, after the success which he had achieved there, either through his skills or through pure chance, he had devised and publicized this plan of travelling down the Danube under these extraordinary conditions! And thus, on this barge which had passed along unnoticed, he had allowed himself to be carried along by the current just like his boat or boats which he had been following day and night, and with which he could remain in contact, and of which he could also oversee the clandestine loading of illicit cargo without giving rise to suspicion... In short, all these arguments were put up against the accused man, and made him out to be the real Latzko and a "forged" Ilia Krusch.

Once the poor man had heard the public reading of this letter, he remained overwhelmed, crushed. A thousand terrors tormented his brain, his eyes no longer saw anything, his ears no longer heard anything, his powers of reason were dimming so that he ultimately came to wondering: "Could I, perchance, be Latzko; might I no longer be Ilia Krusch?"

But he finally came out of his stupor to request that the chairman at least arrange to have enquiries made about him at Racz, his native city, thus allowing the Commission to establish and verify his identity. Chairman Roth, in a condescending and still sarcastic manner, gave him his promise that this would indeed be done with all due expedition, and Krusch was then returned to his prison. But nobody had any doubt but that he was the leader of the smuggling ring, concealing his identity by passing himself off under the name, and in the clothes of, the Danubian Line's prize winner!

However, it is worth noting once again that, though the vast majority of the population of Pest expressed their belief in Krusch's guilt, the vast majority of the population of Buda declared themselves to be of the opposite opinion. Here, the pro-Krusch brigade; there, the anti-Kruschists. A pure affair of local rivalry.

Ilia Krusch spent another bad night; a sleepless one this time. Certainly, he knew that he was as innocent as a newborn babe. But can one really be sure of anything when it comes down to the human administration of justice, and with so many miscarriages of justice, often realised and acknowledged only when it is too late! And the most likely upshot of all this was that he was about to be committed to trial!

A thought suddenly crossed his mind... Mr. Jaeger?... Nobody had said anything to him about Mr. Jaeger... Were they unaware of Mr. Jaeger's presence in the barge with him?

Yes, they were unaware of it. When Jaeger had gotten on board at Ulm, he had virtually gone unnoticed by the public. Subsequently, throughout their river trip, as Ilia Krusch avoided all public displays of admiration, Jaeger had continued to go unnoticed... And finally, he was no longer there on the day when the barge had been seized by police officers at Pest.

"Great God," he said to himself, "suppose Mr. Jaeger was... ?"

But he pushed away this idea, feeling horrified.

"No," he kept repeating to himself, "No! Such an excellent man! Ah! I did the right thing by not speaking about him... After me, it is he who would have been accused of being this Latzko, who Jaeger doesn't know anymore than I do! It's fortunate that that chairman of

the tribunal didn't know that we were sailing together... And I won't say a word about that... No! I won't say it!"

Such was the resolution made by this excellent-natured man. To entertain the idea that Mr. Jaeger might be Latzko... that he might have willingly carried out those deeds that Ilia Krusch was being accused of having carried out... It was a thought that he didn't even want to consider for even one second... And yet, and yet... Mr. Jaeger's constant insistence on closely surveying the Danube's river fleet... and his visits to the various towns... and his absence, right at the very moment when Karl Dragoch's squadron had been routed by the criminal gang? Were there not obvious conclusions to be reached from these circumstances? Well, no! Ilia Krusch would jump to no such conclusions! Moreover, he didn't doubt that if Mr. Jaeger came to Pest, he wouldn't hesitate to vouch for his honesty, just as he had no doubt, at the end of the day, that he would be found not-guilty, as soon as his identity had been verified by the documents due to be sent from Racz.

The next day, Ilia Krusch waited in vain to be brought again before the international commission. The fact that he didn't, however, leave the prison at all, was probably because they were waiting for information which had been sought about him.

Throughout that same day, June 4th, Ilia Krusch was left alone with only his thoughts for company. And as legal proceedings had not yet been taken against him, no lawyer came to consult with him about his case. He was thus reduced to consulting with himself. And so, his thoughts kept coming back inexorably to Mr. Jaeger. Undoubtedly, this case must be enjoying a sufficient level of notoriety to have reached Mr. Jaeger's ears. It was thus certain that Mr. Jaeger could not be unaware of the arrest of his travelling companion, that he would not at all try to rejoin him at some point downriver, but that he would, instead, rush to Pest to give evidence in favor of Ilia Krusch... "Unless," the good man thought to himself, "that he's afraid of being mistaken, in his turn, for this abominable Latzko, just as I myself have been, and, I do declare, the prospect of being locked up has nothing appealing about it."

And never, no, never did he entertain so much as the slightest suspicion abou this companion, a suspicion which would certainly have been felt equally by the chairman, Roth, by the secretary, Choczim and also by many others, if it was to be discovered under what conditions

Mr. Jaeger and Ilia Krusch had gotten acquainted and had travelled down the great river together since Ulm!...

Finally, on the morning of June 5th, the door of the cell opened once again. A coach was waiting outside for the accused man, who was brought to the City Hall with the same legal formalities and officialdom to which he had already been subjected. The fact that he was being brought back before the Commission must quite obviously indicate that some progress had been made in these preliminary investigations of the case. Moreover, the room was overflowing just like the first time, and, just as on that first occasion, the sentiments of those in the public gallery seemed no less hostile. Ilia Krusch was, for them, still Latzko. Moreover, it must be said that, since his arrest, the police had heard no further news of Latzko, and, as far as everybody was concerned, this was explained by the very fact of the imprisonment of the false Ilia Krusch.

The accused thus appeared before the commissioners in an attitude of completely natural discouragement, following four days of imprisonment. Despite how strongly he believed in his innocence, it was only too plain to see how utterly despondent and anxious he was. In vain did his eyes search the packed courtroom for some friendly glance in his direction...Not one friendly look did he encounter, yet, it must be said, it was on the face of Chairman Roth that he thought he perceived some evidence of sympathy. Yes! And also on the face of the secretary, Choczim, and of the other Commission members.

Ah! What effect was produced, when the chairman, taking the floor, expressed himself in the following terms:

"Ilia Krusch, we have made enquiries about you in Racz. I shall delay no further in telling you that the information which has come to us about you, is excellent in every respect..."

A stir of surprise, and, who knows, perhaps of disapproval, ran through the people present at this hearing; the public could see its prey escaping from it.

"Excellent," went on Chairman Roth. "The chief of police in Racz has sent us indisputable proof of your true identity and of your personal integrity. Yes, you are really Ilia Krusch. You really were a pilot, and one of the best on the Danube. You truly are now in retirement in that little city of Racz, where your residence is currently located..."

My goodness, but Ilia Krusch was by now bowing as though he were acknowledging compliments, and he didn't seem any more amazed or satisfied than the day when he received his double prize from the hands of President Miclesco at the Sigmaringen contest.

Then, the sounds of people clearing their throat rang out in the courtroom.

"We have been led astray in our line of reasoning, Ilia Krusch," declared chairman Roth by way of conclusion. "You are free to go, and it only remains for us to offer you our apologies for this mistake, and to wish you every success in your novel journey!"

The case against Krusch was closed, with his honor having been completely restored—he had been the victim of a judicial error, a miscarriage of justice which had been fully and openly acknowledged. He now only had to get back to his barge, though this was not achieved without many public displays of support en route. He was accompanied on his return journey to the barge by whole crowd comprising a mix of different people, tycoons, Magyars, the Slovakians who are so numerous amongst the workmen of the city. Men, women and children came rushing from all parts of the city

Budapest

to see the hero of the hour, now more heroic than ever, and just as embarrassed as ever by so many bravos and tributes. Even though it meant lengthening his journey, he had to pass by the Stadtvallchen, which was packed with crowds of people, and a concert given by Hungarian gypsies, the *tziganes,* which was just about to take place in this admirable park, added its singing voices and musical instruments to the cheers of the crowds.

There was even, at one point, a question of leading Ilia Krusch to the Bruckenbad, those famous public baths, where he would have been brought to the steam room to ensure he was even more thoroughly cleaned of the false accusations which had tarnished his existence. But, as this would have necessitated crossing the Danube upriver from Buda, the citizens of Pest gave up on this idea, so that Ilia Krusch had a lucky escape from that triumphant ceremony which, in any case, he had no need of. Following a three-hour-long procession, Krusch finally reached the little headland behind which the barge, guarded by a police officer, was moored. Ilia Krusch was finally able to get on board his little barge, and plunge his vessel into the current of the Danube which quickly drew him far from that lively, ostentatious city, in which the worthy man had experienced the trials and tribulations of prison while he waited for those of the death chamber! And now, he was experiencing the enormous joy of having been cleared of all charges. For another while yet, a flotilla of boats accompanied him until he had finally lost sight of the last church bell towers of the capital, a few leagues downriver.

However, it would be wrong to think that this whole affair had reached closure through such a happy denouement. No, there were still many arguments to be had, for or against Ilia Krusch. Except that this time, it was Pest which had gone from being anti-Krusch to pro-Krusch, while it was Buda which had switched allegiance from being "Kruschist" to "anti-Kruschist."

Chapter XII

From Pest To Belgrade

Upon leaving Pest, Ilia Krusch had accomplished the halfway mark of his great journey, give or take a few leagues. But it is necessary to acknowledge that the first half of his epic fishing trip, though it had been undertaken without risks or fatigue, had almost had a tragic denouement; it had narrowly escaped coming to a very sorry end indeed. And it was, above all, only when he felt himself to be truly free, when the last gasps of admiration no longer reached his ears, when the barge, solitary and peaceful, was slipping between the riverbanks, that he truly began to perceive just how serious a situation he had been in.

"Me... me!" he repeated to himself, "me, Ilia Krusch from Racz, ex-pilot, me, the winner of the great fishing contest, to be mistaken for this Latzko! And if he's fated to end up at the gallows some day, oh, how close I came to being hanged instead of him!"

Then, continuing to sink ever-deeper into the quick sands of his distressing ruminations:

"After all, I can understand that the justice system could easily have made a mistake in this matter," this excellent man said to himself, "and I bear no ill will towards the tribunal chairman Roth!... It is certain that this leader of the smuggling ring, knowing himself to be pursued, hunted down from all sides, couldn't have dreamt up a more ingenious scheme to sail downriver in complete security while carrying out his criminal activities!... Who would have thought of seeking him out while he was in the guise of Ilia Krusch? Not to worry; I've had a narrow escape, and I shall light a candle at the statue of the Blessed Virgin of Racz!"

Obviously, that was the very least he could do to show his gratitude!

And then, memories of Mr. Jaeger began to return to his mind. He continued to experience a feeling of self-congratulation at never having uttered the name of his companion. If anybody had learnt of the conditions under which Mr. Jaeger had come to be on board the barge, or the type of business proposition which had been agreed between both men—the entire takings of the fishing trip purchased in advance, and at the price of five hundred florins—that would have seemed the behaviour of a madman... or, better still, for the police, it would have seemed like the conduct of an individual who had chosen this very pretext in order to artfully dodge his pursuers,for as long as he was sailing as far as the mouth of the river.

"Certainly," thought Ilia Krusch, "he would have been, understandably, even more of a prime suspect than I myself was, and I did well not to draw any attention to him!"

No! not once did it occur to this fine fellow, Krusch, that Mr. Jaeger could have been Latzko, not once!... such an excellent man as Jaeger, a friend whose friendship he appreciated so much!... He, the head of that smuggling ring!... Come on, now!...

"And as soon as I meet up with him again," Ilia Krusch would say to himself, "because I truly do hope to see him again, I'll tell him about all this, and he shall thank me, and shout: 'Mr. Krusch, you are the finest man I've ever met on this earth!'"

After a bend in the river at a right angle close to Waitzen, a bend needed in order that it can flow downwards from north to south as far as Pest, the Danube continues to send its waters in this southerly direction, which it even maintains for more than three hundred kilometers, taking account of its many detours, until it reaches the village of Vukovar. As Ilia Krusch allowed his barge to be drawn along by the river's current, setting out each morning and stopping in the evenings, he could see the immense *puszta* stretching out towards the east. This is the Hungarian flat, open country, the Hungarian plain *par excellence* which is bordered, at more than one hundred leagues distant, by the Transylvanian mountains. As it travels over this plain, the railway line from Pest to Basiach crosses an infinite expanse of deserted moors, vast pastures and enormous marshes teeming with waterfowl. This *puszta* is like a great dining table which is always generously served, for countless four-legged dinner guests, thousands upon thousands of ruminants, and represents one of the Hungarian kingdom's greatest riches. One encounters only the bare minimum of fields of wheat or of corn. And it is also the historic plain *par excellence,* where the shepherd, or *kanasz,* and the keeper of horses, or *csiko,* reign supreme, and poets of every period have celebrated this plain in their national poems.

At this point, the river is considerably wide. It was animated by the coming and going of boats which carried local riverside dwellers from one bank to the other. And it was no uncommon occurrence for Ilia Krusch to be recognised as he passed by, which led to cordial greetings and very friendly gestures. His trial had made him so famous that he could no longer even dream of fleeing the various events and gatherings which his passage led to, and if he had happened to go into any of the houses of the shepherds or fishermen, or of the farmers who have the appearance of country gentlemen, he would have noticed, above the living room chimney, a portrait—of varying degrees of likeness—of the Danubian Line's prizewinner. But the upshot of all of this was that his fish was being sold at ever-higher prices, something which truly satisfied him. "And it's not for me, it's for him!" he repeated to himself, "and I'm beginning to believe that he won't lose out as a result of his deal!"

Then, always the same refrain which escaped from this good man's heart: "But where is he right now? He's written it to me, and I have his letter which I'm keeping carefully. And in it, he says: 'I don't even know, any more, where and when it will be possible for me to rejoin you… However, I will do so, sooner or later, perhaps around Pest, perhaps around Belgrade!' Well, he certainly didn't come to Pest, and I'm not sorry about that, for he would have got there at a very remarkable moment… So let's hope I shall see him reappear at Belgrade… before that, perhaps… at Mohacs… at Neusatz… at Peterwardein!… and he will be welcome!"

The riverbed was unceasingly enriched by islands, large and small. Some of the islets were of great expanse, leaving, on both sides, two branches at which the current attained quite a high speed. The barge therefore lost nothing of its average speed of navigation which amounted to about ten leagues per day. It would, therefore, most probably reach the mouth of the Danube within the appointed time frame.

Belgrade

These islands were not at all fertile. On their surface, there grew only birches, aspens and willows in the midst of the silt deposited by the frequent flooding. Nevertheless, abundant supplies of hay are gathered on these islands, and the boats, loaded to the gunwale, carry it to the farms and villages of the riverbank.

Even more so than upriver, boats floated along this stretch of the waters of the Danube in large numbers, not to mention the dampfschiffs which sailed up and down the river. The customs officials were also very active at this part of the river, as was required by current circumstances. Ilia Krusch could see, very clearly, that squadrons of police were keeping the riverbanks under surveillance, and not a boat could have berthed without being visited by these officers, with whom he had just had dealings, the memory of which would never be effaced from his memory.

At this part of its onward flow, the river is, at times, lined with sand dunes; but sometimes also, these dunes are suddenly lowered to give way to some fertile plain or other, and this is what can be seen upriver from the little town of Paks, from which the great post road approaches, a road which is opened between Vienna and Constantinople, passing through Buda, Semlin, Belgrade, Andrinople and the Ottoman territory.

No, never had the time appeared so long to Ilia Krusch, as it did during this navigation from Pest to Belgrade, which was due to last about twelve days. Furthermore, the sky was often criss-crossed by large clouds, and rain poured down in wide, heavy showers. There also suddenly appeared some of those very thick fogs which the river rarely spares from the tourists. When these fogs descend, all visibility disappears. It then becomes necessary for the dampfschiffs, and also for the yachts and barges, to momentarily stop sailing until these fogs lift. But the ex-pilot was so intimately acquainted with the twists and turns of his river—and God knows just how many twists and turns there are between Mohacs and Vukovar—that he didn't even dream of dropping anchor, and continued to allow himself to drift along in his barge. In these circumstances, the thing which bothered him most was that, if Jaeger had arrived at this moment on one of the riverbanks, Ilia Krusch would not have seen him, and he would not have seen Ilia Krusch. This was indeed the situation prevailing during the stopover near Mohacs. The city, drowned underneath the hazes, didn't even make visible the tips of its church steeples. And as for its ten thousand inhabitants, not a single one of them knew that the hero of the hour had spent the night at the foot of the quays at the left bank of the river. And when he set off again the following morning, neither did he spot the long flights of crows and storks which were flying off, in a flurry of feathers, towards less dark regions.

It was during this period of the journey that the barge passed in front of Bezdan. Though, from the middle of the river, one can catch sight only of the mills bearing the same name, and which are powered by the river's current, this is not the case for the Apatin fisheries. It is a sort of river village; in sum, a central square dominated by a great flagpole from which the national flag flies, and which is surrounded by a whole group of constructions in all shapes and sizes, from cabins to huts, and in which dwells a population of fishermen.

It is likely that Ilia Krusch wouldn't have been hugely successful if he had tried to sell his catch of fish in such an environment! Fish: these good folk had enough fish to be able to sell some of it themselves. In any case, he didn't have any opportunity to stop at these fisheries.

It was during this same day that he left behind, on the right, the mouth of the River Drave, one of the large tributaries of the Danube, on which the river fleet uses boats of quite high tonnage. The next day, he came to a halt at the quay of the town of Neusatz, built on the left bank, almost at the spot where the Danube, by means of a sharp bend, abandons the north-south direction which it has been following since Pest, in order to follow a south-easterly direction towards Belgrade. It is a free city, which is the seat of a Serbian bishop, who is a suffragan of the metropolis of Karlowitz.[1]

By this date, June 15th, twenty-seven long days had elapsed since Mr. Jaeger had taken his leave of Ilia Krusch in the circumstances which the reader is now familiar with. And the barge was getting closer to Belgrade, which it would reach at the end of that week.

"Well," wondered Ilia Krusch, "is it here that I am going to meet Mr. Jaeger again? Neusatz is a major town! I can certainly envisage the possibility that he may have been brought there on business... Well, from Vienna to Neusatz, I'm sure he wasn't short of any means of transport?... Perhaps he is in this town, and, I do declare, since my arrival there doesn't seem to have been noticed, I have nothing to fear, and I'm going to scour all the various districts of that town... Mr. Jaeger may be perfectly unaware that I'm here in Neusatz, and who knows whether I might not meet him somewhere along the way?"

Ilia Krusch was right, and, as it would not be dark for another two hours, he spent those hours wandering round, this way and that. But all of the steps he undertook to locate Mr. Jaeger proved fruitless, and he had no choice but to come back to take his place, once again, under his solitary tarpaulin shelter.

"Let's wait," he said to himself, "and maybe I'll have more luck tomorrow at Peterwardein."

Along the Danube there are several major cities which stand opposite each other, one on the right bank, the other on the left. Such is the case with Buda and Pest; or Neusatz and Peterwardein, and, finally, with Semlin and Belgrade. And in cases where it is not the great river itself which separates them, it is one of its tributaries. It follows from this that, in order to go from Neusatz to Peterwardein, all Ilia Krusch

---

1.   A suffragan is a bishop appointed to assist a diocesan bishop. Verne gives the name of the city as Carlovitz; the German name, Karlowitz, has been used here.

had to do was to disembark and to take the boat bridge which links those two towns.

From the vantage point now occupied by his barge, he could see the powerful stronghold perched upon its promontory, towering over the flowing river. Peterwardein is known by the name of the Military Borders.[2]

Hardly was the sun beginning to appear over the rooftops of Neusatz than Ilia Krusch was setting foot on the quay at Peterwardein. He had crossed the Danube in his barge. This had seemed more advisable to him, and, should he encounter Mr. Jaeger, all that both men would have to do would be to get back on board the barge together. He hadn't even baited his fishing hook that morning, so possessed was he by the desire to locate, and be reunited with, his dear companion. And so here he was, wandering through the streets, travelling through the various neighbourhoods, and, should he have to devote the entire morning to his investigations, he wouldn't hesitate to do so.

His efforts were, however, in vain, and it has to be admitted that he had had little chance of succeeding. To run into Mr. Jaeger in this city could only have happened by chance, and even then, for that to happen it would have been essential that Mr. Jaeger be there at that same moment.

At about ten o'clock, Ilia Krusch went into a café to rest for a few moments, and ordered a bottle of that excellent wine produced in Karlowitz. That city, the capital of the Serbs, who live under Austrian domination, is only a few leagues away, to the west of the river. It was indeed the least that Ilia Krusch deserved, to fortify and cheer himself with one of this region's finest vintage wines. And he was saying to himself: "If Mr. Jaeger was here, with what pleasure I would offer him a glass of this fine Karlowitz wine!… and he wouldn't have said no to it… and he would have clinked glasses with me, and we would have drunk to each other's good health!"

As he was reasoning to himself in these terms, the disconsolate Ilia Krusch had happened to mechanically cast his eyes downwards

---

2. Today the town is part of Serbia. Jules Verne had left a space at this point of his manuscript, in order to enlarge upon his historical overview of this region, a commentary which he had already written in Chapter II of *Le Secret de Wilhelm Storitz* (Montreal: Stanké, 1996), translated by Peter Schulman as *The Secret of Wilhelm Storitz* for University of Nebraska Press in 2011.

onto a nearby newspaper. It was from Hungary, and his attention was drawn to an article under the headline: "Where is Latzko?"

"Ah," he said, "now that's something that's of interest to me, after all, and I wouldn't mind knowing where he is, this leader of the smugglers, who I was accused of being!… And, I do declare, if they catch him, that will be yet another piece of proof that Ilia Krusch was not at all Latzko!…"

In truth, there was no need of such additional proof, as the identity of the Danubian Line's award-winning, champion fisherman had been duly and thoroughly established!

The article contained no specific information. Ever since that skirmish between the smugglers and the police squadron at the entrance to the Lower Carpathians, there had no longer been any sign, anywhere, of the elusive criminal gang. It was likely that their boats had continued to sail down the Danube, but the police visits to which all of the river fleet were now subjected had yielded no results. Latzko's whereabouts had once again become unknown, and probably, in order to more effectively throw the police officers off his scent, he was following the river banks, sometimes the right bank, sometimes the left, wearing some disguise or other, all the while overseeing the transport of the contraband as far as the Black Sea. As for Karl Dragoch, the chief of police, there was no news of him either, and unless the Chairman of the international commission had been directly tipped off, nobody could have said where he was at this moment.

Ilia Krusch had reached this point in his reading of the article, when he suddenly straightened up in his seat. Through the glass door of the café, which opened out onto a street leading to the quayside, he thought he had just recognized one of the passers-by who was walking quickly back up the street, towards the upper districts of Peterwardein.

"But that's him… that's him!" he exclaimed. And as he had already paid in advance for his bottle of Karlowitz wine, he hastily left the café and rushed outside. In the street, there were two or three people, but not a single one of them bore any resemblance to Mr. Jaeger. It was, moreover, possible that the latter had turned a corner to the right or perhaps to the left. "I can't have been mistaken," Ilia Krusch repeatedly said to himself as he walked randomly along the street, but from whom could he have made enquiries and have been assured of receiving dependable, reliable responses? Who knew Mr. Jaeger at Peterwardein; wasn't it just Krusch alone?

"Ah! What confounded bad luck," he said to himself; "if only, instead of shutting myself up in that café, I hadn't stopped walking around the street, I'd surely have met him! He would have seen me, he would have come to me… and by now, we'd be walking along, arm in arm… and we would have resumed our sailing trip which would nevermore have been interrupted."

The poor man was disconsolate. To have let such an opportunity— which would not offer itself again—slip through his fingers!… How likely was it now that he could find Mr. Jaeger again and rejoin him?… Was he staying at Peterwardein?… Wasn't he going to go to Neusatz?… As for the possibility of Krusch having been mistaken, no! Ilia Krusch couldn't countenance this… It was unmistakably his companion whom he had glimpsed and of whom he could now find not a trace!

In this situation, there was only one remaining course of action to be decided upon, and Ilia Krusch opted for this strategy after he had spent an hour wandering in vain throughout the neighbourhood. It was to go back to the river and wait in the barge. If he couldn't find Mr. Jaeger, well, Mr. Jaeger would find him, and the result would be the same, that is, an excellent one!… Whether Mr. Jaeger was at Peterwardein or at Neusatz, he would surely check whether the barge had dropped anchor there, and it was essential to get back to the barge without a moment's delay. And so, this is exactly what Ilia Krusch did. Public attention had not at all been awakened as to his presence, and this was unfortunate. Some sort of public display couldn't have escaped Mr. Jaeger's notice. But the newspaper, with that air of assurance as to the correctness of its information, which is the hallmark of reporters, had announced that Ilia Krusch had already gone past Belgrade, and nobody was giving him any more thought.

Ilia Krusch waited in vain in the barge, and, in the afternoon, he started to make further searches for Mr. Jaeger on the quays of Peterwardein, and then on the quays of Neusatz, but again in vain. Evening came, but Mr. Jaeger had not reappeared.

And so, it was another bleak night for Ilia Krusch! But in the end, he couldn't afford to delay his journey any longer. Belgrade was not too far from Neusatz, and hadn't Mr. Jaeger said in his letter that he might rejoin his companion in Belgrade, there or thereabouts… perhaps…

Thus, the next day, the barge set sail once again off into the current of the Danube, and Mr. Jaeger was not at all with Ilia Krusch!

Equally bleak were the riverbanks between which the waters of the Danube, wide and monotonous, ran, sometimes stretching as far as the horizon. To the right were clayey swellings, narrow gullies which came to an end at the river itself. Sometimes there were cliffs, and above them, sloping fields over which vineyards were spread out and some trees stood. There was still great hustle and bustle on the surface of the Danube, which was criss-crossed by long streams of barges drawn onwards by the wind or the current, and by numerous boats which the barge managed to avoid by sticking close to the riverbanks.

That evening, June 18th, Ilia Krusch, at about five o'clock, dropped anchor at the mouth of the Theiss, and cast his fishing rod into the bottom of a little creek, whose approaches were quite well-stocked with fish. This important tributary, situated to the left—before it becomes absorbed into the waters of the great river—brings its waters to the little village of Titel, after flowing for nine hundred kilometers starting from its source in the Carpathians, after which it crosses Transylvania and the kingdom of Hungary. And Ilia Krusch would only have had to sail about ten leagues up this tributary to get to Racz.

As the reader will not have forgotten, this was the former pilot's home town, his place of birth. It was there that he had learnt his trade aboard the boats which frequented this tributary. It was in this town also that he had been enjoying his retirement over the past six years, and there that he had first acquired his passion for fishing. It is from there that the information requested by the chairman of the international commission had been forwarded—information which allowed Ilia Krusch's identity and probity to be established and verified, leading to the finding that he was perfectly innocent.

And you may well ask yourself whether Ilia Krusch might possibly have considered, at this point, taking a few days holiday in his home, with his family, shaking hands with his old friends, before continuing his journey, which he had thoroughly resolved to see through to its end.

"No!" he said to himself. "And suppose Mr. Jaeger arrived during my absence, suppose, he was watching out for the arrival of the barge at Semlin or at Belgrade, while it was put into port at Racz! Wouldn't there be a danger that he might never be able to find it again?"

This was sound reasoning, and wasn't it already most unfortunate that the newspapers, by incorrectly reporting that Ilia Krusch had gone past Belgrade, had possibly contributed to misleading Mr. Krusch and causing him to make an error? Thus, Ilia Krusch abandoned the idea of going to Racz, though with regret, and, the next day, after selling his fish at Titel, he set off downriver once again in his barge. The following day, when he came to a halt a short distance upriver from Semlin, in the late afternoon, he wanted to continue, in this town, the searches which he had already undertaken in Neusatz and Peterwardein.

Semlin is built on the confluence formed by the Save on the right bank, and that river separates it from Belgrade. As Semlin is situated at some distance from the river, Ilia Krusch had no option but to entrust his barge to the guard of one of those fishermen whose wooden houses are grouped underneath the shelter of the great trees, and gave him his name, just in case anybody might come enquiring after him.

"Ah! Mr. Krusch," said this fisherman.

"Yes, but that name is for your ears only… Do you promise me?…"

"I give you my word!"

Yet as soon as Ilia Krusch's back was turned, the fisherman had nothing better to do than to disclose the arrival of the famous Ilia Krusch in Semlin. And of course that immediately ended any hopes Ilia Krusch might have had of travelling incognito, and, as he travelled through the streets, he was spotted and recognized, and the Serbs, who form the majority of the population of Semlin, proved themselves to be no less welcoming than the Austrians of Passau or the Hungarians of Pest in paying homage to this illustrious guest. Since it was founded in the eighteenth century on the site of a castle which belonged to the famous Jean Hunyadi, patriotic defender of Hungary against the Ottoman armies, Semlin had perhaps never before launched itself into such triumphal tributes!

But as for Mr. Jaeger, there was still not a trace of him to be found, and most assuredly, if he had been in Semlin, the news of so rapturous applause in the streets would have reached his ears, and he would have rushed to rejoin his companion.

The next day, June 19th, a little before midday, in clear weather, Ilia Krusch saw the outline of the city appearing before his eyes, a city built, in the shape of an amphitheatre, on a hill, with its European-style houses, its steeples upon which the sun projected an aigrette of flame, and the two minarets of a mosque, which didn't stand out too glaringly despite its closeness to the churches. A little to the left, in the middle of a circle of fruit trees from which several tall cypresses soared upwards to the skies, there was what looked like a second, more modern city which contrasted with the old Turkish city.

This was Belgrade, the *alba Graeca,* the White City, which had in bygone days been the capital of the former principality of Serbia, which consisted, at this time, of three very distinct parts: the new city, built for and occupied solely by the Serbs, the suburb, held and occupied jointly by the Serbs and the Turks, and the fortress, the pasha's official residence, on which the Ottoman flag flapped in the wind.

Just at the moment when—his boat having been moored at a quay of the suburb which is the business district—Ilia Krusch was about to disembark, a man suddenly clapped a hand on his shoulder in a friendly manner.

It was Mr. Jaeger.

"So, how's it going, Mr. Krusch?" he asked.

"Not bad… and you?..."

This was all that Ilia Krusch—as stunned as he was satisfied, at the sight of his former travelling companion—could think of to say in reply!

Chapter XIII

FROM BELGRADE TO THE IRON GATES

MR. JAEGER AND ILIA KRUSCH hadn't seen each other since they had become parted from each other in Vienna on May 20th, that is, for a total of thirty-one days. Mr. Jaeger had arrived in Belgrade forty-eight hours ago. Ilia Krusch would certainly not ask him the cause of his long absence, for reasons of discretion. The important thing now was that both men were going to resume their navigation of the Danube, together.

Ilia Krusch's first question had been: "When are we leaving?"

"This very minute, if you are willing," Mr. Jaeger had replied, "and that'll mean you can avoid the public honors you have so little fondness for…"

"Indeed, Mr. Jaeger. So, my arrival?…"

"Has been publicized as not taking place until tomorrow. Sometimes the papers report that you're late; at other times, they state that you're ahead of schedule, and it's high time…"

"I shall follow your orders to the letter, Mr. Jaeger. It's only barely four o'clock in the afternoon, and for the three remaining hours of daylight left to us, we can make some headway on our onward journey, by sailing about two or three leagues downriver from Belgrade over those next three hours of brightness…"

"Agreed, Mr. Krusch, agreed."

To a casual observer, Mr. Jaeger might have appeared in quite a hurry to depart from the Serbian capital. But Ilia Krusch didn't even notice his friend's demeanour; he could see only one thing, and that was, that Mr. Jaeger had been "given back" to him and that Jaeger asked nothing more than to set off again.

However, Mr. Jaeger felt himself duty-bound to add (though with the air of a man who already knew what his companion's reply was going to be): "Unless, Mr. Krusch, you have still some business to transact here at Belgrade…"

"Me, Mr. Jaeger… The only business I have is to get to the mouth of the Danube, and as we still have a further three hundred leagues to travel…"

"There is not a moment to be lost, Mr. Krusch, not a moment to be lost!" replied Mr. Jaeger.

As for that question of curiosity about Belgrade needing to be satisfied, it didn't in the least apply to Ilia Krusch. Over the years during which he used to ply his trade as a river pilot, he had often stopped over at Belgrade, either to load or unload his cargo. The view which can be enjoyed from the esplanade of its citadel; the Konak, or pasha's palace, whose high, thick walls are erected in the form of square pillars; the ethnically mixed city surrounding the great fortress, with its four gates which flank the outer walls; the suburbs in which there is a concentration of important, widespread, intensive business and trade, as merchandise bound not only for Serbia but for all the Turkish provinces is stored there; its streets which, through the arrangement of its shops, and their excellent stock and high volume of customers, give it the appearance of a district of Constantinople, and the new city extending all along the river Save, with its palace, its Senate, its ministries, its wide communication routes planted with trees and its comfortably-appointed private houses; all of this brutal contrast, so to speak, with the old city, meant that Ilia Krusch was at a stage where he no longer felt he knew this bizarre combination of disparate elements which constituted the city of Belgrade. As for Mr. Jaeger, assuming that this was the very first time that he had ever arrived in this curious capital of Serbia, had he not already had the opportunity to visit it at his leisure over the previous forty-eight hours? Neither man had any motivation, therefore, for prolonging his stay in Belgrade. As Ilia Krusch had rightly pointed out, there was still a long distance to be travelled to get to the mouth of the river. From Belgrade onwards, big cities would become rarer in number—the few there are, include Nicopoli, Rouschtchouk, Silistrie and Ismail and, taking the essential stopovers into account, the onward journey by boat could take place under optimal conditions of speed.

That afternoon, the barge—having avoided coming to the notice of an enthusiastic public—thus resumed its negotiation of the Danube's current, at about five o'clock. Those two cities which had, in the past, been such sworn enemies, but which now enjoyed such amicable relations, quickly disappeared from sight—the current friendship between these two cities means that the reprimands and admonishments once addressed to them by the composer of the *Orientales* poems, quoted by Lancelot, could no longer be justifiably applied to them:

> Please see reason, Turk and Christian!
> Selmin and Belgrade! What's your affliction?
> God give me strength! Not a moment's sleep—
> Without being rudely woken—it makes me weep—
> Upon hearing jealous insults fire, between Belgrade and
>   Semlin
> What woeful ire![1]

When the Danube becomes angry these days, its wrath is no longer directed at Semlin or against Belgrade, whose canons it threatens to silence, but rather, it is because terrible winds assail its wide, deep bed; it is because it has "like the sea, its swell," and at such times, it is sailors who have cause to dread its furious passion.

One thing which would have been surprising, is if Mr. Jaeger and Ilia Krusch hadn't spoken of the various incidents which had marked the period of their separation. And, to begin with, as soon as the barge only had to allow itself to drift freely along:

"Ah, Mr. Jaeger," exclaimed Ilia Krusch, taking both his companion's hands in his, "how long they seemed to me, those days without you! In every town or village I came to, I kept hoping to meet up with you again... and each time, nobody! I feared that you might have come to some harm..."

"No, Mr. Krusch," replied Mr. Jaeger, "No! I'm afraid I was detained in Vienna by important business which came up unexpectedly, and I only barely had enough time to let you know through a few scribbled

---

1. By Victor Hugo.

Belgrade

words in a note! I found that really frustrating, but it was impossible for me to do anything other than that, and by the time you had my note in your hands, I had already left Vienna…"

"And as for myself, Mr. Jaeger, I didn't exactly put down roots there either… From three in the morning onwards, as soon as I'd taken back in my grapnel, I was sailing towards Pressburg…"

"And why the hurry?"

"First, so that you wouldn't be looking there in vain for me, if by any chance you had wished to rejoin me there… and second, to avoid public ovations from the Viennese…"

"So they knew?"… asked Mr. Jaeger.

"They knew I was there, because the bearer of your letter must have gossiped about my being there, but it was too late when they found out, and I was already a good distance away from them…"

"Always the same, Mr. Krusch!"

"Always the same, Mr. Jaeger, and always happy to be back in your company."

"I feel the same, Mr. Krusch."

"And we won't separate again before the end of the voyage?"

"I have every reason to believe that we won't be separated again."

This answer brought a radiant glow of happiness to Ilia Krusch's kind face.

"And now, Mr. Jaeger, you know what happened to me in Pest?"

"Indeed I do, Mr. Krusch! Your arrest... your imprisonment... To think that you were mistaken for that notorious Latzko who they are decidedly unable to lay their hands on..."

"I ask you," said Ilia Krusch, beginning to get a little worked up, "do I look like a criminal?"

"No, most certainly not, and if the most honest man in the world looks like anybody, it has to be... like you!"

"Well, for nearly four days, Mr. Jaeger, I was assumed to be that head of the smuggling ring, and the chairman Mr. Roth didn't seem to be in any doubt on that score..."

"Mr. Krusch," said Mr. Jaeger at that point, "please believe that if I had been free, when I got wind of the word of your arrest, I would have rushed to Vienna to testify in your favor... But unfortunately I wasn't free, and by the time I was once again at liberty to act, the matter had ended... And I didn't even know about this whole unlikely story until it was too late to be able to write to the chairman of the international commission and tell them what I had to say about you..."

"Oh, Mr. Jaeger, though I was extremely annoyed to find myself confined within the four walls of a prison cell, believe me when I say that I didn't feel any worry over it... I was sure of my innocence, wasn't I, and I was well aware that the information sought at Racz would be favorable to me... I... I... a Latzko!"

"The truth is that the whole thing was totally contrary to common sense, and I think you've already forgotten this unpleasant experience..."

"It's as if it had never happened to me, Mr. Jaeger..."

"By the way," Jaeger asked, "was there ever any mention of myself during that case?"

"Never, Mr. Jaeger... It was not known, and it is still not known, that I have a travelling companion... If by chance you have been seen with me in the barge, it must have been assumed that it was just a temporary arrangement... a favor I was doing for somebody..."

"So, my name wasn't mentioned, not even once?"

"Not once, Mr. Jaeger... I was the only one who knew about you being with me in the boat, and, as you can well imagine, I wouldn't have been so naive as to mention it..."

"Yet, Mr. Krusch, did it perhaps occur to you that I could have backed you up with my evidence?"

"Yes... I did indeed think of that, but I knew that I would get out of that distressing spot of bother on my own, and I also felt that it could have caused unnecessary inconvenience and strife to you..."

"Strife, and why so?"

"Because the Commission would have been capable of thinking that you were this Latzko fellow..."

"I?"

"Yes, you, just as easily as they thought I was him! You could have been taking advantage of this situation to travel downriver in complete safety... and they might even have assumed that I was your accomplice... No... I preferred to say nothing."

"And you were perfectly right to do so," replied Mr. Jaeger, who seemed to have listened especially carefully to what his companion had just told him. "Yes! You were right, Mr. Krusch, and I thank you for your discretion..."

"It was the most natural thing in the world, Mr. Jaeger, although, when all is said and done, you would not have had any more difficulty than I did in proving your identity and getting the case dropped..."

"Evidently, Mr. Krusch, evidently!"

When evening came, the boat dropped anchor, as usual, close to the river bank, at the foot of a village in which Mr. Krusch was able to sell his fish and stock up afresh with bread and meat.

The next day, after a successful spot of fishing at the break of dawn, the current carried the barge off again, downriver, and it floated with a certain degree of speed. Around the Austrian side of the riverbank, flat and low-lying, subject to flooding, there could be seen a lot of guards, close enough to each other to be able to communicate among themselves. This personnel belongs to the frontier regiments, half-soldiers, half-local countrymen, who receive no salary in peacetime, the so-called *grenzers,* armed at the expense of the government. As one can well imagine, the severity of Austrian discipline makes it quite difficult to disembark on that side of the river. Thus, in order to avoid any trouble, Ilia Krusch gladly berthed at the opposite side of the river.

It was also at that side that the numerous boats which didn't want to expose themselves to any danger on the open river during the night, tended to stop over. At that moment, there were about thirty of them, sailing along in a row, one behind the other. That well-steered, well-piloted boat which Mr. Jaeger had already noticed in the narrow pass at Strudel, still stood out among them.

"As far as our fishing is concerned," said Mr. Krusch, "it's just as good on one side of the river as on the other, and when all is said and done, up to now, Mr. Jaeger, I've been fairly fortunate in the amount of fish I've caught… The fish I've sold since I set out have earned me—or, I should say, have earned *you*—one hundred and twenty-seven florins and seventeen kreutzers, and I don't think you shall have any cause to complain by the time we get to the end of this river journey…"

"That has always been my opinion, Mr. Krusch," replied Mr. Jaeger, "and it's you yourself who shall have lost out as a result of our deal!"

Throughout the four days which it took the barge to sail down the river as far as Orsava, it navigated on a bed which was most unpredictable in its twists and turns, but which maintained its general easterly direction, and which bordered the Military Frontiers to the left. The barge passed before the city of Smederevo, which had in the past been the capital of Serbia, a city whose fortress is built on a promontory which blocks part of the Danube, and which is defended by an entire crown of towers and a dungeon.[2] In this place, the great river compensates marvellously for the wildness and aridity of the rural regions which border it further upriver. Everywhere, there are fruit trees brimming with full yields of their delicious fruit, orchards enriched with diverse sorts of tree plantations and a succession of lush vineyards stretching as far as the mouth of the Moravia. This smaller river reaches the great river through a magnificent valley, one of the most beautiful in Serbia. At the mouth a certain number of boats were displayed, some of which were sailing downriver, while the others prepared to sail back upriver by means of tugboats or attachments.

After Smederevo, there was Basiach, which is where the railway line connecting Vienna to Orsova still came to an end at that time, though by the time Ilia Krusch and Mr. Jaeger passed alongside Basiach, its railway line was shortly to be extended as far as Orsova; then they came to Columbacz, with its magnificent ruins, then caves which were the stuff

---

2. Verne gives the name of Smederevo as Semendria.

of legend, including the cavern in which Saint George apparently left the body of the dragon which he had slain with his own hands. At each bend in the river—and it had countless twists and turns—there rose up, from all sides, steep promontories, against which the current's foamy waters swept urgently. Above, dense woods gather, rising in terraced rows up as far as the mountains, which are higher on the Turkish side of the river than on the Hungarian side. A tourist would have certainly stopped on numerous occasions along the river journey, to gaze more closely and at length, at the magical sights which the river offers along this stretch. A tourist would have temporarily disembarked at the defile of Kazan, one of the most remarkable along the entire route; he would have followed the towpath, so as to examine that famous Tabula Traiana or Trajan's Tablet, that rock upon which can still be seen the inscription recalling the campaign of the celebrated Roman emperor.

But neither Mr. Jaeger nor Ilia Krusch allowed themselves to be distracted by the whimsies of tourism: one of them was still completely absorbed in his observations of the movement of goods vessels along the river, while the other—depending on differences in the current— was uniquely concerned with sailing close to the appropriate bank of the river, now the Turkish riverbank, at other times, the Serbian side of the Danube.

And it was thus that, during the afternoon of June 24th, in quite rainy weather, they crossed that Carpathian mountain range which stretches from Poland as far as the Balkans, and which is crossed by the Danube at the point where its fourth basin opens.

There are two Orsovas, the old and the new, on the border, and beyond, the Valasian territories extend. The Danube has by this point entered into Ottoman territory, or at the very least, the Turkish provinces, and doesn't exit from them until it reaches the estuary which pours its waters into the Black Sea. Orsova is, quite naturally, a military post, occupied by Valasian soldiers, among a population of two thousand inhabitants. It is at this place that travelers—and with greater unpleasantness than they have encountered at earlier stages of their journey—are subjected to tyrannical treatment by the police and harassment by customs officers.

Obviously, Ilia Krusch and Mr. Jaeger, who didn't have any merchandise to load or unload, weren't banking on suffering any delay on this score. Their small barge wasn't one of those larger vessels and,

Orsova

unless a new tax had been introduced on fishing rods, hooks and floats, they were not at all liable for customs duties which would require two or three hours to be paid, so they confidently expected to be able to leave as soon as they thought fit, at any hour of the day or night.

However, what ought to have initially caused Mr. Jaeger some surprise, was the large number of barges which had halted at Orsova. There were about thirty of them, and on each one there could be seen a Valasian sentry standing guard, while customs officers subjected each boat to an extremely rigorous inspection. Mr. Jaeger quickly learned that, upon orders from senior sources, a complete embargo had been imposed upon all boats wishing to sail past Orsova. This extremely harassing measure had just been implemented by the international commission. Very strict orders had been given to its officers. No barge could continue its navigation downriver until the Customs officials had assured themselves that it wasn't carrying any smuggled goods, even if it meant having to completely unload its cargo. "Good!" Ilia Krusch remarked, "this must be a stroke executed by police chief Dragoch, and he must have reason to believe that he's finally about to get his hands on Latzko, or at the very least, that he'll seize one of his smuggling vessels!"

The Iron Gates

Mr. Jaeger made no reply. His lips tightly pursed, he stood on the barge, the anchor of which had by now gripped the riverbank, and was watching all this hustle and bustle, listening to all these shouts, all of these reprimands which burst out from every direction, protesting against a measure which was so damaging to the Danube's river fleet.

Mr. Ilia Krusch then added:

"In any case, that can't possibly affect us… and I don't see what type of smuggled goods could possibly be on our barge!… What's more, they'll have it completely inspected within ten minutes tops, if they wish."

Well, the good man was sadly mistaken! He had not reckoned with the routine measures of harassment which the governments of all countries take delight in applying, and more particularly, in the Danube provinces.

This provoked a fine outburst of anger on the part of Ilia Krusch, inasmuch as that peaceable line fisherman's nature was susceptible to feeling anger; though let the reader be reassured, Krusch's anger did not go so far as to cause him any heart spasms! And he added: "After all, Mr. Jaeger, what I'm saying is not so much for me as for you, and if this delay doesn't offend you…"

"But no, it doesn't," replied Mr. Jaeger, "and I don't mind seeing how all this is going to turn out, if they end up seizing one of this Latzko's barges—this Latzko whom they did you the honor of mistaking you for, Mr. Krusch!"

In actual fact, there was a stopover of only twenty-four hours at the market town of Orsova. And during this period of time, the boats were detained. The sentry guards who had been positioned on board each boat didn't allow any stranger to come near, and none of the bargemen was allowed to leave his boat. The cargo had to be moved, upon which the officers would visit each barge throughout the entire length of its hold. They satisfied themselves that there was no double back, that the planks couldn't at all be moved. After the holds, it was the superstructure supporting the upper bridge that was thoroughly scoured in every nook and cranny, and also the personnel's accommodation, set out at the back of the boat, as in all of the large Danube vessels.

As soon as this inspection was completed, none of the boats was yet given permission to leave. They would only be allowed to leave all together at the same time, following payment of customs duties.

Obviously, this operation did not take place without leading to disagreements and quarrels. But the numbers of police were sufficient, especially when supplemented by the soldiers from the Orsova garrison.

Mr. Jaeger was extremely interested in these inspections and his attentiveness did not waver a single instant. To such an extent that Ilia Krusch ended up saying to him: "Eh, Mr. Jaeger, up to now, nothing's been discovered?"

"No, and I'm afraid that this whole operation may have been a complete waste of time..."

"Have you noticed amongst all these barges, Mr. Jaeger, that one we've already come across in the narrow pass of Strudel, and which was so adept at forcing its way through the entire flotilla?"

"Yes, Mr. Krusch, it is that one that is there, against the wharf... I know it only too well... It was one of the first to be inspected, but nothing suspicious was found on board..."

"Indeed, Mr. Jaeger, and it is ready to set sail again, but it'll have to wait, just like all the others. Well! I'm not worried about it! It obviously has a good pilot, and it'll be well able to make up for lost time and end up being ahead of schedule once again!"

And indeed, this barge was there, and all of its cargo had been put back in its place. There was nobody to be seen on board, and its crew was probably either on dry land or in the cabins. Only a single Valasian soldier walked up and down the deck, his rifle at his shoulder.

It was the head of the Orsova customs services who had, in accordance with the instructions given to him by his superiors, initiated this general inspection, which was due to continue for a few more days on all of the barges which would arrive from upriver. But as regards those boats which had been detained there for the past twenty-four hours, the inspection came to an end during the evening of the 25th. Police had been unable to uncover any contraband and so an authorization to continue their journey—known in customs terminology as transpire—was granted to all of the boats.

Some of them thus set off that evening, and, all in all, they would not be in any danger during this night-time sailing. The others preferred to wait till the next day, and among them was the boat that had come to Ilia Krusch's particular attention. However, for whatever reason, it set off during the night, for, the following day, as soon as dawn broke, it was no longer to be seen at Orsova.

After a few fruitful casts of the whip line—allowing Ilia Krusch to strike some large fish; amongst others, some quite fine salmon—the barge was launched into the current. The next day, at about four in the afternoon, it dropped anchor at the Giurgiu quayside, and twenty-four hours later, having passed the mouth of the Tcherna which comes from the Transylvanian Carpathians, it had arrived at the entrance to the famous narrow pass known as the Iron Gates.[3]

This is quite a dangerous part of the Danube to negotiate, and has been ripe in catastrophes. Over a stretch of the river of almost one league, between walls four hundred meters high, the river flows, or rather rushes, over a bed which is less than half a league in width. At the foot of these walls, enormous rocks are piled up; these have fallen from the ridges above, and the waters break against them with extraordinary fury. It is from here onwards that the waters take on that rich golden hue which allows that great Central European River to be more accurately known as the Beautiful Golden Danube.

---

3.   Verne gives the name of Giurgiu as Giurgevo.

Chapter XIV

Nicopoli, Rouschtchouk, Silistria

THE FOLLOWING MORNING, while Mr. Jaeger was still sleeping, Ilia Krusch had a fruitful spot of fishing. It would not have been wise to spend the night in the narrow pass of the Iron Gates, where the Danube is fifty meters deep. It is difficult to land there, and boats are exposed to the danger of their cables breaking under the pressure of the furious waters. Therefore, boats usually drop anchor above or below this point, along the river banks, in complete safety. Thus, Ilia Krusch—after a crossing lasting an hour and a half—had gotten back to the wider part of the river and had taken his position a little below the small modern town of Turnu-Severinu, which, by virtue of its strategic location, seems destined for a very profitable future as a business center.

When Mr. Jaeger came out of the tarpaulin shelter to breathe in the fresh morning air, the barge had already set off again along the river. A little more than three quarters of the journey had been completed by this date of June 27th, and there still remained another two hundred leagues in order to reach the mouth of the Danube. In sum, both Ilia Krusch and his companion had thus far managed to avoid both danger and exhaustion, and there was every reason to believe that this fortunate situation would continue right up until their destination was reached.

"Nothing new?" Mr. Jaeger had asked, after he had first taken a close look upriver and downriver.

"Nothing, Mr. Jaeger, but the weather doesn't seem very settled… I think we may possibly be about to have a storm, and after the storm, there'll be a few hours of showers and gusts of wind…"

"Okay!" replied Mr. Jaeger, "we'll be able to stay clear of the storm by taking shelter under the riverbanks. What about the other barges?"

"You can see them over there… twelve of them in a row. But their number will diminish according as we travel further downriver… Most of them will hardly be going any farther than Silistria or Galati, and they're rarely headed for the ports at the mouth of the river."[1]

After subjecting those boats to his customary scrutiny, Mr. Jaeger came back to take his place at the rear of the barge.

Over the course of the week which followed, the journey was not marked by any incident. The sky was changeable and unsettled in appearance. At times, there were actual gales on the surface of the river, which grew wider between flat banks which offered it no protection against the westerly and easterly winds, as it was flowing in a southerly direction. But the barge, well piloted, didn't suffer any damage.

It passed by the famous Trajan bridge, or rather, the two pieces of stonework which are all that remain of it. The two companions did not at all waste their time discussing the question as to whether or not these ruins are authentic. That is a matter for the scholars who, in any case, know no more about this subject than the great unwashed.

After Trajan bridge, Korbovo is a border post, the end point of a road which local engineers have boldly constructed through the mountains, then Radouievatz, the last outpost of the Serbian side of the river, where the dampfschiffs stop. Finally, there appeared Filordine, a pretty Bulgarian town, and Calafat on the left bank, where Ilia Krusch successfully sold a large quantity of fish, despite the fact that his arrival had not at all been known about in advance.

Moreover, as he went further and further away from the main Austrian and Hungarian cities, his degree of fame seemed to be following a downward trajectory. It is likely that the trumpets of Renown, despite their great power, didn't reach quite that far; one would have needed, instead, those trumpets which are due to resound on the day of the Final Judgement; but Ilia Krusch didn't have any of those on his person. Was that something he regretted? No, most assuredly not, and as long as he could continue to sell his wares at good prices, he wasn't asking any more than that. And in any case, if his sales hadn't been successful in Calafat, all he would have had to do was transport himself to the other side of the river. On the

---

1.   Verne give the name of Galati as Galatz.

right bank stands another Turkish town, quite a prosperous trading center, with its squares, cafés, bazaars, and there he would easily have sold the products of his fishing, on condition that he canvassed his potential customers at a slightly livelier pace than the Orientals, whose idleness, indeed, torpor, is a well-known characteristic of theirs.[2] Mr. Jaeger, who had arranged to be brought to this town while Ilia Krusch attended to his fish-selling in Calafat, had great difficulty acquiring some changes of clothes, even though he was not at all unwilling to pay very expensive prices for them.

The banks of the Danube—from the point at which its waters bathe, at Sattchi, a Valachian coast to the left and a Bulgarian coast to the right—take on a very different appearance. The ground is infertile over a very extended territory, completely furrowed by ravines and hills which are linked to the mountains of the north. There is also a significant contrast from the point of view of the hustle and bustle. On Valachian soil, there is no shortage of towns and villages, of which there is a whole succession, sheltered by trees and, at times, washed by the Danube's waters. Ilia Krusch was even able to observe that at this side of the river, line fishing was a hugely popular and honored occupation. Men were engaged in this noble pursuit, and women also, sheltered from the showers as well as from the sun's rays by a wide red Moorish-style umbrella. But were they as well kitted-out with fishing equipment as Ilia Krusch, member of the Danubian Line? No, most assuredly not, and the fish would have had to be extremely accommodating to accept such rudimentary tools as those employed by these primitive fishermen and women.

If he had been able to speak Turkish, or if they had understood Hungarian, the good man would have willingly given them some advice, in addition to some choice hooks. But, being unable to converse with them, he had no option but to give up on this idea.

---

2.   For contrasting views of the Far East, see (most famously) Verne's novel *Le Tour du monde en quatre-vingts jours* (*Around the World in Eighty Days*, 1873), and also its stage version, co-authored with Adolphe D'Ennery, which amplifies the importance of Asian characters and settings. The play first appeared as a book publication in English translation in the Palik series as *Around the World in 80 Days—The 1874 Play*. Less known but more directly concerned is *Les Tribulations d'un Chinois en Chine* (*The Tribulations of a Chinese in China*, 1879), set in the titular country. Placed in Turkey was Verne's *Kéraban-le-têtu* (*Keraban the Inflexible*), a novel that he adapted into a play, with publication and staging in 1883.

Moreover, the waters of the river, very well-stocked in fish, are frequented by very large sturgeons, from three to five meters in length and weighing up to one thousand and twelve hundred pounds. Sturgeon is eaten in all forms, fresh or salted, and its eggs are used to make caviar.

As they sailed along, Mr. Jaeger and Ilia Krusch encountered several of these fishermen, and took a keen interest in observing them.

"Eh, eh!" Mr. Jaeger went so far as to remark, "if one of those enormous beasts was to throw itself onto our barge, our poor vessel would risk being demolished, and ourselves along with it…"

"You're right," replied Ilia Krusch. "So it's wiser not to wander out into the middle of the river, which is where the sturgeon prefer to be. Along the river banks, on the other hand, the waters are not at all deep, and there's no danger at all."

And, very prudently, Ilia Krusch did not distance himself from the banks any more than was strictly necessary in order to benefit from a faster current.

When the barge reached the town of Racova, which is Bulgarian, the Danube was even wider. It was like a real stretch of sea, with its swell and white waves at their crest. One could barely distinguish the outline of the Valachian coast. Thus, just as the barge was doing, the larger vessels sailed as close to land as possible. With their flat backs and heavy forms, they are not at all constructed to cope with the open sea, and could suffer significant damage if they were caught in the middle of squalls. Moreover, there were now only five or six of them which were still pursuing their navigation downriver, something which quite astonished Ilia Krusch, who did not at all conceal his surprise from Mr. Jaeger, who asked him: "When you were a pilot, Mr. Krusch, did you never sail right as far as the mouths?…"

"Sometimes I did, Mr. Jaeger, but what precautions I had to take!"

"And you never met with any calamity?"

"Never, no, never, for I know my Danube well!"

"And do some of these barges go beyond Galati?"

"Yes… some of them! Beyond the mouths, there are small inlets, where sailing ships and steamers come to collect their cargo for the different ports of the Black Sea."

"Are there many of these mouths of the river?" asked Mr. Jaeger.

"There are two principal ones, which are separated by Leti Island, and the biggest one is that of Kilia."

"You know them all?..."

"All of them, Mr. Jaeger, and there's hardly a pilot on the Danube who doesn't know them the same as I do..."

"So, it's likely that these boats which are going in the same direction as ourselves, are headed for the Black Sea?..."

"It's possible, Mr. Jaeger, and, I do declare, I wouldn't be surprised if one of them—you know, the one that's being so well-steered—doesn't sail right up to one of the mouths."

"You really think so?" insisted Mr. Jaeger, who seemed to accord quite singular seriousness to this exchange.

"I do think so, and what's more, we'll soon know what's going on. That boat can no longer use its sail—as that would risk falling across the waves, and, loaded as it is, it could capsize... I can assure you that its pilot will not commit an error of that nature... Well, the current is there for us all, and it won't bring that boat downriver any faster than us... So if it's really headed for the Black Sea, we'll arrive there together."

And then, Mr. Jaeger asked this final question:

"As for customs or police inspections, that barge will probably not have any more of them to undergo?..."

"No, Mr. Jaeger, no more inspections. Surveillance is hardly possible along the lower course of the river in the way that it is along the upper course... The river becomes ever-wider, and what do you expect the officers stationed along the banks to be able to do?"

"That's what I was thinking, Mr. Krusch, plus, these boats have already been subjected to the embargo at Orsova, and the fact that the customs officers allowed them to continue en route means that they weren't involved in smuggling..."

"Correct, Mr. Jaeger, and Latzko isn't about to get himself caught on one of those boats..."

"As you say, Mr. Krusch!"

It was quite late in the evening of the 4th of July when the barge dropped its anchor at the post of a small landing stage at the quay of Nicopoli, which is situated at the confluence of the Alula on the right bank of the Danube. This city, built by Augustus, links the East to Italy. The Transadriatic telegraph line currently comes to an end at this point. This city is the seat of a Greek archbishopric and a Catholic bishopric.

The darkness was already so deep that Mr. Jaeger and his companion could have seen nothing of Nicopoli. This would have been a source of disappointment to a tourist who would probably have extended his or her stay by a few hours. It is worth visiting this city. It has a population of twelve thousand inhabitants and is built in a picturesque location between two hills, on one of which there stands a dungeon, on the other, a fortress.

Ilia Krusch thus asked Mr. Jaeger if it would suit him to spend the following day there. They could afford a stopover of twenty-four hours.

Mr. Jaeger thanked Ilia Krusch for his offer, but he was already acquainted with Nicopoli, which no longer held any secrets for him, and the best thing to do would be to leave at sunrise, since the weather conditions were favorable.

"As you please, Mr. Jaeger… We shall raise anchor at dawn… But perhaps, you might like to stay in Rouschtchouk for a day…"

"Yes, I'd prefer that, Mr. Krusch, for I have only very vague memories of that city…"

"That's agreed, then."

"How far is it from Nicopoli?"

"About twenty leagues, and the day after tomorrow, we'll get there in the evening."

As soon as daylight appeared, the barge set off along the current, along the Bulgarian bank of the river, while the fishing line floated in the waters simultaneously.

Ilia Krusch might, perhaps, have feared that his travelling companion could end up being overcome by boredom. Unlike Krusch, Mr. Jaeger was not motivated by the lure of an undertaking—however bizarre it might seem—which he intended to bring to a successful conclusion. Furthermore, one needs the wonderfully-balanced soul of a line fisherman to be interested in the vagaries, surprises and joys of this noble profession, over many months, on a journey of nearly seven hundred leagues.

Well, no! Mr. Jaeger was not bored for one single moment. He was becoming increasingly interested in what he saw around him, especially as regards the river vessels. Ilia Krusch even wondered if he might not be preparing some dissertation on that very topic, in which he would discuss all of the questions relating to the river fleet which is constantly increasing in volume, and might this not be, in sum, the whole purpose of his journey?…

And, when Ilia Krusch sounded him out on this point, Jaeger replied, with a smile: "Something like that…."

"So, Mr. Jaeger, I hope you'll reap the benefits of your sailing expedition…"

"I hope so, Mr. Krusch, and I like to think that my time won't have been wasted."

"So, the time isn't dragging too much for you, then?"

"Oh, Mr. Krusch, in your company… in your company!…"

And the good man felt deeply moved by this response. Without a doubt, he would be able to push this friendship he felt towards Mr. Jaeger, to the point of devotion, should the opportunity to do so ever present itself!

During the two days which it took the barge to reach Rouschtchouk, the sites to be seen along the river showed little variation. Nothing but a monotonous procession of cabins and huts, on the Valachian bank as on the Bulgarian one, and also the posts of the border guards; at times, a village, a few scattered houses, overlooked by the great towering lever of the commonplace mine. On the Bulgarian side was a long cliff which supported a layer of rock, which continues as far as the town which has given its name to a *livah* of the principality.

Just as Ilia Krusch had declared, both men arrived at Rouschtchouk on the evening of July 7th.

The river is very wide at this point. On the Valachian riverbank, opposite Rouschtchouk, there rises up the town of Giurgiu, in the middle of an arid plain. Travellers disembark here because this is where the road leading to Bucharest, the Valachian capital, situated to the north of the Danube, begins. However, its business activity is not unimportant, and is concentrated in the district in which the winding, narrow, dirty streets intersect, streets containing warehouses full of merchandise and taverns full of customers.

But it wasn't at all Giurgiu which Mr. Jaeger wished to visit, but Rouschtchouk, and, as had been agreed, he was going to spend the whole of the following day there.

Thus, in the morning, having taken his leave of Ilia Krusch whom he left to his usual occupations, he set foot on the Bulgarian riverbank. But just as he was about to walk off, he turned round and said to his companion:

"While I come to think of it, will you have dinner with me this evening?"

"I'd be delighted to, Mr. Jaeger."

"Good… so, see you at five o'clock on the main square…"

"See you at five."

Rouschtchouk is a city of thirty thousand inhabitants, on the right bank of the river. It belongs to the province of Silistria and therefore is part of European Turkey. It is the seat of a Greek bishopric. It is badly constructed and poorly maintained, and the buffalo-drawn carts can barely get round its narrow streets. Most of the houses are built of clay. In this city, can be found numerous cafés, warehouses of merchandise, bazaars at which are sold fabrics, woollen garments, fruit, pipes, tobacco, drugs and medicines of all sorts. The city is dominated by a fortress and here and there stand the pointed minarets of the synagogues and mosques. The only building worthy of notice is the Governor's palace.

It is likely that Mr. Jaeger's memories of this place returned to him quickly, for he showed no hesitation in finding the road which led to the post office. There, he found a dated letter from Galati, the contents of which he immediately noted.

"Decidedly," he said to himself, "I've arrived at the right time!"

He put the letter into his pocket, walked about for an hour and had lunch in the hotel where he was due to dine that evening with his guest. At about one o'clock, he resumed his stroll through the business district in which the crowd of merchants, customers and shippers was buzzing. Several commercial ships, sail ships and steamships, moored all along the quayside, were in the process of loading or unloading merchandise.

It is there that Mr. Jaeger, at about three o'clock, was accosted by a man—a Bulgarian, most probably, judging from his dress and his quite pronounced facial features. Both of them already knew each other and did not seem surprised to be meeting each other in this city, situated practically at the edge of Eastern Europe. They began to converse, and Mr. Jaeger even made this man aware of various passages of the letter he had just received. The mysterious interlocutor seemed to nod his assent, and when they took their leave of each other, it was with the following words, repeated by Mr. Jaeger:

"Yes!… We've arrived at just the right time!"

At five o'clock, Ilia Krusch, whose arrival was not at all known to the general public, was on the city square, from whence Mr. Jaeger brought him to the hotel. The menu of their dinner included caviar, sauerkraut, and chicken with paprika, all washed down with Hungarian wine. Ilia Krusch did honor to his host by eating copiously, and Mr. Jaeger, despite being perhaps a little preoccupied, wasn't outdone by him.

By nine o'clock, both men had gotten back to the barge, and the next day, they were sailing quite rapidly downriver, along the Bulgarian coast. The proximity of the Black Sea was by now already apparent from the appearance of the surrounding countryside. If the Danube had flown directly towards the east, it would have encountered that Sea's coastline at about forty leagues from Rouschtchouk. But, after following the forty-fourth parallel right as far as the town of Tchernavoda, the river turns round sharply towards the north, bordering Moldavia. It is at Galati that it resumes an easterly direction, as far as its mouth.

Navigating this stretch of the river is thus sometimes a consistent struggle, difficult and even dangerous along this part of the Danube, at least for the barges. However, of all those barges which had sailed downriver since Vienna, at the same time as Krusch's barge, there still remained three. Were they due to stop at Silistria, the biggest place before reaching the Moldavian border? In any case, they were following the Bulgarian riverbank, and hugging it as closely as possible, so as to be able to find a speedy refuge there in case the weather changed for the worse.

The state of the sky was hardly reassuring. Great, wild clouds, dragging enormous fragments of fog along the surface of the river, scudded along from the east, completely laden with the humidity of the nearby sea.

Ilia Krusch was looking at the sky with a rather uneasy expression. It was not at all that he had any fears for his fragile boat, as he could also find shelter for it under the river banks. But the navigation of the river could be delayed, and who knows if he might not take more time to travel over these final six hundred kilometers than it had taken to travel the two thousand kilometers covered since Sigmaringen!

However, throughout all of that day of the 9th, he was not at any stage obliged to drop anchor, which he didn't ultimately do until the hour when the sun was beginning to disappear beneath the western horizon.

The night passed without incident. The wind died down for a few hours, while torrential rainfall beat down. It became necessary, on several occasions, to empty out the water which had accumulated in the barge. But the wind ultimately began to rage once again with the same violence as before, and by sunrise, it had become obvious that there would be no change in the adverse weather conditions.

Ilia Krusch was forced to abandon his plans to get some fishing done that morning, so troubled were the waters of the Danube, and in any case, he would have been unable to maintain his rod steady in the correct position. By the time he was raising the grapnel, the three barges which had dropped anchor near to the bank of the river had already set off again, and were heading for the other side of the river where, no doubt, sailing would be easier, the wind having risen a little towards the north-east.

Mr. Jaeger, noticing this manoeuver, with which, moreover, his companion agreed, asked whether the barge couldn't cross the river so as to follow the three boats.

"That's the best thing we can do," replied Ilia Krusch, and, an hour later, he was sailing along the Valachian riverbank.

The day was quite a rough one, for the sailors and for the fisherman. However, at around five o'clock that evening, they arrived opposite Silistria, which is a Bulgarian city, the chief administrative center of a cyalet, which includes the whole of eastern Bulgaria and the fortresses of the lower Danube, and which is one of Turkey's three great fortified towns. Its citadel, situated at the western extremity, is added to by a very high wall. The town has a population of two thousand souls. It trades in wool, timber and livestock with Valachia, which supplies it with salt and hemp. Narrow and winding streets, low houses, no monuments. That explains why Mr. Jaeger didn't ask to visit it; in any case, this would have necessitated crossing the river again, since, like Rouschtchouk, it is situated on the right bank. He made do with pacing up and down on the riverbank, passing back and forth beside the boats which had dropped anchor there.

The next day, they departed at the usual time. But what was especially noticeable was that, out of the three barges, two were now heading towards Silistria where they were probably set to unload their cargo.

Only the last boat—the one whose pilot had so manifestly

exhibited his professional skill—continued to sail downriver, despite all the indications that the weather was becoming increasingly worse.

The barge set off again en route, hugging the right bank much more closely. The only noteworthy incident was that, in the course of the morning, a boat which had sailed out from a little village of Bulgarian fishermen, at one stage drew alongside that third barge. One of the men carried by the boat then got on board the barge which immediately turned round. During the afternoon, the weather became so bad, the squalls so violent, the swell so strong, that Ilia Krusch didn't believe he should risk going any further.

"And what is that barge going to do?" asked Mr. Jaeger.

"Most likely, what we ourselves are going to do," answered Mr. Krusch. "I believe its pilot to be too practical a man to continue sailing in these conditions. With the swell that's rising, he would risk having a serious collision and sinking on the spot."

Ilia Krusch was right, and while his barge was taking refuge at the end of a small cove within the shelter of a headland, the other, third barge drew close to the riverbank so as to find a refuge there, until such time as a lull in the storm would allow it to set off again.

Except that, when that boat had dropped its anchor, Ilia Krusch seemed surprised and said to Mr. Jaeger:

"The pilot would have been wiser to drop anchor closer to the riverbank… He's at least twenty fathoms away from it, and it's not very safe… If his anchor failed to take hold, or if it was caught abeam… It's true, it's not very deep here, but at the end of the day, that boat can't draw more than three to four feet even when it's fully loaded, and he could easily have come closer so as to keep his anchors on dry land. So what can the pilot be thinking of?…"

However, the pilot did not change his mooring place. Mr. Jaeger was able to notice that the man who had been brought, that morning by the boat, and the sailors positioned to the front of the boat, were carefully observing the situation. And yet, in the final analysis, they didn't alter their mooring place.

Darkness quickly descended—it was a black, rain-soaked, moonless night. Mr. Jaeger walked on the riverbank until eight o'clock, even though the gusts were raging with extraordinary fury. But the rain soon redoubled in intensity, and he was forced to rejoin his companion.

At half past eight, both men were stretched out under the tarpaulin shelter, well protected from the elements. But they were unable to get any sleep, so violent was the storm which raged outside; and at about two o'clock in the morning, it was not without a keen emotional reaction that they suddenly heard cries of distress in the midst of the howling tempest.

Chapter XV

From Silistria to Galati

At about eight o'clock in the morning, after that terrible night, the larger barge, which had been moored close to the right bank, brought its anchor back on board and was beginning to sail off along the water once again. To the rear, a man, helped by two sailors, held in his hand the long helm of a rudder; to the front, three other men—including the man who had gotten on board the previous evening—were observing the current state of the river.

The swell was not as strong now, and the wind, blowing in a westerly direction, was beginning to die down. A few bright spots, sometimes furrowed by bright rays of sunshine, were emerging out at sea. The sky, gradually becoming clearer, displayed long strips of azure blue on the horizon.

From the place where Ilia Krusch had sought shelter the previous evening, one could see the Valachian riverbank and the mountains which overlook it in the background.

The larger barge was now sailing down the course of the Danube, alone. By evening, it would have reached that bend in the river which drives the waters back in a northerly direction, more or less at the corner where the small town of Tchernavoda stands, a town which is lined by a small railway line to the coastline at Kustendjé port, on the Black Sea.

And so, where was Ilia Krusch's small craft at the moment? Had it been struck violently by a swell during the night and smashed to pieces against the riverbank? Had Ilia Krusch and Mr. Jaeger perished, almost at the end of their journey, and had that journey, therefore, ended in tragedy?

Whatever the case may be, if the Krusch vessel was no longer to be seen along the Bulgarian riverbank, neither was it visible along the Valachian side… And if it was the case that Ilia Krusch and his travelling companion had managed to cheat death, it is in vain that either one of them would have been sought on the bank or in the village underneath which the little craft had taken shelter until daybreak.

Here is the story of what had taken place, and of how—to his great surprise as well as to his great strife—the Danubian Line's prize-winner now found himself launched into an adventure whose outcome risked being most prejudicial to his interests.

That storm which had so profoundly disturbed the tranquillity of the river, to the extent that it was no longer possible to sail on it, had lasted all night. Ilia Krusch and Mr. Jaeger had taken shelter underneath the tarpaulin covering, against the torrential downpours, having first ensured to increase twofold the length of the anchor which held their vessel fast to the riverbank. But the jolts occasioned by the swell were so violent, that it was virtually impossible for them to sleep.

It was, therefore, about one o'clock in the morning when cries of distress pierced the night air. Were they coming from the river bank or from the bigger barge moored below the Krusch vessel?

Both men, emerging from the tarpaulin covering, sought to distinguish what was going on, in the midst of this deep darkness.

The cries which could be heard weren't coming either from the bank or from the village. They were actually coming from the mysterious barge itself, upon which men could be seen coming and going, holding lighted lanterns, now to the sides of the boat, then to the front, at other times, to the rear.

And these fragments of sentences reached the ears of Mr. Jaeger and Ilia Krusch:

"Over here… over here!"

"He fell from over there…"

"To the water—the lifeboat, to the water!"

And, from the noise, Ilia Krusch recognized that a vessel was being hastily lowered into the river by means of a cable.

"It's one of their men," he said, "who must have been swept away by a swell!"

If this is what had happened, the skipper would do everything possible to save this unfortunate victim. And indeed, at the risk of capsizing, the small open rescue boat was already sailing downriver, for the man could only have been carried off in the direction of the current. Ilia Krusch could do nothing for the victim, and to set his barge adrift would have meant pointlessly exposing it in the midst of the tumultuous waves.

Both men waited. The lanterns were still moving about on the upper bridge of the barge. After half an hour, the lantern which had been lighting the way for the rescue boat, reappeared; that vessel was being rowed back to the barge, and it didn't seem as though the rescue attempt had been successful, because one of the sailors could yet be heard crying out:

"He's lost!… He's lost!"

This was, indeed, only all too likely.

"And how could they have rescued him?" said Ilia Krusch.

"And the current must have swept him out to sea very quickly," added Mr. Jaeger.

"Yes," replied Ilia Krusch, "from this headland onwards, the current goes towards the left bank."

Moreover, it seemed that it was all over, completely over, for the rescue boat, having struggled to draw alongside the barge, had just been hoisted back on board. The lanterns were then extinguished, and everything fell back—if not into silence—at least into darkness.

Ilia Krusch and his companion had to go back underneath the tarpaulin shelter, and it was in vain that they tried to get a few hours sleep.

Moreover, hardly had the first light of dawn broken over the horizon—and the storm had considerably died down—than Ilia Krusch heard his name being called from outside his boat.

He went out, followed by Mr. Jaeger. A boat with six men on board had drawn alongside Krusch's vessel.

One of these men, who seemed to be in charge of the others, was standing—a man of about forty years of age, with harsh features, bright eyes under eyebrows which constantly tensed up, a face with brutal energy, a curt manner, of medium build, wide-shoulders, which were the sign of remarkable robustness.

Addressing Ilia Krusch, he didn't say to him: "Are you Ilia Krusch?" instead, he said: "You are Ilia Krusch…"

"Yes," replied the latter, a little taken aback, both by the question and by the tone in which it had been asked.

The other man continued speaking, all the while proceeding through affirmation rather than question:

"You are the prize-winning fisherman at Sigmaringen."

"Yes."

"You are a former Danube pilot."

"Yes... but, now it's my turn to ask you who you are?"

Throughout this exchange, Mr. Jaeger remained completely uninvolved and reserved, in the background, observing this individual who he was looking hard and extremely carefully at.

"I'm the skipper of the barge moored below yours... We've had a unfortunate accident this night... our pilot has been swept away by a tremendous swell... he fell into the river, and despite our best efforts, we've been unable to save him. Since you are a pilot, I've come to ask you to be his replacement."

Ilia Krusch was so completely unprepared for this proposition that, at first, he didn't know how to respond. Finally, after looking over at Mr. Jaeger, as though he wished to consult him on the matter, he said:

"Would this be just to guide your barge to the nearest Bulgarian or Valachian port, which it would reach within a few hours?..."

"No... I wouldn't be able to get hold of another pilot there, and I need one," added the skipper, whose tone was becoming increasingly peremptory. "Oh yes! I need one, at all costs..."

"Until we get to Galati or Ismail?..."

"Until we get to the Black Sea."

"Through which mouth?"

"The Kilia mouth."

Mr. Jaeger, his arms folded, was waiting for whatever response his companion was about to make.

"Well?" the skipper continued.

"It's impossible," declared Ilia Krusch.

"I said, I'll pay any price, whatever it takes!... and I won't think twice about paying a sum of two or three hundred florins..."

"It's impossible," repeated Ilia Krusch. "I've begun a particular journey and I can't simply abandon it..."

"Four hundred florins," the skipper went on, "and you can earn them in about a week or so..."

"I refuse," retorted Ilia Krusch. "I have a travelling companion with me, whom I can't just leave alone in my barge..."

"Your companion will get on board our barge with you," the skipper insisted, his voice now trembling with anger, "and as for your barge, we'll tow it behind ours. Your final word?..."

"No!" replied Ilia Krusch.

And, indeed, it couldn't possibly suit him to give up on his plans, and to complete his navigation of the Danube on board this larger barge. If it had been merely a case of piloting it for two or three hours, he would have done so out of the goodness of his heart. But eight to ten days of sailing, as far as the mouth of the Danube... as he had said: impossible. And it seemed plain to him that Mr. Jaeger couldn't but agree with him.

What happened next was quick. On a sign from their leader, his men forced Ilia Krusch and Mr. Jaeger to get into their vessel; then they started to float Krusch's barge, attached a tow cable to it and, a few minutes afterwards, it had drawn alongside the larger vessel, and was immediately hoisted onto its bridge.

Ilia Krusch's objections were futile. There were fifteen men against two. Any resistance was impossible, and if Ilia Krusch had refused to serve as pilot, he would have been locked up in the bottom of the hold and detained there until he consented to do these men's bidding.

Moreover, Mr. Jaeger, who had not put up any resistance, seemed to say to his companion, instead of being stubborn:

"But do as they say, then!"

Ilia Krusch therefore had to go up onto the upper bridge, and was led to the helm, near to which there stood two sailors.

The skipper immediately joined him, and said:

"You would have been wiser to have accepted my offer which was a lucrative one... You have left me with no choice but to use force... Too bad for you, Mr. Krusch... And now, sail straight onwards!... and in the right direction... and don't make any mistakes in direction!... Do you hear me... otherwise..."

The skipper didn't finish his sentence, which was accompanied by a gesture whose meaning was unmistakable.

In any case, Ilia Krusch had made his mind up to co-operate, and he asked only one question:

"What draft?"

"Seven feet," replied the skipper.

A quarter of an hour later, the anchor had been brought back up to its cathead and, with its new pilot at the helm, the barge was following the river's current, which was by now very rapid.

As for Mr. Jaeger, nobody was paying any heed to him. He was completely at liberty to come and go as he pleased. He thus remained on the bridge, sometimes watching the Bulgarian riverbank from which the barge never strayed far, at other times seated on a spar, lost in thought. He didn't make any attempt to converse with his companion, even though he wasn't at all forbidden to do so.

Indeed, at mealtimes, they were served together, apart from the others, and at nightfall, while the barge was berthed near to the riverbank, both men were consigned to a cabin which was part of the accommodation to the rear, and the door was locked behind them.

Where had they gone, those oh-so-peaceful, happy days of that novel sailing trip, when Krusch's barge would stop at the quayside of the various towns, while Krusch gave himself over to the delights of line fishing and sold his fish at each stopping-off point!…

The days of the 12th, 13th, 14th and 15th went by, without any change occurring in the situation. The reluctant pilot, erect at the helm, guided the boat, with the air of a man who was perfectly acquainted with his profession. It was obvious that the skipper, in kidnapping Krusch in the circumstances which have just been reported, knew who he was dealing with. For many weeks already, his men had noticed this little barge which was sailing downriver in convoy with their own barge. And like most of the boatmen, they knew that it was Ilia Krusch, whose renown was no secret to them. At the same time that the identity and innocence of the famous prize-winner had been established at the trial at Pest, it had been learnt that he had once been a professional pilot on the Danube. This explains how, in the bothersome situation in which he had found himself after the loss of one of his men, the skipper had had no hesitation—even if it meant having recourse to violence—in guaranteeing himself the services of Ilia Krusch in person.

As for his behaviour and manner of proceeding, the reader is free to assess them according as they deserve, and he who does what he pleases with the freedom of one of his fellow creatures, in defiance of the other person's wishes, is always unforgivable. And in fact, the skipper of this barge truly seemed to be one of those people who never seek forgiveness or excuses for their manner of behaving.

It is worthwhile noting at this point that, without having confided in his companion, Mr. Jaeger was entertaining certain suspicions about this boat. As he was aware of the major smuggling case—and, in Austria, in Hungary, in the Turkish provinces, who hadn't heard tell of it?—a conviction had taken firm hold in his mind, that this barge was engaged in smuggling. It didn't seem impossible to him that Latzko might currently be on board—and he might even be that very man who had embarked a few days previously.... Yes! This Latzko, whom the international commission was having pursued, and whom Karl Dragoch hadn't yet managed to seize!...

Whatever the case might be, Mr. Jaeger resolved to strictly keep his counsel and disclose nothing, even to Ilia Krusch. If any circumstance should arise which would make it necessary to inform him, he would inform him... In the meantime, throughout these days of navigation, he would observe everything that was taking place on board, without doing anything that could make him look suspicious, and, depending on what transpired, he might resolve to swing into action.

And indeed, if, given his naturally affable nature, Ilia Krusch's suspicions were not as keen as his companions, there was, nevertheless, one detail which had struck him and impressed itself upon his mind.

And, while the boat was moored on July 15th, in a conversation which he had with Mr. Jaeger, taking particular care not to be overheard, he said:

"Have you noticed, Mr. Jaeger, the type of cargo that this barge is carrying..."

"Of course, wood; planks, beans..."

"I know, Mr. Jaeger, but what I also know is that it's not a heavy load..."

"Certainly, and what are you getting at?"

"This: I don't understand how, in these conditions, this barge has such a strong draft..."

Mr. Jaeger looked at his companion without replying, and the latter added:

"When I asked the skipper how much water the barge drew, he answered me: 'Between six and seven feet'... Well, that's the thing that seems unexplainable to me..."

"Unexplainable, indeed."

"If it was loaded with stones or ingots of ore, it wouldn't be drawing more than this…"

"But after all, what does it matter to you, Mr. Krusch," replied Mr. Jaeger, after a moment's thought. "What do they want of you? That you bring this barge to its destination… Well, steer it, and once you've reached journey's end, claim the price of your navigation."

"That? Never! Mr. Jaeger," cried Ilia Krusch. "What I'm doing now, I'm doing it under duress! As soon as we arrive, I'll definitely find out who this skipper really is… and I shall prosecute him… I will see that justice is done to me!"

"As you please, Mr. Krusch!"

And most assuredly, he would do just what he was saying! One may very well have the blood of a line fisherman coursing through one's veins, but a man worthy of that name doesn't suffer, lying down, the indignity of being treated as he had just been treated!

There was also another observation which Ilia Krusch felt he should make: it was to do with the deal which had been struck between himself and Mr. Jaeger.

"You can see," he said, "that I'm now unable to fish as I've been doing up to now, since we set out… So no more sales of fish means no more profit. Well, under those conditions, your five hundred florins are at extreme risk, and I shall not at all keep them, I shall give them back to you as soon as this accursed journey has reached its end…"

"Without a doubt, Mr. Krusch," replied Mr. Jaeger with a smile, "you are truly the most honest man in the whole world!… But don't worry, and who knows whether all this might not end better than you think!"

And Mr. Jaeger shook Ilia Krusch's hand with a level of cordiality which particularly moved the latter.

It should also be pointed out that, since his kidnapping, Ilia Krusch never had any opportunity to enter into communication with anybody at all. There were rarely any vessels to be seen on the lower course of the river, sailships or dampfschiffs. In any case, the skipper used to intervene to ensure that he distanced himself from their route, and they passed each other only at a fair distance, which prevented them from "reasoning with each other," as they say in seafaring slang. As for the towns and villages, the same precaution was taken, and the barge never stopped at their quays. It always sought anchorage at several hundred toises below the quay. Neither did they ever moor at a riverbank, or drop anchor at the mouth of tributaries such as the Jalomitza, the Bouzeb and others. As a result, it was not only impossible to communicate with anyone, but also impossible to escape during the night. When, during the afternoon of the 16th, the barge came abreast of Braila, a town on the left bank, where the river is considerably wide, it passed at such a distance from the town that it was impossible to distinguish the houses, overlooked by the high mountains to the west.

And, in this regard, once evening came, when the barge had dropped anchor, before they were enjoined to return to their cabin, Ilia Krusch said, with a deep sigh:

"Do you see, Mr. Jaeger, I'd have done good business, nonetheless, at Braila… I've always seen fish being sold there very successfully… But on this boat, which seems to dread Bulgarian or Valachian towns as if they had the plague, there's nothing for it!"

"One must be philosophical, Mr. Krusch," his companion made do with replying to him, "and if a line fisherman isn't philosophical, who is?"

It is worth noting that no liaison had been forged between the former passengers of Krusch's barge and the crew of this larger barge. None of the sailors ever spoke a word to them, and they were always kept apart. Moreover, these men didn't have a very engaging appearance; robust fellows, but clearly rather coarse and uncouth in nature; it seemed that the majority of them were, like their skipper, from Hungary or Valachia originally. Only the skipper used to question Ilia Krusch about his navigation of the barge, or used to give him orders when it was time to stop over. Outside those occasions, there wasn't so much as "Good day" or "Good evening," as they say.

As for Mr. Jaeger, nobody seemed to be taking a blind bit of notice of him, and, from his own point of view, he kept himself removed from everyone else as much as possible. When, at times, the skipper happened to fix him with a stare, he would turn his eyes away and affect total indifference.

In sum, no untoward incident had occurred thus far during this navigation. The storm, which had raged so furiously during the night from the 11th to the 12th, had been replaced by mixed weather with a rather low breeze. At this mid-point of the month of July, the temperature was already very high, the sun unbearably hot when the

clouds weren't there to moderate its heat. True, the sea breeze was generally felt in the afternoons, and did not die down till evening. But the nights were warm, and most of the time, the sailors used to stretch out on the bridge in order to get a better night's sleep.

This relief was refused to both Ilia Krusch and his companion, and after the barge had dropped anchor for the night, they would have to return to their quarters at the rear.

During the afternoon of July 17th, the barge came within sight of Galati, a Romanian city situated seven or eight leagues below Braila, at the right angle taken by the Danube in order to resume its final direction towards the west. This city has no fewer than eighty thousand inhabitants. It houses the headquarters of the European Navigation Company at the mouth of the Danube. It is a free port, into which the Pruth flows, and it exports wheat, corn, rye, barley, oats, linen, flax, hides and tallow. Its annual turnover amounts to between fifty and sixty million francs. There are lots of Greeks there. Communication with Constantinople is dealt with by Lloyds'. It is divided into two cities; the old city, paved with wood, with winding streets; and the modern one, rising in terraced rows on the hills overlooking the river.

The barge did not stop in front of Galati. It passed by it at a distance of at least a quarter of a league from it, and dropped anchor on the right bank, on the other side.

The night passed off without incident. But the next morning, when Ilia Krusch left the cabin to come and take his place at the helm, Mr. Jaeger had already left the room while his companion had still been sleeping. Ilia Krusch therefore assumed that he would find him on the bridge, and, when he couldn't see him there, he called him…

But Mr. Jaeger was no longer on board the barge, and, during the night, he had disappeared without anybody noticing.

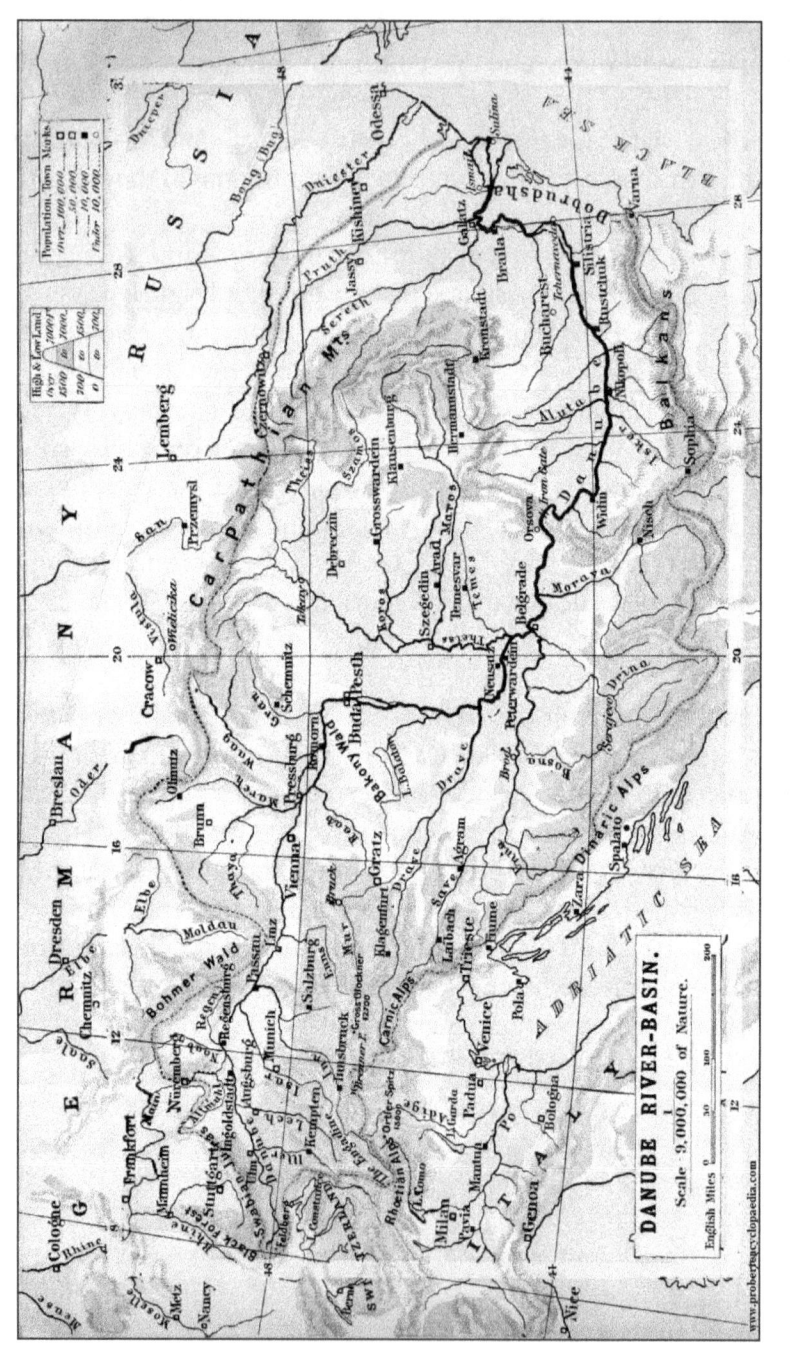

DANUBE RIVER-BASIN.
Scale 9,000,000 of Nature.

English Miles

Chapter XVI

FROM GALATI TO THE BLACK SEA

WHETHER MR. JAEGER had been the victim of an accident or whether he had intentionally escaped, nobody could say. And it would also have been necessary to explain how—given that he had been locked up in the cabin—he had managed to leave it during the night, even though two or three men had been standing guard outside the cabin door until daybreak.

The skipper made no attempt to conceal his feelings on the subject of Jaeger's sudden disappearance. He sent for Ilia Krusch and harshly questioned him, but could get nothing out of him. Ilia Krusch had not at all heard Mr. Jaeger getting up, nor had he seen him leaving the cabin. He was just as surprised as the skipper, and no less anxious, but probably from a different point of view. As far as Krusch was concerned, Mr. Jaeger must have fallen into the river and drowned, even though the barge was no more than half a cable's length away from the riverbank. As for the possibility of his having run away of his own free will, why would he have done such a thing, and especially, without informing Ilia Krusch who would probably have asked nothing better than to follow him.

Every nook and cranny of the barge was searched, but Mr. Jaeger was nowhere to be found.

The skipper then went back to see Ilia Krusch.

"Who was this Jaeger guy?" he demanded, in a voice shaking with anger.

Ilia Krusch, feeling rather awkward, could only reply: "Mr. Jaeger had been my travelling companion since I left Ulm… It was there that

251

he got on board my barge in order to sail down the Danube with me, as far as its mouth, having bought all of my fishing catch from me for a price of five hundred florins… I don't know anything more than that about him."

"And since he joined you, he has never left you alone on the barge?"

"Yes, he did leave me in Vienna, and after an absence of thirty-one days, he rejoined me in Belgrade."

"And what nationality is he?"

"Most definitely, he is Hungarian, just as I myself am."

And that is as much as the skipper was able to extract from the pilot, who resumed his position at the helm.

The barge, its anchor having been brought back on board, set off along the river once again, and as the wind had begun to blow in a north-western direction, the sail was raised, which had the effect of adding two or three knots to the speed of the current. As the distance separating Galati from the Black Sea is only about one hundred and thirty kilometers, it shouldn't take the barge more than three days to reach the mouth of Kilia.

As he continued to carry out his piloting duties, what distressing thoughts assailed poor Krusch! No! He couldn't accept the possibility that his companion's disappearance had been intentional!… If Mr. Jaeger had conceived a plan to flee at all costs, would he have hidden his intentions from Ilia Krusch? And moreover, why would he have done this? No, alas! He had been the victim of some accident… For one reason or another, perhaps because the atrocious heat which dominated the cabin had proved very uncomfortable to him, he must have managed to pry open the cabin door, and, in the midst of the darkness, he must have lost his footing and fallen into the river… And he must have been swept away very quickly indeed, given that his cries for help weren't heard! And he must not have been able to reach the safety of the riverbank!

Less than two days later, and without any change having taken place in the situation, the barge came within sight of Ismail, during the afternoon of July 20th.

Ismail is a port in Moldavian Bessarabia, on the left bank of the river. It is a port of a certain importance, since it has a population of forty-two thousand souls. A merchant port which is supplied by the various products of Moldavia, it is under Russian domination, practically a military port, and at the very least it acts as a stopping-off point at which part of the river fleet of the Danube puts into harbor. It is downriver that the river branches out into multiple arms.

When the barge came abreast of Ismail, Ilia Krusch was ordered to stay as close as possible to the right bank. No doubt the skipper was not at all anxious to receive an inspection by customs authorities, something which he avoided by floating at a good distance from the city. Then, just as was done every evening, he dropped anchor a league downriver.

During the night, Ilia Krusch wouldn't have been able to leave his cabin to breathe the night air outside. Ever since Mr. Jaeger's disappearance, he felt that he was being guarded more severely than ever. As his services were needed, he wouldn't be allowed to escape… Therefore, under these conditions, his only desire was to reach the required destination and to immediately disembark.

It so happened that an incident then occurred which would make Ilia Krusch aware of what the situation was.

At about one o'clock in the morning, as he wasn't managing to fall asleep, he overheard a conversation which was taking place near to the door of the accommodation to the rear of the barge. It was two sailors who were chatting, most probably having been assigned to guard him, and here is what he overheard of their exchange.

These two men were speaking about the imminent arrival of the barge at the Black Sea, and one of them said:

"The steamer will be waiting for us there…"

"Definitely," said the other man… "It's been notified in good time, and the customs officers will never think of searching it at the mouth of Kilia…"

"Good," the first man continued, "it'll take us two hours to unload all our merchandise."

Thus, there was a steamer waiting for the barge at the mouth of the river… And in the space of two hours, it would have loaded all of its merchandise on board? Therefore, the merchandise in question couldn't be this cargo of wood, beams and planks which were cluttering the deck and the hold, and which would have taken more than two days to be transferred to another vessel.

And it was then that a particular name struck Ilia Krusch's ears… a name uttered by one of these two men, the name of the skipper of this barge... and that name, was none other than that of Latzko!...

What a revelation now took place within Ilia Krusch's mind! The skipper of this barge was the head of the gang of smugglers! And the contraband must be hidden in a double hold!... Yes! No doubt about it, a double hold, the existence of which nobody could have suspected!... And that was the reason why the barge was drawing more water than is ordinarily drawn by boats of similar tonnage and size!...

Ilia Krusch had thrown himself back down on his bed. But there was no way he could have slept now. He was thinking. It was he who was piloting this barge to the mouth of Kilia where this Latzko's accomplices would be waiting for it! What should he do now, this honest ex-pilot of the Danube, and what could he do?... Was he not at the mercy of these men, who, were he to refuse to co-operate with them by lending them his services, would be well able to force him to do their bidding, even if it meant a pistol being applied to his throat!...

Ilia Krusch didn't want to make any hasty decision... He would, instead, wait and see how circumstances evolved and act accordingly, and, when dawn broke again, he resumed his customary position at the rudder, without giving any hint of what was going on in his mind, without even casting a more curious glance than usual at this daring leader of this criminal fraternity.

That day, nothing new occurred, and, with the help of the fully hoisted sail, the distance covered amounted to about twelve leagues.

There are multiple mouths of the Danube, and its delta is covered by a sort of network of rivers. The two main mouths are separated by the large island of Liti, a triangular landmass whose apex is at the point at which the two mouths branch out. The mouth which borders the island to the south is the bigger one, and most boats prefer to follow this mouth in order to reach the Black Sea.

The mouth which borders the island to the north, less travelled over, takes the name of Kilia, which is also the name of a small fortified town built on the left bank.

It is this branch which the barge had to take to reach its destination, and, during the morning of the following day—favored by a fairly rapid current—it was sailing closely to the right bank in such a way as to pass by Kilia at a far distance from it.

Ilia Krusch now understood why the skipper always passed at a significant distance from the towns built along the banks of the

Danube. As for Krusch himself, he had still not made any definite resolution on a course of action; instead, he observed with as close a level of attention as he himself was being observed on board. At all times, two sailors were beside him to help him in manoeuvering the helm. The barge was no longer merely letting itself be carried along by the drift of the current, and with its sail mounted high, it was taking advantage of the westerly breeze. That day, it would have reached the mouth of the river before five o'clock.

Latzko, unable to control his mounting impatience, worried by this disappearance of Mr. Jaeger, was coming and going on the deck; then, standing at the front of the vessel, he scrutinized the horizon.

Finally, one of the sailors who was stationed close of the flag mast, cried out:

"The Black Sea!"

Indeed, thanks to the widening of the river at the Kilia mouth, it was now possible to see a horizon formed by the line of sky and water.

Ilia Krusch had already spotted the sea. In an hour's time, he would have reached his journey's end, but not, alas, under the conditions in which he had hoped to complete it!

But what he could also now detect was a steamship cruising on the open sea, which was now alongside Leti island.

And it was not at all a warship, flying a Turkish or Russian flag, but rather a commercial vessel which displayed no signs of what country it originated from.

"It's that rogue of a smuggler that they're expecting, and who's expecting them," said Ilia Krusch to himself.

He wasn't mistaken. Signals were now sent by this steamship, which shot up a flame at its foremast. The barge replied by lowering its flag three times.

The steamship immediately altered its direction and began to steer a course enabling it to come close to the barge.

"Let's do it," murmured Ilia Krusch, "it's time for me to do my duty!"

And he turned the helm lightly towards port side, in order to make, obliquely, for the north-east.

Neither Latzko nor his companions could have detected anything suspicious about this manoeuver, and what is more, they had no option but to rely on the pilot who had been so skilfully steering a course for them along the Danube over the past ten days.

Moreover, the steamship was sailing on towards the channel of Kilia, and within half an hour or less, it would have drawn alongside the barge within the shelter of the island of Leti, in its calm waters, where the transhipment of the merchandise would then take place.

Suddenly, a tremendous scraping sound was heard, one which shook the barge to its very depths. Its mast had broken at its base, and the sail came crashing down, covering, with its wide folds, the sailors who were standing to the front of the vessel.

The barge had just run aground on a sandbank which cut across this part of the Kilia mouth; this area of the river was, of course, well known to Ilia Krusch.

What oaths then broke out from the mouths of the sailors, and with what violence did Latzko now rush forward towards Ilia Krusch!…

In actual fact, that man, so simple and courageous, had been under no illusions about the fate which now awaited him; he had sacrificed his own life.

Latzko didn't seek any explanations from him for his action, but, with a tremendous blow, laid him out on the deck.

It was now necessary to act with all possible haste; all was not lost. The barge had only run aground on a sandbank. Its bases had not been torn open, it wasn't taking in any water, and by the time the steamer would have drawn alongside it, the cargo of contraband could be removed undamaged and loaded on board.

But imagine the disappointment and shock of Latzko and his men when they saw what happened next! Instead of making its way to the barge and its crew in order to help extricate them from this difficult situation, the steamship had just tacked and was now heading for the open sea, full steam ahead.

A quarter of an hour later, the barge was invaded by the crew of a customs dispatch boat which the steamer had glimpsed just as it was overtaking the headland of the island of Leti. Realizing that the game was up, and knowing that it wouldn't even be possible to take Latzko and his gang on board, it had taken flight from the scene, heading eastwards.

One of the people who had been on board the dispatch boat, running in front of the others, rushed onto the deck of the barge and, while the sailors, who numbered about thirty, seized Latzko and his companions, in spite of the strong resistance mounted by them, he ran towards the rear of the vessel where Ilia Krusch was lying unconscious. He then lifted him up, freed his head and restored him to consciousness, and, when the pilot opened his eyes:

"Ah! Mr. Jaeger!" he cried.

"Not Jaeger, my good Krusch, but Karl Dragoch, the international commission's chief of police!"

For indeed, it was him. In order to throw the smugglers off the scent, and to be in a better position to survey the river without raising anyone's suspicions, he had conceived the idea of accompanying Ilia Krusch during his sailing trip, and the reader can now guess why he had paid so much attention to all the boats which had been sailing downriver. Whenever he used to go back onto dry land, police officers or letters would keep him briefed and updated on everything that was happening in the case. It was thus that, in Vienna, he had been tipped off that Latzko's gang were carrying out a heist at the entrance to the Lower Carpathians, and he had gone to lead the police squadron in that skirmish which, as we now know, had gone against him. Then, Mr. Jaeger—or rather, Karl Dragoch, to give him his real name—had rejoined Ilia Krusch in order to continue the river journey. We now know the circumstances in which his suspicions had become aroused regarding this mysterious larger barge, suspicions confirmed by Ilia Krusch's observations. And so, during the night of the 17th to the 18th of July, he had had no hesitation in fleeing the barge, even without notifying his travelling companion. Having been able to get out of the cabin—as its lock, which was in bad condition, had yielded when forced—he had slipped back to the rear of the barge, and, at the risk of drowning, he had managed to slide down into the waters of the Danube. His daring ploy had been successful, and he had been able to reach the bank of the river. He gained admittance to one of the little houses of a nearby small village, wherein he had his clothes dried, and then left the house before daybreak; then, having crossed the river, it took him twelve hours to reach Kilia. There, he made himself known, and the customs discharge boat, which, by a stroke of good fortune, happened to be available in the port, was placed at his disposal. But if the barge hadn't run aground on that sandbank at the entrance to the channel, Karl Dragoch might have got there too late to capture its illicit merchandise, and Latzko and his cronies, collected by the steamship, would probably have escaped the sentence which now awaited them.

And then, Karl Dragoch told Ilia Krusch the whole story of all that had taken place, adding:

"In any case, the fact that the barge ran aground at such an opportune moment was a fabulous stroke of luck..."

"Which we did our best to help bring about!" Ilia Krusch modestly retorted.

And Mr. Jaeger-Dragoch, kissing him on both cheeks, cried out:

"Ah! The good man! The good man!"

And so, the final resolution of this story can be guessed: Latzko and his accomplices were sentenced to imprisonment in the penal colony; their merchandise, which had been removed from the double hold of the barge, was confiscated, and it proved to be a very successful outcome for Karl Dragoch, of whom the international commission was not sparing either in its favors or in its praise; and finally, Ilia Krusch received a reward of two thousand florins which, combined with the florins previously won by him as the Danubian Line's prizewinning fisherman, amounted to a tidy sum, not to mention the great glamour and commotion which now, more than ever, surrounded his name. However, he didn't make any changes to his lifestyle, which was as happy as it was simple. He continued living in his house at Racz, where his friend Karl Dragoch comes to pay him visits every so often. Honored by the considerable respect which he enjoys from his fellow citizens, he spends his leisure hours fishing in the waters of the Theiss.

And, after hearing this story, who would now dare to ever make fun of that wise, prudent and philosophical man that, in every era and in every country, is the line fisherman?

THE END

ILLUSTRATIONS

ONE OF THE CHALLENGES in the Palik series is selecting illustrations. Most are derived from the first French publication of Verne stories in the 19th century and the beginning of the 20th century. They are selected either from the stories with which they appeared, or from others, choosing images to match the new context, with the source work noted in the captions. Only those depicting actual historical locales, persons or events are from other sources.

For *Golden Danube*, all engravings, unless otherwise noted, are by George Roux from Michel Verne's version of the novel, *Le Pilote du Danube*, although in most cases they are in different order given the narrative changes Michel made from Jules Verne's original manuscript. Other illustrations, especially photographs, are from various sources, but in all cases correspond to the temporal setting of the novel.

We are particularly indebted to Bernhard Krauth, chairman of the German Jules-Verne-Club since 2005, for providing the illustrations from Verne stories. A deep sea licensed master working today as a docking pilot in Bremerhaven, Germany, Bernhard has published several Verne-related articles in France, the Netherlands and Germany. Intensely interested in the illustrations of the original French editions of Verne's work, he has been deeply involved in a project to digitize the illustrations, more than 5,000 in all. The project is for common, non-commercial use, and most of the illustrations in the Palik series were made possible through his generosity.

Additional thanks are due to J.A. Marquis for assistance in providing scans of covers of the original Hetzel volumes of Verne stories. Scans from various editions have been provided by Frits Roest of Het Jules Verne Genootschap (the Dutch Verne Society).

❀

Acknowledgements

THE PALIK SERIES, while spearheaded by the North American Jules Verne Society, represents a cooperative effort among Vernians worldwide, pooling the resources and knowledge of the various organizations in different countries. The Society is grateful for research assistance to Frédéric Jaccaud, curator of Jean-Michel Margot's Verne Collection at the Maison d'Ailleurs (House of Elsewhere) in Yverdon-les-Bains, Switzerland.

The City of Nantes (France), whose Municipal Library has placed all Jules Verne manuscripts online, helped make this publication possible, and the Society would like to thank the City of Nantes and its Bibliothèque municipale (Agnès Marcetteau, director) for their ongoing assistance.

Elvira Berkowitsch provided invaluable geographical assistance with the various place names given by Verne.

The Society also appreciates the efforts of members who have contributed to this volume, and further assistance has been provided by Jean Frodsham and Pachara Yongvongpaibul.

CONTRIBUTORS

KIERAN O'DRISCOLL was awarded his Ph.D. in Verne literary translation, by Dublin City University, in 2010. His doctoral thesis was entitled *Around the World in Eighty Changes: A Diachronic Study of Six Complete Translations (1873-2004), From French to English, of Jules Verne's Novel, Le Tour du Monde en Quatre-Vingts Jours (1873)*, and explored the multiple causes of Verne retranslations. The monograph version was titled *Retranslation Through the Centuries: Jules Verne in English*, published in 2011 by Peter Lang Ltd. Kieran holds a B.A. in Applied Languages (French and Spanish) with International Marketing Communications (2003) from Waterford Institute of Technology, and an M.A. in Translation Studies (2005) from Dublin City University, both degrees with First Class Honours. His Master's dissertation focused on the translations into French of J.K. Rowling's Harry Potter series. He has lectured in French at third-level, and in Advanced English as a Foreign Language, and has also done professional literary translation. Before entering academia, Kieran worked for almost twenty years in Irish local government, and also holds academic qualifications in Public Administration, Law and Music (Pianoforte).

BRIAN TAVES (Ph.D., University of Southern California) has been an archivist in the Motion Picture, Broadcasting, and Recorded Sound Division of the Library of Congress since 1990. He is the author of over 100 articles and 25 chapters in anthologies. Taves has also written books on P.G. Wodehouse and Hollywood; director Robert Florey; the genre of historical adventure movies; and fantasy-adventure writer Talbot Mundy, in addition to editing an original anthology of Mundy's best stories. In 2002-2003, Taves was chosen as Kluge Staff Fellow at the Library to write the first book on silent film pioneer Thomas Ince, published in 2011. Taves's writing on Verne has been translated into French, German, and Spanish, and he is currently writing a book on the 300 film and television adaptations of Verne worldwide. Taves is coauthor of *The Jules Verne Encyclopedia* (Scarecrow, 1996), and editor of the first English-language publication of Verne's *Adventures of the Rat Family* (Oxford, 1993), as well as the Palik series.

THE PALIK SERIES

THE LAST TWO DECADES have brought astonishing progress in the study of Jules Verne, with new translations of Verne stories, including the discovery of many texts. Still, there remain a number of Verne stories that have been overlooked, and it is this gap that the North American Jules Verne Society seeks to fill in the Palik series.

The North American Jules Verne Society (NAJVS) was formed in 1993, and a decade later, underwrote *Journey Through the Impossible*, the first complete edition in any language of Verne's 1882 science fiction theatrical spectacle, *Voyage à travers l'impossible*. With this experience, and thanks to the generosity of the Society's late member, Edward Palik, a series was commenced to bring to the Anglophone public a series of hitherto unknown Verne tales.

Ed Palik had a special enthusiasm for bringing neglected Verne stories to English-speaking readers, and this will be reflected in the series that bears his name. In this way the Society hopes to fulfill the goal that Ed's consideration has made possible, along with the assistance of a variety of Verne translators and scholars from around the world. The volumes in the Palik series will reveal the amazing range of Verne's storytelling, in genres that may surprise those who only know his most famous stories. We hope to allow a better appreciation of the famous writer who has, for more than a century and a half, been the widest-read author of fiction in the world.

PREVIOUS VOLUMES IN THE PALIK SERIES:

The Marriage of a Marquis

Foreword by Brian Taves; Introduction by Walter James Miller; *The Marriage of Mr. Anselme des Tilleuls* translated by Edward Baxter, with a preface and notes by Jean-Michel Margot; afterword by Edward Baxter; Appendix: *Jédédias Jamet, or The Tale of an Inheritance* translated, with a preface and annotations, by Kieran M. O'Driscoll.

Jules Verne is the acclaimed author of such pioneering science fiction as *20,000 Leagues Under the Sea* and *Journey to the Center of the Earth*. Yet he also wrote much more, and foreshadowing such classics as *Around the World in 80 Days*, this inaugural volume focuses on two of Verne's earliest humorous stories, *The Marriage of Mr. Anselme des Tilleuls* and *Jédédias Jamet, or The Tale of an Inheritance*. Mr. Anselme des Tilleuls, in the featured story, is a ridiculous young man seeking a bride, following the advice of his Latin tutor to utilize the maxims of that language in his courtship. Translation is provided by Edward Baxter and Kieran O'Driscoll, two of the leading Verne experts; critical commentary by Jean-Michel Margot, Walter James Miller, and Brian Taves examine both stories, and why some of the author's tales were overlooked for so many years.

Shipwrecked Family: Marooned with Uncle Robinson

Translated by Sidney Kravitz; Introduction by Brian Taves.

Castaway by pirates on a deserted island… without tools or supplies to survive… a mother and her children have only a kindly old sailor to help. But what explains the strange flora and fauna they find? The second volume in the Palik series was rejected by Verne's publisher, so rather than finish it, he began to rewrite it with new characters—and that became the classic, *The Mysterious Island*, where Captain Nemo made his last appearance. Here, then, is Verne's first draft of that novel, one which is very different from the book that it became.

Translation is provided by Sidney Kravitz, also translator of the definitive modern edition of *The Mysterious Island* (Wesleyan University Press, 2002). The introduction by Brian Taves discusses the influence of the Robinsonade on Verne's oeuvre, while an appendix comprises Verne's own prefaces to two of his novels in the genre, describing the influence of the form on his writing.

Mr. Chimp and Other Plays

By Jules Verne with Michel Carré, Charles Wallut, and Victorien Sardou; Translated by Frank Morlock; Introduction by Jean-Michel Margot.

Long before Verne stories had formed the basis for such movies as *Around the World in 80 Days*, many of his plays were theatrical blockbusters on the 19ᵗʰ century stage, including several from his novels. Even as he became a novelist, the stage remained crucial to Verne. In this volume, expert scholarly research by Jean-Michel Margot introduces four of Verne's plays written early in his career, from 1853 to 1860. The four plays are translated by Frank Morlock, one of the most prolific modern translators of 19ᵗʰ century French drama. Included in this volume are: *The Knights of the Daffodil* and *Mr. Chimpanzee*, co-authored by Verne with Michel Carré; *An Adoptive Son*, co-authored by Verne with Charles Wallut, and *Eleven Days of Siege*, co-authored by Verne with Charles Wallut and Victorien Sardou. The works range in content from romantic comedies to a scientist's discovery that there may not be such a difference between human and ape after all!

The Count of Chanteleine: A Tale of the French Revolution

Translated by Edward Baxter; Introduction by Brian Taves; Notes and maps by Garmt de Vries-Uiterweerd; Afterword by Volker Dehs.

This adventure, first published in France in 1864 but never before available in English, is for everyone who has thrilled to *The Scarlet Pimpernel, A Tale of Two Cities*, or *Scaramouche*. A nobleman, the Count of Chanteleine, leads a rebellion against the revolutionary French government. While he fights for the monarchy and the church, his home is destroyed and his wife murdered by the mob. Now he must save his daughter from the guillotine. This exciting swashbuckler is also a meticulous historical re-creation of a particularly bloody episode in the Reign of Terror.

Commentary by an international team of experts including Garmt de Vries-Uiterweerd, Volker Dehs and Brian Taves explores the historical background, composition, and generic context of *The Count of Chanteleine*, translated by Edward Baxter.

The Count of Chanteleine is also available in a full-length professional reading by the noted vocal artist, Fred Frees, on audible.com.

Vice, Redemption and the Distant Colony

By Jules Verne with Michel Verne; Translated, with an introduction and annotations, by Kieran M. O'Driscoll.

Literary fraud or filial devotion? This is the question at the heart of a firestorm that erupted when manuscripts and letters were discovered proving that Jules Verne's son, Michel, significantly revised over a dozen of the stories published under his father's name, and even originated some himself. It was a collaboration that had begun while both were still alive, and continued as Michel saw to the posthumous publication of many of his father's books.

In this volume will be found two different versions of a story, as written by Jules (*Pierre-Jean*), and expanded by his son (into *The Somber Fate of Jean Morénas*)—a tale Michel even made as a full-length movie in 1916! Also in these pages is the first English translation of a novel Jules began, *Fact-Finding Mission*, but which his son finished, and hitherto has been only available in the completed version by Michel Verne.

The English rendering and notes are by a leading authority on Verne translations, Kieran O'Driscoll.

Around the World in 80 Days—The 1874 Play

By Jules Verne and Adolphe d'Ennery; The original translation commissioned by the Kiralfy Brothers; Introduction by Philippe

Burgaud, with Jean-Michel Margot and Brian Taves; Afterword: "The Meridians and the Calendar" by Jules Verne, Translated and Annotated by Jean-Louis Trudel; Appendix: The Play on Screen, by Brian Taves.

Jules Verne's most famous novel was originally conceived as a play— and had its greatest 19th century success as a stage hit the author himself adapted. Running for thousands of performances in many different countries, including the United States, here is the original playscript, translated directly from the French by the producers of the original Broadway presentation, and only issued in the most limited form in 1874. Like filmmakers after him, Verne understood the need to make changes for the stage, and in collaboration with Adolphe d'Ennery created a distinct variation, a play with many different characters and episodes than are in the novel. Included in this volume are an introduction about how the play was created and staged, together with the first translation of Verne's 1873 essay, "The Meridians and the Calendar," by Jean-Louis Trudel, explaining how Phileas Fogg accomplished his feat. Background on the production of the play, especially its staging in the United States, is provided by Philippe Burgaud, Jean-Michel Margot, and Brian Taves, along with an appendix on films of the play.

Bandits & Rebels

San Carlos and *The Siege of Rome* translated by Edward Baxter; Introduction by Daniel Compère, translated by Jean-Michel Margot with Brian Taves; Appendix: *Martin Paz, or The Pearl of Lima*, the 1852 translation by Anne T. Wilbur of the original French edition.

Captain Nemo's *Nautilus* in *Twenty Thousand Leagues Under the Sea* was not the first undersea craft imagined by Jules Verne! A decade earlier, the prophetic author wrote *San Carlos*, imagining a Spanish smuggler who utilizes a vehicle capable of diving beneath the surface of the waves. This newly-discovered story is published here in English for the first time—together with Verne's final words before his death on the future of the submarine as an instrument of war. Also in this volume is another never-before-translated tale, *The Siege of Rome*, a historical adventure of love and betrayal as Garibaldi's revolutionaries are defeated in 1849.

Sorbonne professor Daniel Compère introduces the expert translations by Edward Baxter.

Since *Bandits & Rebels* emphasizes two Verne stories written early in his career, but which remained unpublished during his lifetime, this volume includes *Martin Paz*, another story of the same genre but which did appear in the 1850s, in both France and the United States. Reprinted here for the first time from that original translation, this preserves in unvarnished form Verne's own first version of *Martin Paz*, as well as the manner in which it was presented to American readers. Previously, only the more polished version rewritten in the 1870s has appeared in book form.

Additional volumes are underway.

IN 2003, the North American Jules Verne Society also co-published (with Prometheus) the Verne play, **Journey Through the Impossible**. A tale of fantasy and science fiction, *Journey Through the Impossible* ran for 97 performances in Paris in 1882 and 1883. In three acts, the characters go first to the center of the Earth, then under the sea, and finally into outer space to the planet Altor. Characters from *Journey to the Center of the Earth*, *From the Earth to the Moon*, *Twenty Thousand Leagues under the Sea*, and *A Fancy of Doctor Ox* appear again in *Journey through the Impossible*. The players include Captain Nemo, the lunar travelers Barbicane and Michel Ardan, Doctor Ox, and Professor Lidenbrock, after his trip to the center of the earth. Translation of *Journey Through the Impossible* is by Edward Baxter, with introduction and notes by Jean-Michel Margot, along with reviews from the play's first presentation. Roger Leyonmark provides new illustrations in the style of the 19th century woodcuts that first illustrated French editions of Verne works, and the original engravings from the play are also featured. This is the first complete edition and English translation of a surprising work, by the popular French novelist whose works continue to delight readers—and audiences—to this day.

❀

The North American
Jules Verne Society

JULES VERNE WAS A FRENCHMAN, born in Nantes in 1828, who lived most of his life in Amiens, where he passed away in 1905. Despite his nationality, Verne has always had an exceptional popularity among English-language readers, one which the North American Jules Verne Society celebrates today as the successor to previous organizations.

The first group of Verne enthusiasts was formed, not in Verne's own France, but in England. The Jules Verne Confederacy began in 1921 at Dartmouth Royal Naval College, publishing *Nautilus*, a literary magazine in tribute to Verne and his son Michel, with whom they were in regular contact until Michel's death in 1925. The most permanent legacy of the Confederacy came with the publication of the Everyman's Library edition of *Five Weeks in a Balloon and Around the World in Eighty Days* in 1926, reprinted as late as 1966. Not only did it contain some of the first new, corrected translations, but the introduction by members of the Confederacy offered one of the earliest thoughtful critical overviews and bibliographies of Verne.

In France, the Société Jules Verne was formed in 1935, but their work would be interrupted by war and did not resume until 1967. Meanwhile, the American Jules Verne Society began a 20-year association. It was initiated when Willis E. Hurd penned an article, "A Collector and His Jules Verne," for the August 1936 issue of *Hobbies*, recounting his discovery that most of Verne's novels available in English had received many different translations, under widely divergent titles. A number of enthusiasts read Hurd's pioneering analysis, and a network formed. Hurd's retirement allowed him to take an interest in authoring English versions of some of Verne's untranslated stories. His collection would be willed to the Library of Congress and the volumes of another American Jules Verne Society member, James C. Iradi, were deposited at Indiana University's Lilly Library.

Iraldi was still active in the late 1960s when the Dakkar Grotto was formed by Ron Miller and Laurence Knight, publishing two issues of a journal entitled *Dakkar*, after Captain Nemo's original Indian name. A mid 1970s effort to re-establish an American Jules Verne Society led by Ron Ulrich, Gary Kraidman, and Dennis Larson built up a mailing list and finally issued a single bulletin.

In 1993, the North American Jules Verne Society (NAJVS) formed, and has steadily grown with annual meetings in increasingly prestigious venues and a peer-reviewed newsletter, *Extraordinary Voyages*. Although founded largely by collectors, the group now includes scholars and readers generally, to span all types of Verne admirers. In 2003, NAJVS undertook its first book publication, Verne's science fiction play, *Journey Through the Impossible*, with the Palik series of first-time translations commencing seven years later.

The Society is a not-for-profit corporation with these goals and objectives:

- To promote interest in Jules Verne and his writings.
- To provide a forum for the interchange of information and materials about and/or relating to Jules Verne and his works, such as annual meetings with workshops and presentations.
- To stimulate Jules Verne research.
- To publish a newsletter, *Extraordinary Voyages*, with articles about Jules Verne and Society related issues.

Information on membership and activities, along with our various educational activities, may be found at our website, najvs.org.

✸

For additional details, and links to order the books, see the North American Jules Verne Society's website: www.najvs.org.